Red

THE NURSERY

JUDI CULBERTSON

THE NURSERY

ST. MARTIN'S PRESS ✠ NEW YORK

For Tom, Andy, and Robin,
with love

A THOMAS DUNNE BOOK.
An imprint of St. Martin's Press.

Design by Nancy Resnick

Library of Congress Cataloging-in-Publication Data

Culbertson, Judi.
    The nursery / Judi Culbertson.—1st ed.
      p. cm.
    "A Thomas Dunne book."
    ISBN 0-312-14692-2 (hardcover)
    I. Title.
PS3553.U2849N87   1996
813'.54—dc20   96-21700
                                   CIP

First Edition: November 1996

10 9 8 7 6 5 4 3 2 1

THE NURSERY

ONE

The sound, when it crackled over the nursery monitor, was so ordinary—the creak of a floorboard in a house a century old—that only a new mother would have been awakened by it. Three rooms away, Caroline Denecke's eyes opened. Pulled out of a dream of finding kittens in grocery bags, she made herself look at the clock on the night table. Was it really only 2:25 in the morning? Babies weren't supposed to wake up every two hours!

But at least he wasn't crying yet. She willed Zach to go back to sleep, imagining him in his new room. The bookcase was lined with toys from her own childhood, a zoo of new stuffed animals, and the books she had used in her classroom for years: Ezra Jack Keats, Maurice Sendak, the Little Bear series, Dr. Seuss. Even Tuggy—the limp cloth tugboat with a boy's face that she had carried everywhere with her as a child—was next to Paddington. He was fragile now, frayed at the joints, but she wanted Zach to have the comfort of Tuggy, too.

The baby shower they had given her at school had supplied everything else an infant would need. She smiled a little, remembering how she had burst into the house wearing the silly hat made of bows from the packages, her arms filled with stretchies, a folding stroller, and a huge Raggedy Ann doll.

"Look," she cried to Joe, her eyes getting watery. "Look what they did!"

He had looked surprised—all this for an adopted baby?—then pointed out that, after all, they owed it to her. She had taught at Crane Island's elementary school for thirteen years, and developed their whole Special Education program. "They know when they've got a good thing."

"But they didn't have to do all *this*." One of the few things she disliked in Joe was the way he kept a ledger book on life. "You should have seen the cake!"

The cake had been in the shape of a stork carrying a blue-blanketed baby, and covered with pounds of white cream icing. Even the parents of the little group of children she taught had sent in gifts—Sesame Street nursing bottles, tiny plush animals, a crib bumper pad set.

Several weeks before leaving she had started to prepare her class, explaining that she would be adopting a tiny baby and staying home for a while to take care of him. "You could bring him here," Tiffany protested, nodding her pretty, cornrowed head. "We could *play* with him."

Much as she loved them, she could not imagine her class let loose on an infant. But she hated to leave Tiffany. The others had parents, but Tiff was already in her fourth foster home. Left to herself she would hum tunelessly and stick her hand inside her underpants to rub herself to climax. On her first day she had terrorized a shy little boy by pushing him down in her quest to mount him.

Sometimes she felt guilty about not taking Tiffany home herself. If you really want a *child*, why should it matter what color she was or what her problems were? But she could not imagine Joe's reaction to the little girl or how to fit her into their lives. It was better to start with a baby, as nature arranged.

2

As it was she felt guilty about leaving her class in midyear. She didn't have to, she knew. Joe had encouraged her to keep on teaching, and if she did they could afford a nanny. But she had been waiting for this for so long! Her own mother was urging her to stay home, a message she would be hearing again in a few hours, when she and Zach arrived in Myrtle Beach. She worried that the baby was too young to be flying. But since his retirement her father had already had one heart attack and did not want to travel. Besides, they had her sister, Ruthie, with all her problems, still living at home.

She shifted again so that she could see if the crackling noise had wakened Joe. Every morning he complained that he had slept badly, a complaint that made her feel defensive. She slept fitfully too, but she had wanted the baby more than he did. Maybe she should just put a cot for herself in the nursery. But then Joe would feel abandoned. And Joe, sprawled on his back, his gray curls matted down, was certainly sleeping now. It would help if his family had been more supportive. Unlike her own parents, Joe's father had wondered out loud why he would want to take on such a responsibility at *his* age. And Maureen, Joe's sister, had wanted to know why he would even consider another child after losing Lisa.

The nursery monitor sputtered again, this time amplifying the creak of a dresser drawer. What was that kid doing, getting himself a clean diaper? Smart baby. She smiled at the idea. Not likely at ten days old—but someone was moving around in there. The thought made her bolt up. Maybe it was the crib, not the dresser. Maybe he had gotten caught in the covers and was thrashing around, unable to breathe!

Pushing off the weight of the comforter, she was across the room in seconds, yanking the door open. She was beyond caring if she woke Joe or not.

The hall was a long, dark tunnel, lit only by a night-light shaped like the moon. Her feet felt trapped by the thick shag carpet. They should have kept Zach in the bedroom with them. They had given

3

him the best room in the house, the one with all the windows, but they could have moved him into it later on.

Reaching the door, she slowed herself, as if braking. There was no reason to wake him if he was okay, if he had already drifted back to sleep. She touched the door with her index finger; it opened part of the way. In the nursery a seashell-shaped plug-in light picked up the shine of the oak crib and the row of jars and lotions on the dresser top. The covers in the crib were a dark mound. But where was Zach's head? He had smothered! Her heart banging, she closed in and jerked back the blue gingham comforter. There was only the white empty space of the sheet. Where was her baby? The appliquéd Pooh grinned up hopefully at her, but the cotton sagged beneath her hand. *Where's Zach?*

She dropped to her knees, and swept her arm wildly across the floor under the crib. But why would he be there? He couldn't get out of the crib, he couldn't even turn over yet! She remembered a terrible story about a four-year-old who took her newborn twin brothers out of their cribs and played with them in the darkness until she crushed their skulls. The kind of child who would end up in one of her classes. But she didn't *have* a four-year-old. There was only Joe and herself. For a hysterical moment she imagined Tiffany finding out where she lived, then creeping up the stairs to do away with her rival.

But that was preposterous. Joe! She must have fallen back to sleep without realizing it, Zach had cried, and Joe had come in and gotten him.

Clinging to that explanation, she raced back down the hall. She pushed open the bedroom door and circled to Joe's side of the bed. But he lay motionless, a mummy under the ivory comforter.

"I can't find Zach," she gasped, pulling at his shoulder. "I thought *you* had him."

"What, Caro? What?" He was instantly awake, shaking his silvery curls as if to clear his head.

4

"Zach's not in his crib!" She felt her teeth chattering. "Don't—don't you have him?"

"No. . . ."

"Then someone took him!" She turned and limped frantically back to the nursery. As she stopped at the nursery door, Joe bumped into her softly. Her hand flailed against the inside wall to find the switch.

Then the room was lit against the night. Joe's hands squeezed her shoulders. It was the way her father had grasped her as a child when he wanted her to notice something—the constellations of the starry skies, the way fish swam in schools at the end of their backyard dock. "Caroline. Look."

She stared at the crib, at the firm mound of covers and the tiny dark head. "Oh!" She must be going crazy. It was like the trick in which you suddenly saw a face where there had been only a mirror or vase before. An optical illusion.

"You new mothers worry too much."

"But—he wasn't there before. I *felt* the empty covers! I guess, it was just—" She let herself sag against Joe, knowing he would hold her. Could she have only dreamed of leaving the bedroom and coming in here? Finding the crib empty? She must have. She had not been sleeping much, the line between waking and sleeping stretched dangerously thin.

"He was probably scrunched down at the end," Joe said magnanimously.

"I guess." But even in her dream she had felt the bed all over. "The part where I came running to get you—that seems so real!" And why did she still sound out of breath?

"It *was* real. You came in here half asleep, he wasn't where you were expecting him to be, and you panicked. That's all." He pressed his body against hers, rubbing his chin on her hair. "Anyway, he's fine, he's asleep. Now can we do the same? I have a hell of a day coming up."

"Sure." She felt his erection graze her nightgown politely, but knew they wouldn't act on it. Before, they would have. If frequency had counted for anything, they would have had a dozen kids. Maybe they still would. But instead of responding to Joe, she moved to the crib to her new love. "Precious baby, I was so worried about you!"

"Don't wake him," Joe warned. "He should be sleeping through the night."

"Not yet!"

Zachary was lying on his side facing the window, one fist raised as if giving a playful punch. What a wonderful little boy! She refrained from risking Joe's annoyance by scooping him up and kissing him all over, but reached out to tuck his arm under the quilt. It didn't move. She tried again, then squeezed his hand, disbelieving. "Joe, he's freezing! Did the heat go off?" She was chilly too, but not with that solid deadweight cold. Snatching him up, she pressed her face against his. Where was the warm, milky smell around his mouth, the bubble of saliva? Why didn't his eyelids even flicker when she touched him?

Joe pushed her arm aside to look at Zach, then cupped his hand across the baby's forehead. "Christ!" He reached for him, then moved away. "I'll call the ambulance!"

Oh no oh no oh no. Without thinking, she knelt down with him on the braided rug beside the crib. Gently she put her lips over his cold, cold mouth and nose and began breathing in. Was she doing it right? She had learned CPR in her first year of teaching. There had been children with seizures, children who held their breath when enraged, but never . . . this. *Breathe in and listen. Breathe in and listen.* In her mind she saw herself rushing into the bathroom and immersing him in hot water. Could you—unthaw someone? Instead she checked his nose for mucus, tapped all over his chest. But she could not create any answering breath.

She did it mechanically again and again. Finally she picked him up and stumbled over to the rocking chair. He felt like, *oh God,* the dolls she had played with growing up, dolls with hard plastic arms and bent, dimpled knees. If only she were still eight, back in Lindenhurst! Dropping into the seat she rocked him, her tears scalding her hands, dropping on his dark hair. He felt different now, larger and heavier. He didn't even look the same. Did death make you heavier?

She rocked faster in the pressed-back oak rocker. One runner slipped off the braided rug, but she did not bother to adjust the bumpiness. *Don't cry.* She made herself focus on the chair. *I bought it at that auction right after I came to the island. They dragged it out of a shed with some broken wicker at the last minute, and I didn't even get a chance to look at it first. But it was only eight dollars.* It had taken her forever to get the green paint off, though. She suddenly smelled the harsh odor of varnish remover, and saw the pale green blistering as the layers retreated from the wood. *Once she had something she kept it forever. Only—what happens when forever ends after a week?*

She tried to return her mind to the chair, but instead heard Joe's father. *I told you no woman gives up a perfectly good baby.* . . . *She must have known there was something wrong with him.* . . . *Something was sure wrong with her.* . . . *Crazy.* . . . *That's the kind who gives up her own.*

That's not true, Caroline protested. *Zach was perfectly healthy! So was Susan. She talked about using the money to go to college.*

College? The only college she'll see is the school of hard knocks.

You only had him a few days, Maureen argued. *It's not like you carried him nine months under your heart.*

You can always get another baby. Whose voice was that? There would never be another Zachary!

You're still being punished for what you did. She recognized that voice as her own. "Joe! Where are you? I *need* you." But as she was calling him her throat closed up. She let herself be sucked down into a dream.

Although they had not called them, although Joe had dialed "911" and begged for an ambulance, the police arrived first.

She was still sitting in the rocking chair, cuddling Zach, when the two men pushed into the room. The first man was stocky, no taller than she was, with a pale crewcut and a thick navy overcoat. He came toward her, his arms out, the way people did when they were asking for a hug. But she understood that he wanted Zachary. Maybe he could make him okay! She pushed herself up, holding the baby out. That felt familiar too, a picture from Sunday school of Jesus healing the sick. Please, God, help him!

The man squeezed Zach's bluish cheeks together gently, forcing his lips open with a pop, then put his ear to the baby's chest. Frowning, he ripped away the fuzzy blue sleeper, pressed his hand all over the baby's bare skin, then moved quickly with Zach toward the crib. She saw him push the baby's eyelid up roughly. Too roughly. Then turning to her, his eyes narrow and mean, he opened his arms over the crib. The baby bounced against the mattress, banging his head with a hollow crack at the crib's end.

The man was crazy! She heard herself scream and saw the younger officer's soft brown eyes widen with shock. Frantically she threw herself against the crib then knelt beside it, reaching through the slats to stroke what she could of Zach. "What's the matter with you?" she shrieked.

He turned on her. "What's the matter with *me?* When was the last time you remembered you had a kid?"

Before she could answer he was slapping the crib rail with his open palm and firing words at her. What kind of idiots did she think they were? She might think she could fool someone who didn't know any better, someone like Donald here, but *he* had spent years in a precinct in New York City before coming to the island and knew all about times of death. She was maybe expecting someone who could raise kids from the dead?

Caroline pressed her forehead against the slats. Above her head he raced on like an out-of-control truck, talking, talking, about a boy who had almost drowned in a Batman pool last year, six god-damned inches of water, he had revived him and kept him breath-

8

ing until they reached Jefferson Hospital; about a little girl who choked on a peanut butter sandwich whom he *would* have saved if the baby-sitter had gotten help right away instead of running around the yard screeching in Spanish. And where was the mother? Out *working* somewhere.

"Same goddamned thing." But, like one of her kids after an episode, he was winding down.

"We called you as soon as we found him!" Joe sounded angry.

"And when did you last see him alive?" The cop was deadly calm.

This was a question she could answer. "When I fed him at midnight, he was fine." But her throat was aching, bloated with tears. Her baby was gone; truly gone. She had fed him in the dark, rocking him in the chair until he burped gently, spitting a little milk on the diaper across her lap. *Why* hadn't she gotten up right away when she heard that noise? *I'll never forgive myself.* . . . She looked at the clock of dancing rabbits on the wall. It was almost three hours ago that he had eaten.

She jumped as the policeman banged his palm against his temple to pantomime disbelief. "You're telling me that at midnight— tonight—this kid was alive and fine and drinking milk."

What was surprising about that? Mutely she pointed to the almost empty bottle of Enfamil on the dresser. He strode over and unscrewed the nipple. After a cautious sniff inside, he stuck his finger into the bottle and tasted the tip. Quickly he screwed the top back on without saying anything.

She pulled herself up holding onto the slats, hand over hand, swaying a little; then she reached over the rail and pressed Zachary's bare chest. Cold, so cold! He looked different already, his nose a different shape, more pointed . . . or something. "I don't know how we could let him get so cold," she confessed. The man was right, it was their fault. Could he charge them with child abuse for keeping the heat too low?

The policeman was writing in a small black notebook now. He was close enough for her to read his photo ID—Rafe Millar—but not to see the words he was putting down. She smelled tobacco; did people still smoke? Not around my baby.

But then she remembered and could not stand it. Reaching into the crib, she picked him up. As she did, something crackled under her fingers. Puzzled, she stuck her hand inside his sleeper. It felt like a disposable diaper. Quickly she lay Zach back on the mattress and pulled the sleeper to his ankles. He was wearing a tiny triangle of blue plastic. "But I use cloth! *Joe*—"

Where was he? She whirled around and found him leaning against the wall in front of the blue schoolhouse quilt. His arms were holding his maroon wool robe closed, his eyes shut. *Is he dead, too? Carbon monoxide poisoning . . .* "Joe!"

She saw his shoulder twitch.

"Joe, look at this," she pleaded. As he came closer she pointed at the unfamiliar blue. "Look at this—you know I use cloth diapers!"

Joe looked into the crib, then back at her, as if he could not understand what she meant. What was the *matter* with him? They had had this whole discussion about not polluting the earth any further, of opting for cloth diapers and rubber pants.

The policemen looked in, too. "What's your point?" Rafe Millar asked her coldly.

"I never put this diaper on him. Either someone else did—or it's someone else's baby!" Until she said it out loud she hadn't known it, truly known it herself. Now, other things made sense. "See? These pajamas are brand-new, they still have the creases in them from being folded. And I heard noises in here, over the monitor!"

"They call it denial," the younger man, Donald, said softly to Rafe Millar. "It's the first stage of grief. Or the second, I forget which."

"Yeah, yeah, I had that training, too. You believe all that shit?" But Millar peered at the fuzzy blue material of the sleeper, squinting at the teddy bear appliqué. The folds that always remained until the first washing were still visible. "How come you didn't notice those creases before?"

"Because he has a pair just like them! They sell them everywhere, even in the hospital gift shop. Listen, the hospital *gives* them away!"

Millar snorted, then peered at her sternly. "Maybe you *had* to put new pajamas on him. To hide the blood on the others."

"Blood!"

She felt Joe come back to life and wrap his arms around her from behind. God, she needed him so much! But being held made her realize how frigid the room seemed. "Caro, it's *okay.*"

"No, it isn't! He doesn't realize this is another baby. Tell him!"

Millar was staring at her uncertainly, his fleshy lips pursed. Then he said to Joe, over her head, "Maybe she really does believe it. We've seen stuff like this before. Donald, you remember that woman a few months ago. I guess it is denial. Maybe that's why you waited so long to call," he said to Caroline.

"But I didn't. Anyway, what about the noises?" She pointed to the ivory plastic monitor; with its baby blue grille it looked like another toy.

"Just what is it you think you heard?"

"Creaking, like the crib moving. And somebody walking around."

"Those things"—he jerked his head at the monitor—"magnify everything. You probably just heard the house settling, a house this old. Or the trees rubbing on the window."

"I know it wasn't that. We'd be hearing those noises all night if it was that."

"What about blood tests?" Donald asked. He had the fresh, cheerful look of an apprentice; he was probably not more than twenty. "They could check if this baby has the same genetic markers. That would clear up any mix-up."

Millar wheeled and stared at him, as if he should have thought of it himself.

Caroline felt Joe's grip loosen just a little. "He isn't our own baby," she explained. "We adopted him. We've only had him eight days."

"He's not your baby?" Millar sounded disgusted. "No wonder you can't tell the difference!"

"That's not true!"

"What about footprints?" Donald persisted. Evidently he had learned something in criminal justice college. "Doesn't the hospital keep them on file?"

Millar sighed. "Not on Crane Island. They take footprints in the city, but not over here. Even you should know that."

The wail of the ambulance sounded a block away. She stared at the rabbit clock. Had it really only been five minutes?

"You want a moment with your baby before they come up?" Millar asked. He sounded resigned, as if he could only do so much to save the world from itself. From somewhere he produced a hat, an old-fashioned fedora, and held it in front of him like a respectful mourner.

"I don't think so," Joe murmured.

"He's not my baby!" She knew she was screaming it. "I want you to find *my* baby. Zach!" She turned to Donald. After all, he was a policeman, too. "Help me find him," she begged.

"I'll get back to you after the autopsy." And then Rafe Millar left the room. Caroline held tightly to Donald's black raincoat sleeve. He looked at her sadly.

"Someone must have taken Zach and left this baby in his place," she pleaded.

"Things always seem weird at night." One brown eye was smaller and set higher than the other, but both eyes were kind. "But if there's anything I can do . . ."

"You can help me find Zach!"

"You have a family doctor? Or a minister?"

It was no use. It was sensitivity training at work, nothing else. She let him go.

Millar appeared suddenly in the doorway. "I'll be back," he warned.

TWO

As Diana Larsen turned into the driveway of the maternity home, she felt an unfamiliar uneasiness. Her mouth flooded with saltwater; a buzzing like an insect trapped under glass began inside her head. Approaching Heart's Retreat for the first time three weeks earlier, she had felt fine. Now she fought to keep from pulling her car to the side of the gravel road and vomiting up spinach pizza and Coke. Was the food around here tainted, like the fresh mangoes in Delhi? Or was her stomach responding to the hopelessness of her quest?

She had accepted the assignment gladly enough. With abortion under a fresh attack from the right, the magazine she wrote for was doing a special issue on reproductive rights. She was supposed to be exploring adoption as an alternative—a flawed alternative, in the editorial point of view, one which exploited young women. She had spent a frustrating two weeks being stonewalled at the largest baby factories, including the Margaret Ritter Pease Home and the Golden Cradle. As soon as they heard she was from *Women* magazine they had nothing to say. They would barely let her pet the cat.

Bruised, she had limped back to her last choice. Heart's Retreat and Crane Island Social Services, which operated it, were innocently welcoming; but it would take major creative writing to make it into the kind of material she needed.

The maternity home, huge and white in the March drizzle, looked like one of the Newport mansions modestly known as cottages. Its green shutters were cut out in a sailboat design and it was easy to imagine faces behind the glass of the gables. She had heard a story about a girl inching out one of the top windows and throwing herself from the peak of the roof, but the current housemother pooh-poohed it. Still, it was a great way to start her story.

Heart's Retreat, opened in 1922 to serve the daughters of New York's richest families, had brought girls secretly to its doors at night by boat. They had been spirited out the same way, leaving their babies behind like boardwalk toys. The girls had not been allowed to know one another's last names or leave the premises. A Vanderbilt or a Frick, imagined to be in school in Switzerland, could not risk being spotted so close to Manhattan. A collection of wedding rings had been kept in the hall drawer so they could slip one on before leaving for the hospital.

Crane Island had been an ideal place for sheltering secrets. Situated in the Sound between Long Island and Connecticut, it had been accessible only by a ferry that ran once a day until 1958 when the Carpenter Bridge was built. Until then, except for some wealthy New Yorkers who owned summer estates along the water, the residents had been a mix of lobstering and farming families. With the bridge, the population had ballooned to its current size of 75,000.

But it was the increased availability of abortion and the relaxing of social mores that had done Heart's Retreat in. Over the years its exclusivity had seeped away. When the private teacher was replaced by a tutor from Martinville High, the doctor and the Episcopalian chaplain stopped making daily calls as well. Currently there were only three girls in residence. They were being pressured, Diana knew, into giving up their babies, but for her story's sake she wished that there were more of them. The year before, the maternity home had lost its private status altogether and had come under the jurisdiction of Crane Island Social Services. That took away even more from its mystique. Well, she could always focus on the past and give the present a gloss.

Diana parked in the semicircle in front of the house. Climbing out of the leased blue Sentra she marveled at the broken white clamshells that crunched under her feet. Someone had taken the trouble to walk down to the bay, collect bushels full, and carry them back. Why didn't the sharp edges puncture tires? Checking the porch steps for ice, she climbed to the front door. Several rocking chairs painted the same forest green of the shutters were tilted backwards against the house to indicate they were not in season.

As she reached for the black dot of the bell wedged in layers of white paint, the heavy front door was pulled back.

"I thought it was you." Eileen Norris, the housemother, must have heard the car tires on the shells. For editorial purposes Diana had transformed Eileen into a tall, white-haired woman with gentle ironclad habits. But the real Eileen actually reminded her of a childhood toy, a plastic, round-bottomed Dutch girl who, no matter how hard you pushed her down, bobbed right back up. She had the same shiny black bowl haircut and round red cheeks. She was bottom-heavy, too.

"Back again," Diana agreed.

"Well, come in."

Eileen had been eager to tell her story. As a teenager she had been a novitiate in an Irish order, but it had been mutually decided, she said, that she would not be happy with convent life. She had gone on to become a WAC, and then taught gym at a girls' boarding school before coming to Heart's Retreat. As openly as Eileen laid out her life history—"You can use my real name," she kept saying hopefully—Diana knew there had to be more. Forget this *Sound of Music* fantasy. Why had she been kicked out of the convent? Eileen had never married; she talked constantly about her

15

nieces and nephews, as if they were her own children. And why leave a teaching job to baby-sit a bunch of pregnant girls? She wasn't *that* old.

"To the kitchen!" Eileen, wearing a purple sweatsuit with a Notre Dame insignia and elephant-legged pants, winked at her. Then, raising her arm as if holding a parade baton, she led Diana down the hall. They passed the living room, which still held brown wicker settees, an upright piano with chipped brownish keys like neglected teeth, and glassed-in bookcases. Even the painting over the fireplace, a hunter and two red setters stalking their prey through dark woods, made Diana think of the 1920s. The rest of the doors along the hallway were closed.

Life at Heart's Retreat had been reduced to living in the large kitchen. The modern stove and refrigerator looked tiny and out of scale, like toy furniture dropped between the wide double sinks and tall cupboards. Bookcases and pieces of overstuffed furniture had been overlaid like a double negative. Someone with a sense of humor had framed a "worklist" from 1933 and posted it above the stove. The list of character-building chores that each girl had to perform began with "Polish silver napkin rings" and ended with "Pick and arrange flowers for the commode."

On her last visit the current girls had been slouched in the alcove at the far end of the room watching TV. Today the brown plaid couch was empty, though the television was on. A host demonstrated an electronic flea collar on the shopper's bargain channel.

Diana looked questioningly at Eileen.

"I've got them upstairs on the rack."

Housemother humor. It was axiomatic that an observer's presence changed the reality being studied. Still, maybe she could work the quote in somewhere.

She sat down at a white wooden table whose matching chairs had fairy-tale spires—more dollhouse furniture.

Eileen placed a cup of coffee on the yellow-checked vinyl tablecloth in front of her, and shoved over an open box of Munchkins

16

from Dunkin' Donuts. Diana chose a doughnut hole; her stomach turned over as she bit into the glaze.

"This bunch *hates* getting up in the morning," Eileen added, sitting down across from her and taking a sip from a floral cup that proclaimed her World's Best Mother. "Girls used to be more ambitious. This bunch just doesn't care."

"Don't they have to follow any schedule?"

"Only if they have a tutor coming. Shane lost another one last week with her fresh mouth."

"What happened?" But she didn't listen to the answer. Shane wouldn't deliver her baby for another month and Diana would be gone before then. Besides, Diana thought that a thirteen-year-old should give her baby to someone more capable of caring for it. "How's Crystal?"

Eileen let her eyes wander to the TV and back. "I guess I can tell you."

"What?" Crystal Andresen was the girl Diana had chosen to track, following her from life in the maternity home to signing surrenders and placing her baby with an adoptive couple. Had she decided to keep the baby herself? A wave of coffee licked at her stomach, then subsided.

"Her baby was born Tuesday night. But it was stillborn."

"What?" The room pulled in on Diana, sharpening the colors of the orange doughnut box and red mug in her hand; the TV voice, now advertising a shortwave radio, exploded in her ears. *There goes the whole story. And I really need the money!*

Eileen lowered her voice to a husky whisper that Diana had to strain to understand. "The baby only weighed four pounds."

"But why didn't you call me?" Instead, this woman sat here drinking coffee and chatting about Shane.

The housemother was shaking her dark head sadly—at her own negligence? "I wanted to. But Crystal made me promise not to say anything to anybody. She was so upset that I went along with it."

"But why didn't she want me to know?" She thought that she

17

and Crystal had a good relationship. At least, Crystal seemed to admire the way Diana lived. And despite what Eileen said, she was ambitious. Crystal floated above the whole situation as if the home were a boarding house and she a career girl on her way to better things—she was civil to the common folk, but in a way that indicated she would soon be leaving them behind.

"Who can say?" Eileen dropped her voice again. "Between you and me, she's embarrassed. She thinks she let you down."

"Well—she couldn't help it! But why didn't you call me when she went into labor? I thought that was the deal. That I would be there when the baby was born."

Eileen pouched her lips defensively. "Well, I would have. But I had no idea how to reach you at one A.M. You're not in the phone book. By the time the agency opened, it was all over."

"Didn't I give you my phone number?" She knew she had.

"If you did, I don't know what I did with it."

Yeah, right. "Crystal's still at the hospital?"

"No. She's upstairs."

"Upstairs here? They discharged her *already?*" She put down her cup and stood up to go see her.

But Eileen waved her back down. "I don't think she's up to seeing anyone."

"But I have to see her!"

Eileen wavered.

"At least to say good-bye. She'll be leaving, won't she?"

"Oh." It was as if she hadn't thought of that. "I'll see what she says." But first she brought over the glass pot from the coffeemaker and poured fresh cups for them both.

When Eileen had disappeared, Diana crossed to the alcove and snapped off the TV, then sat back down at the table. It did not compute. The night before last Crystal had gone to the hospital and had a baby. The baby, after what everybody assured Diana was at least a year of pregnancy, weighed four pounds. Crystal didn't want her to know anything about it.

18

Maybe Crystal was feeling guilty now about not wanting the baby. Maybe she thought that her attitude had caused the stillbirth. At last week's visit, she had patted the enormous expanse of red jersey that read PIGGING OUT FOR TWO, and complained, "My due date was three weeks ago! I want the little creep *out.*"

"It'll be over soon."

"I know I'm going to have stretch marks!"

Diana dumped milk into her coffee morosely. Sometimes she thought she had connected with people, then found out they didn't even like her. Crystal wouldn't be the first—it had started with her own adoptive mother. And growing up in a small farming town where decent women and their daughters prided themselves on blond home permanents, Scottish lineage, and flat chests, everyone had looked askance at her long black hair and olive skin. People around there were always on the alert for Mohawk blood. Her well-curved body had confirmed people in their prejudices. *She'll sleep with anyone, that girl.*

College and living abroad had, at least, made her more discriminating in who she slept with.

Eileen came clumping back down the servants' stairs. Wearing the doorway like a picture frame, she announced, "She'll only talk if nobody asks her about the baby."

Diana laughed. There was always the weather and the home shopping channel. Where do you buy those cute T-shirts, Ms. Andresen?

As if she had been waiting on the steps, Crystal moved quickly into the room, shaking back her long apricot hair. A tight black T-shirt advising READ MY HIPS in gold emphasized her milk-swollen breasts; the metal fastener to her jeans was undone at the top. She still looked healthy, all-American, but the skin around her delicate nose and chin was pinched. For the first time Diana noticed that she had freckles.

"Hi," Diana said.

"Right." Crystal sat down gingerly in a chair on Diana's left. As

19

Eileen planted herself across from the girl, Diana gave her a questioning look. She was used to interviewing the girls in private.

Crystal intercepted the message. "I *want* her to stay."

Had she offended this girl so badly that they needed a referee? "Is it my mouthwash?"

"No, no, it's not you; it's *me*. I'm just—pissed off. I can't stop bleeding and my body is all screwed up. They never said it would be like this." She turned her green eyes on Diana. *You didn't say it would be like this, either.*

"She's learned her lesson, right, kiddo?" The housemother gave Crystal's arm a gentle sock.

"Christ!" Crystal rolled her eyes at Diana and rubbed at her elbow. "You can write about how we get beaten up around here." Then her expression turned dramatically mournful. "They said he was all wrapped up in the umbilical cord. He was probably dead for weeks."

So much for not talking about it.

"Crystal!" Eileen demanded, jerking up in her seat with surprise. "Who said that?"

"The doctor. *You* weren't there." She took her hand and demonstrated with a loop of hair around her neck, then bugged her eyes and let her pretty head droop.

"That's not funny!" Eileen was horrified. "You're talking about a soul precious to Jesus."

"Right. Sorry."

"But didn't I see the baby kick on my last visit?" They both looked at Diana. "I just mean, it couldn't have been weeks. What did your boyfriend say?"

"What boyfriend?" Crystal gave a rapid look at Eileen, then returned to her chipped orange nails. One had what was left of a palm tree decal.

Diana reminded her. "Your high school sweetheart. The one who was dying of leukemia." You said you slept with him only once, so he could have the experience of love before expiring.

20

Crystal, slumped down so far in her chair that the white wooden spires gave her a Viking crown, then rallied. "He got better."

Eileen was looking frankly disbelieving. Maybe she should have been sitting in on the previous interviews to keep the teenagers honest.

Diana had liked the dying boyfriend herself. "Crys, if you weren't having the baby 'so that his spirit could live on' "—and all that other crap you told me—"why didn't you just get an abortion when you found you were pregnant?"

As expected, Eileen inhaled sharply at the word.

"My mother wouldn't let me."

"But you're seventeen."

Crystal made a rueful face. "We went to the doctor, and he talked about how he treated all these women who wanted babies and couldn't have them—so he didn't think he could abort a baby when there were all these great homes waiting."

"I should hope not!" Eileen, scandalized, all but crossed herself. "Nine months is a short time in a girl's life when there's a life at stake."

"This is Dr. Hazelton?" Diana asked. She already planned to see him to get the names of some of the adoptive couples who had profited from his advice.

"He said we would have to go over to Long Island, that no one would do it here. He made it sound really horrible. But it couldn't have been more horrible than this!" She looked tearful.

Diana nodded. "So what are you going to do now?"

"Oh—who knows? Get on with my career, I guess." She pinched the bulge at her waist. "As soon as I get rid of this!"

"Your *career?*" What did a pencil line of fat have to do with finishing high school and college and becoming a psychologist? Or a journalist?

"Well—I'm really into modeling. I met someone from the city who said he could get me a job."

Crystal's prettiness made it more than a come-on, but less than

21

an offer from the Ford Agency. "But what about school?"

"I have it all planned. As soon as I can, I'll get my high school equivalency, then take college courses at night. Money's no problem."

"Money's *always* a problem. But I have some contacts in the city. My boyfriend's a photographer with *Vogue*. Let's go get pizza and talk."

"Really? That's cool. But you just want to fatten me up so I'll stay in school." Still, she started to get up. Eileen's hand darted out, pinning her wrist to the table.

"I don't think she's well enough yet. She just had a baby, remember?"

Crystal sat back, compliant. Diana realized that, for all her brave ideas, Crystal could not challenge adults.

THREE

Caroline lay on the rug in the nursery, surrounded by the blanketing scent of gardenias and roses. When she opened her eyes she could see the notched tails of white and yellow ribbons and look up at the shiny, cut-out words: *Beloved Grandson; An Angel in Heaven;* and, simply, *Regrets.* Lying below them, it felt like being dead herself. After the funeral, instead of taking the arrangements to the cemetery, she had brought them home. Joe was worried that she was wallowing in grief. But you had to feel it, to know everything there was to know about something, before you could go on.

Lifting her head, she felt the impression of the stiff braided rug along her cheek. Yesterday, driving to the funeral on Long Island, she had been distracted for a moment by two clowns whose balloon-filled van had broken down—headed to a birthday party? a circus?—and had forgotten for a minute where she was going. Then this morning in the kitchen she had panicked, thinking *It's past time to feed the baby,* before she remembered. Each time it came back to her, the shock was as strong as when she first discovered him.

She became aware of a pounding downstairs, a leisurely, rhythmic knocking. No doubt it was UPS at the door. Like a faucet nobody could turn off, baby gifts kept flowing in. Joe had told her not to open them, that he would mail them back with a note. But she was resisting that. She wanted the presents waiting for him when Zach got home.

That was the real thing she could not get over, that her baby was out there somewhere. They had buried a baby that was not Zach. That was the truth. The time in between when she had gone into the nursery and there had been no baby in the crib now seemed the key. But she had known at once, even in the rocking chair, that he felt heavier and looked different. And yet . . . she knew that shock could do strange things. There were all those experiments where a "gunman" comes in carrying a banana, shoots someone, and the witnesses swear afterward they saw him holding a gun. What if she had been half asleep, out of cloth diapers, and put some sample disposable on him without even noticing it?

But if she truly believed it was Zach dead, they would have had a very different service. They would have played children's songs, inspirational songs, and released white balloons into the air; instead of stiff funeral parlor flowers, donations would have gone to UNICEF or the Sudden Infant Death Association. It would have been sad but uplifting, instead of . . . murky.

At the funeral mass, during the litany in which the baby's soul was consigned to paradise, Joe had kept his arm tightly around her, as if he was afraid she would flail out of control. But it had also felt, she realized now, as if he were holding her down, as if he were afraid that she was going to turn around and start yelling that the baby was not Zach. She would never have done that, of course. The baby in the tiny white box, whoever he was, deserved a dignified burial. Yet when she first came in and saw that the funeral director had propped a photograph of Zach in a white ceramic frame on top of the casket, she had moved rapidly to take it down. Joe, watching, had not stopped her; but no doubt it added to his fears.

Tightening the Winnie the Pooh quilt around her shoulders, she

24

watched the shadow of the flowers on the ceiling. Suppose they *had* buried some other baby—where were his parents? Why hadn't she read anything in the paper about a child being kidnapped? He had to belong to someone. Maybe she should go to the papers herself. If she gave them Zach's description . . . Yes, that's what she would do!

The pounding continued. It wasn't UPS; they knocked once, then left the package propped up against the door. This knocking indicated that someone had recognized her car and knew that she was home. One of her friends from school probably, though she had not encouraged anyone to come by. As quickly as she could, she pushed herself up off the floor, teetering for a moment on her weak leg. She bunched the quilt around her and limped down the stairs and through the hall.

Opening the door, trying to make herself smile, she was startled by the man in the navy overcoat. That short sandy hair and flattened face . . . Rafe Millar, of course. She felt a twist of fear in her stomach. She remembered how he had seemed to despise her.

Yet he seemed agreeable enough today; he was actually smiling. "Wake you up?"

"No—I don't know." No need to be polite. Her hand brushed at her twisted blond hair. He was seeing her unkempt again, wrapped in a blanket, with a strange pattern across her cheek. "Come on in."

Then a small, dark-haired man she hadn't noticed before, a man with the pointed face of a dachshund, appeared behind Millar. She saw that he wore a herringbone overcoat with a brown velvet collar, the kind of coat she had not seen in years.

"Mr. Denecke home?" Millar asked pleasantly.

"No. He had to go back to school today."

"No kidding."

"They only allowed him two days." Pass Days, they were called. The amount of days off depended on who had died. To the Saint David's administration, losing an adopted child so soon after birth

25

was an inconvenience, not a tragedy. Of course, they had seen Joe lose Lisa to leukemia years before Caroline knew him. How had he survived that? At the cemetery yesterday they had seen her small alabaster stone, with its carved lamb and a photo inset of a smiling child with brown bangs.

Seeing Lisa's grave had been a shock, putting the baby's death in a context Caroline had not considered before. She had remembered that Joe's mother would be buried there—but not his daughter. Odd to think she herself had only been in high school when Lisa died.

Had he dreaded seeing Lisa's grave? The morning after they found the baby he had sat in the den for hours without the lights on, without speaking. Caroline had moved in and out of the room, pausing so that they could hug each other. Yesterday at the funeral he had talked to everyone without saying anything. But this morning he had eaten his usual breakfast of bran flakes, and read the sports page. He had actually laughed at something in the comics, and smiled when he kissed her good-bye. In truth he seemed relieved to be getting away from it all and going back to school. Didn't he realize that the baby had been a tiny version of the boys he taught—but one who would never grow up?

The two men came inside, bringing a rush of March air. She saw that the other policeman was carrying a black satchel like a doctor's bag.

"Last room on the left." Millar pointed the man toward the stairs.

Why were they checking the room out? Maybe they did believe someone had broken in! "What did you find out?" she asked Millar.

But he gestured her deeper into the house, as if directing her to a place where they could talk. Obediently she led him through the hall, the kitchen, and into the octagonal greenhouse that jutted into the backyard. The orange straw placemats from Barbados and her coffee cup remained on the glass-topped table. Even though it was nearly noon, the grayness of the day was like a blind drawn. The winter ivy outside, the stockade fence around the pool, and the remains of the rose garden seemed misted in. "Can I get you anything?"

He stared at her with lidded eyes. "I'll take tea. If you have it."

"Sure." She moved across the threshold back into the kitchen, and set out two thick white mugs. Draping the tea bags inside, she tried to cope with a leaden disappointment. Surely if he had found Zachary, he would already have said so. Unless . . . Filling a black kettle spotted like a cow, she fought the terrible idea of another dead baby.

Without waiting for the tea to steep she carried the cups into the greenhouse, then went back and cut two pieces of the apple cake someone had brought to the house after the funeral.

Millar, shifting his stocky frame against the white wire gazebo chair, looked resentful. As she put the cake down in front of him, she saw that his gray suit jacket was stretched out in the elbows. He did not acknowledge the food. "How come you're limping?"

"I hurt my foot when I was a child." She was used to explaining it to her classes. "Some boys were chasing me when I was seven, just playing, but I darted in front of a car." The fender had only grazed her, knocked her down, but the tire had crushed her toes. They had ended up amputating part of her foot.

When she finished the story he looked through the glass table, as if he could see into her slipper sock. "Not that bad," he diagnosed. "My brother lost half his leg to a tractor. Went right on playing football."

Well, I didn't do that. "Doctor, will I be able to play football after my operation? That's wonderful, I didn't know how before." Actually she loved sports, she and Joe both did. Sometimes she thought he had forgotten her foot completely.

"Your limp has nothing to do with what happened to your kid?" Millar was saying.

"Of course not. How could it?" But she smiled; she didn't want to offend him.

27

There was a pause. He seemed to be cataloging the plants in the room, the Christmas cactus and umbrella trees, the two Red Lion amaryllises still in bloom. Then he got up and walked into the kitchen. She watched, puzzled, as he went over to the refrigerator. Didn't he see that there was already milk on the table? He seemed to be looking at the farewell drawings her class had made her, and Joe's magnetized school notices. Then he extracted a photo of Zach in a small red metal frame and brought it over. The baby was yawning, eyes squinched together. She had taken it just after he finished eating. *Sweet baby, my Milky Mouth.*

"Cute kid."

Now she couldn't keep back the tears. Pressing her hands against her face like a child, she wept, shoulders shaking, for several minutes. It was all so unfair! Finally she pulled a napkin out of the wooden rooster holder and ran it all over her face.

"A tragedy," Millar pronounced. The words were right, but the voice sounded somehow insincere. He propped the photo up against the side of his hand, Zach facing her. "He give you any trouble?"

"Trouble?" What kind of trouble could a newborn baby give you?

"I bet he cried a lot."

"No. Just when he was hungry. Or when he wanted company. He *could* be demanding. But that was part of his charm."

"Kept you on your toes, I'll bet," he smiled. "They always do. Hubby, too?"

"Well, Joe didn't actually get up with him in the night. But it woke him up."

"So tell me about the day it happened. Monday. Did you go out? Anybody see you?"

She tried to think. This was important. Had she gone out for groceries or to the one-hour photo shop again? Had she answered the door for UPS while holding Zach? Closing her eyes, she put herself back into Monday. It had been overcast, much like today. The ground, when she went out to the mailbox, had seemed damp. That morning she had washed a load of diapers, and written some thank-you notes, then read the paper. When Zach was awake, she played with him. Hadn't she done anything else? "I talked to my mother in the afternoon," she said finally.

He perked up. "She live around here?"

"No. South Carolina. It was on the phone."

"Pretty isolated, huh?"

"No, not really; it's a retirement community. They—"

"I meant you."

"But—I wanted to stay home!"

He hadn't touched his tea. "It's not always like you expect." He said it conversationally, as if he were commenting on the weather.

"It was quiet, that was true. But—"

"An educated type like yourself, a teacher and all, I bet you thought you knew all about it."

"I didn't—"

"Listen to me!" He leaned across the glass table. His breath close to her face was warm, a little musky. "Real life isn't like books. In real life when the kid cries, sometimes he won't stop. Hubby keeps complaining he needs his sleep, you put a pillow over the kid's face—not to hurt him, just to turn down the volume a little. Something like that happens before you know it."

"What?" The pounding she had heard before had started up again, but this time it was inside her head. "You think I did that?"

"It happens before you know it," he said soberly. "You can't believe it happened. I see it all the time, guys get pissed at their wives, before they know it, bam! You can't believe it happened."

"No! That's sick." She meant the accusation, not the action. The whole idea was ludicrous; a "hubby" who needed his sleep!

"It was an accident," he suggested. "One of those things."

"But you said—I thought—it was a crib death."

He ran a stern hand over the gray-blond bristles of his hair. "I never said that."

"But what did he die from then?" She had to remind herself that it was not Zach, it was a different baby.

She felt him watching her, a camera ready to snap her reaction. "Preliminary autopsy says he was smothered."

"Oh, *God.*" She felt something inside her slip and give way, a boat loosed from its moorings. Growing up on the water she had seen that happen often. "But—how could they do that to a baby?"

"How could Susan Smith do it to two babies?" He flipped open a small black notebook and began to read. "Contusions around his mouth and his nose, Mrs. Denecke. Other signs of asphyxiation. You'd better pray the same material doesn't show up in the crib."

"What?" She spread her fingers around the mug of tea, clutching its warmth.

"Woman out west, kept smothering her daughters when she had girls instead of boys. Told the police they had been 'kidnapped.' She's in jail now."

"But I didn't—I could never, *never*—"

He stood up. "Not like it was your own kid."

"That's a terrible thing to say!"

"We'll see what the forensics from upstairs tell us. Anytime you want to talk . . ." Taking out a thick black wallet held closed by a rubber band, he extracted a business card. "I'll be back."

He left her sitting there, staring at the reflection of the white rectangle in the glass tabletop.

She stayed in the greenhouse for long minutes, unable to even consider moving. How could he think—he was lying about the baby being smothered, he had to be. But he certainly wanted to blame her for something.

What finally made her able to move was her need to call Joe. He would still be in class, but she could leave a message to have him call. Stumbling past untidy stacks of cookbooks and half-made herb wreaths to reach the wall phone, she wondered if Millar had condemned her for sloppiness as well.

At the phone her finger slipped and she pressed a nine instead of a six. Depressing the switch hook, she started dialing again. If Joe was there it would mean it was all a mistake and would turn out to be nothing. And if he wasn't? For several seconds she could not take a breath. Then she reminded herself that looking for signs was just a silly game.

This time the call went through. When the school secretary answered, she heard herself ask for Joe.

"Is this Caroline? I'm sorry, but he's left for a swim meet."

"Where?"

"On Long Island. If he calls in, I can have him call you. Otherwise, he'll be back about four. Is something *wrong?*"

For a moment she wanted to tell Jean what had happened, and hear her disbelief that anyone could think that Joe or Caroline would hurt a child. She needed the outrage, Jean's shocked, "The idea! Why I'd trust you with my own grandchildren!" But she held back. Thirty-seven years had taught her that people had a dark place inside that wanted to believe the unthinkable, a darkness that wanted to be shocked, to believe that even people who appeared above reproach were no better than they themselves. "No. Thanks, Jean." She hung up quickly.

Next she wanted to call her parents. *They* knew she was not capable of hurting a baby. She started to dial their number, then stopped. Hearing that she was being accused by the police would make them frantic. Her father with his heart patch; her mother with her protective sympathy. She was the good daughter. Amazing how she remembered her own childhood as so happy when Ruthie's memories were so bitter. Sailing with her father, baking with her mother, cocoa before bed. A cliché of a childhood. She had let them down only once, in college, but they had not even known about it.

No, she could not call them. Shakily, she returned to the table in the greenhouse. Was it possible that Susan had taken her baby back? It didn't make sense, she had never wanted him! But still . . . She swirled her finger through a drop of spilled tea.

31

Susan had come at the end of their journey, after the calls to the agencies, after her visits to Dr. Hazelton and the discreet mention to their friends that they were looking to adopt a baby. Caroline had first called Crane Island Social Services and been told that there were few adoptable babies and a waiting list of years. By that time she would be close to forty and Joe in his late fifties. And since he had already had two daughters, they could not be given priority as "childless."

The private agencies were worse. Some objected to the fact that Joe was Catholic and she was Lutheran, and that he had been married and divorced; others minded the sixteen-year difference in their ages and that Joe was over fifty. All advised her that to adopt an infant could take years. Since the medical examination had not discovered any reason why Caroline had not become pregnant, Dr. Hazelton had counseled patience.

But Caroline was not a patient person—at least not when she wanted something so badly. Joe had been against placing an ad, but she had persisted, and it ran in the local *Pennysaver* and the *Crane Island Advance:* Happily married professional couple want to provide your newborn with a warm and loving home. Expenses paid. Please call Alicia and Jeffrey at 447-2928. The woman at the newspaper office had advised her not to use their real names. She had also told Caroline not to get her hopes up.

So she had been unprepared when Susan called the next night. She was already six months gone, she said, and needed to "make arrangements."

Their first meeting had been the night after that in a salmon vinyl booth at the Sunshine Diner. Susan turned out to be a small, thin girl with blunt-cut black hair and a businesslike frown, her narrow fingers covered with silver rings. While they watched, she devoured two wedges of lemon meringue pie—then looked up suddenly with a radiant smile. Caroline had been captivated. Imagine a child with that smile. It was an expression that could enchant the world!

"It's a boy," Susan said with satisfaction. "That's what the sono-gram said."

"Ooh," Caroline sighed.

"Who's the father?" Joe demanded.

Caroline felt herself wince.

"Just a guy."

"What does he think about the baby?"

She frowned, annoyed. "He doesn't *know.*"

"No good. How do we know he won't show up afterwards and decide he wants the child?"

"He won't. I don't even know his last name!"

"How about you? Any drugs? Or alcohol?"

Caroline gave Joe an imploring look. Why was he doing this? She wished she had met with Susan by herself, but that would have been impossible.

"I do a little grass once in a while. But that's all."

Eventually she agreed to have an HIV test. But the sticking point had been money.

"Somebody told me I could get thirty thousand dollars. I'm miss-ing a year of school."

Joe had put down his cup of tea and stared at her, his blue eyes cold. He acted like she was one of his students who had gotten out of line. "Medical and living expenses. That's what's *legal.*"

Why was he treating her that way? Caroline held her breath, pressing her palms together in prayer. *Please, please, please, don't let him scare her off.*

Susan sat, dark head bent so far that they could see her white part, her chin on her palms. "Twenty," she said finally. "But you have to pay the hospital. I mean, you have to put me on your medical insurance."

"How do you expect me to do that?"

"They admit me under your wife's name. That way your names are already on the birth certificate, see? It won't even have to go to court. He'll just be yours."

Then, like a salesperson reeling in a deal, Caroline thought, Susan had gotten up and gone to the ladies room, leaving them to talk. Her sandaled feet, wide for such a small girl, slapped the floor, ducklike, as she moved past them.

"It's too much money," Joe said flatly. "She won't even give us her last name or tell us anything about the father."

"But she *says* she's healthy," Caroline pleaded. "She looks fine!"

"She may be fine, but what about him? We don't even know what color he is."

Was that what this was all about? "So we'll ask." Remembering her feelings for Tiffany, she realized the answer wouldn't matter to her. But she would have to respect Joe's feelings.

"We'll save on lawyers' fees," she added, half joking. "Joe, *please.*" *If you do this for me, I'll never ask for anything again.*

When Susan came back he was more civil. She told them that the baby's father was Italian—or maybe Polish. They settled on hospitalization and $18,000. Coming up with the money after so recently buying the house had wiped out their savings. But that didn't matter. Seeing Susan's belly, round with new life, it seemed to Caroline like the only thing they could have done. Susan had left the maternity ward on Joe's arm and in the parking lot he had taken Zach from her. She had gone to another car and gotten in. They never had found out her last name.

Caroline put her head down on her arms. Susan had been no weepy teenager having doubts about giving up her child. Caroline had been ready to send her photos and progress reports, to stay in touch. But Susan had not been interested. It had been more like a sale to her than anything else. Besides, if Susan had changed her mind, she would have just kept Zach.

Unless she was greedy and wanted the money and the baby, too. Or unless she had promised him to another couple, as well. *Find Susan.*

The wave of fatigue that came over her then was so strong that she could barely stay upright in the chair. She fought the urge to curl up on the blue ceramic tile floor and sleep. Pushing herself up, she headed for the bed upstairs. That was what she needed, sleep.

Caroline was mashing potatoes when she heard the front door open. On waking she had decided it was just as well that Joe hadn't called. They should eat dinner, drink some wine, before they discussed it.

She saw him take in the scene from the kitchen door, blinking at the paisley placemats set on the table in the greenhouse, the white candles flickering against the glass. Then he moved to hug her, lifting her slightly from the floor. She laughed, protesting. His turquoise windbreaker smelled of the smoke from someone's chimney, and his cheeks, next to his silvery hair, were unusually rosy. Something moved far inside her, but she pushed it away. *Not now.*

But soon another reason for his exuberance emerged. His team had won all six events, including the butterfly relay, which was a complete upset. "I've been pushing these kids for months and they finally did it! We *may* just have a team."

She drained the peas and took the fried chicken out of the oven. Comfort food, she realized, squishy and familiar.

"Even wine!" Joe said when they sat down and he saw the bottle of Beaujolais she had opened. "Just like old times."

Old times? Now that Zachary had come and gone, a glorious sunset that glowed briefly before the sky turned black, how could there ever be old times again? As she lowered her head to spoon gravy, her eyes swamped with tears. Replacing the spoon, she fingered her fork but could not pick it up.

She heard Joe sigh. "Caro?"

"I'm okay."

"You have to eat."

"I will." But she could not move.

Gently he pressed the spoon into her potatoes and made a gravy pool. He added peas to the side.

"I'm okay," she wept. "It's just—the police were here today. They think we smothered Zach."

"What?" He put down his wine glass and stared at her. "What are you talking about?"

She wiped at one eye. "That policeman, that Rafe Millar was here today. I tried to call you, but you'd left."

"And he said we *smothered* the baby?"

"Well, he tried to get me to say it."

"But that's crazy!"

"He said there were marks around his face. But that may have come after, when I tried giving him first aid. Maybe that . . . left something."

Joe nodded slowly.

She leaned forward. "But if the baby wasn't Zach, if he had been left there in his place, then it doesn't matter. I mean, like he said, he had been dead a long time. Wasn't that what he was so mad about that night?"

But he waved that aside as irrelevant.

"How did you leave it with him?"

She shrugged. "He said he'd be back."

He pushed back the metal chair. "I'm calling Martin!"

"Martin Lenihan?" Martin, Joe's boyhood friend, had handled his divorce. When he drew up their wills after the wedding, he had treated Caroline's contribution to the estate as negligible, even though her public school salary was higher than Joe's.

He paused, hand still on the edge of the table. One of the candles flickered. "What's wrong with Martin?"

"You know he doesn't like me."

"It's nothing personal. He doesn't like any women." He moved into the kitchen toward the white telephone. "He's my best friend. Do you know how much it costs to call a lawyer you *don't* know?"

My God—the money! She hadn't even thought about having to pay a lawyer. Joe was right, it could cost thousands. If they were arrested . . . Even if they had a trial and were found innocent, they'd still have to pay someone. It was a nightmare they would never wake up from.

Joe turned away from her so she could not hear what he was saying. But he was back very soon. "Marty said not to talk to the police anymore."

"Really?"

"Not without an attorney present. He's going to refer us to someone good. But he thinks this Millar is just trying to kick ass. They all do that when they don't know what else to do." Talking to another good old boy had evidently calmed Joe.

"But . . . won't it look suspicious if we don't cooperate?"

"Look—just do what he says."

"But I'm not sure he's right! Won't it look like we have something to hide? Anyway, he's not a criminal lawyer."

"That's why he's going to get us the name of one."

"But won't someone else be expensive?"

Glumly he picked up the platter of chicken. "Let's hope it doesn't get that far."

She sat with her chin in her hands. When he came back for the potatoes and vegetables, she said, "Rafe Millar asked me who saw Zach alive that last day and I couldn't think of anybody. Any other day I probably could have! But you saw me feed him at midnight."

Joe rubbed the back of his neck. "Did I?"

"Didn't you?"

"I may have been already asleep."

"You didn't hear me get up?" She pressed her palms against the glass table. "But you saw him at nine-thirty," she prompted. "I brought him downstairs. You were watching TV."

His face went blank. "What was I watching?"

"I don't know!" she screamed, surprising them both. "Try and remember!"

Joe pursed his lips. "It must have been basketball. Saint John's basketball. You used to watch it with me."

"But you saw us," she begged.

"I know I played with him *sometime* that night."

She felt herself exhale. "And he was fine."

"Of course he was fine. They have to be wrong about the time."

"It's not the time! This has nothing to do with time!"

"Stop shouting, please."

"Then don't say stupid things!"

He moved behind her, kneading her shoulder with one hand. "Caro, look: They're just trying to scare you. They're fishing. Don't talk to them again without Martin. That's all."

He picked up the wine glasses and Beaujolais and walked back into the kitchen.

The wax from the candles was starting to drip on the table. Caroline blew out the flames but kept sitting there. Suddenly furious, she yelled, "I feel like you're leaving me to handle this by myself."

That brought him back out quickly. "What are you talking about? I called Martin, I told you what to do. He thinks they're on a fishing expedition."

She started to ask Joe if he had told Martin about the autopsy, then realized she hadn't told Joe. Well, she didn't have the strength to do it now. She knew that he was thinking that they had been happy before with each other, that they should have left well enough alone. That if she hadn't pushed to have a child, none of this would have happened.

She couldn't deny that.

FOUR

Crane Island Department of Social Services was located in a building that had once been the island's central high school. The lobby still held a brass eagle and World War I Honor Roll, as well as the names and initials of vanished students carved on the oak windowsills. But now, instead of trophies, the glass cases lining the walls held posters about AIDS testing and food stamp eligibility. Rows of orange plastic bucket seats had been bolted to the fine marble floor. Since smoking was prohibited in public buildings and no ashtrays were provided, people ground out their cigarettes under their shoes.

Diana was amused and scandalized by the signs put up by Public Assistance workers. Taped to the receptionist's glass booth was the notice: "This is not Burger King. You do not get it your way. You get it our way, or not at all." Another sign, photocopied crookedly, showed a poorly drawn woman, grinning and pointing a gun: "Go ahead. Lay one more thing on my desk!"

As she came in, a skeletal man on crutches was pleading with the receptionist. She heard him mention food stamps. There was no question that he was very ill. Watching him, she backed into a young black woman in a white knit cap with racing stripes.

The woman grabbed at Diana's red parka. "Listen, motherfucker, where did you put my kids?"

A smell of urine. "Your kids?"

The woman edged closer. "You've got fifteen minutes to give them back. Phyllis Clapp don't mess around."

"What happened to them, Phyllis?"

But curiosity was the wrong approach. The woman stared at her, then retreated, mumbling, to lean against the wall.

Diana walked to the grand staircase in back, and up past the second floor that housed Child and Adult Protective Services. On the top floor, where Foster Care, Day Care, and Adoption were located, the tone of the posters changed. Diana had copied some of them into her notebook: "Those who haven't seen the dead come back to life have never been here at 5:00 o'clock" and "The only difference between this place and the *Titanic* was that they had a band."

Stepping into the Adoption Unit was going from black and white into Kodacolor. It was a surprising and different world. On the walls were Renoir prints and calendars showing photographs of English gardens. A small white table held a coffeemaker, napkins, and a tin of Scottish shortbread. Every desk but the one loaned to Diana was dense with plants and interesting accessories, though Marci Potamkin's focused on the theme of snakes. Except for a Magritte poster of blue sky and clouds, left by someone else, her own area was bare. She could at least buy a blotter, she was starting to spend enough time here.

Although her assignment was to scrutinize adoption in the nineties and illustrate it by statistics and strong case histories, she had hopes of going beyond the magazine article. What she really needed to establish herself was a book. Something like *House* by Tracy Kidder or the one about the welfare mother. Adoption was a topic that, like tossing water on hot coals, brought forth a rush of response.

The unit seemed deserted. Diana wondered if Howard had forgotten their lunch date. Only the secretary, Pearl Kong, was sitting at her desk, her tomato sandwich dripping all over the *New York Post*. She didn't look up or speak to Diana. She never did.

Without bothering to unzip her parka, Diana picked up the island phone directory and found Sidney Hazelton listed under "Physicians and Surgeons." She knelt on her padded vinyl chair and dialed quickly.

"Surgery."

At first she thought she had dialed the wrong number, then remembered that the obstetrician was English. "Yes. Dr. Hazelton, please."

"Are you a patient of Doctor's?"

"Not yet."

"We require that new patients come in first for an interview," the voice warned.

"I'd like that."

"Well—good!"

"As soon as possible."

"Hold on." A flapping of pages. "I have a cancellation today at five-twenty. Otherwise it will be four weeks."

"I'll come today."

"Name?"

"Diana Larsen."

"Health insurance?"

"Yes." She hung up.

Crane Island was still a small place. Only one other obstetrician was listed with that specialty. The Great Man's wife, Dolly Hazelton, worked in the Adoption Unit and, in fact, was coming through the door. It was a strong temptation not to disguise Dolly, but to leave her in the article just as she was: a cheerful Lady Bountiful whose life was a Martha Stewart moment. Her perfectly cut golden hair and round rosy cheeks gave her the glow of Buster Brown. The skin around her bright blue eyes was unlined. Evidently Dr. Hazelton did a few face-lifts on the side.

"Diana, hello!" Fishing a gold compact out of her Mark Cross bag, she continued, "How's our Crystal?"

Diana stared at her. *Do I just blurt it out?*

"Didn't you see her this morning?" Dolly prompted. "She must be ready to pop."

Diana fiddled with her canvas bag. "You didn't hear?"

"Diana, no!" Marci Potamkin, coming in at that moment, clutched her molded Styrofoam container of salad as if it were being threatened. Her chartreuse raincoat gaped to show a tan sweater with a roaring tiger's face. A red headband in her salt and pepper curls matched the tiger's tongue. "What happened? She's keeping the baby?"

"Worse than that."

"What?" Dolly.

"He was stillborn."

"When?"

"Tuesday night."

"But—" She shifted through the papers on her desk and retrieved a pink message slip. "Eileen *did* call yesterday afternoon. I guess that's what it was about. But she could have said something!"

"Diana, we really needed that baby," Marci wailed. "The family will be devastated."

"I don't believe it," Dolly said. "When I saw her last week, he was kicking up a storm."

"That's what I thought," Diana agreed.

Marci gave a brave sniff. "How are the others?"

"I don't know. I didn't see them."

"Stillborn!" Dolly could not get over it. "And she had such wonderful prenatal care."

"Right from the beginning she was going to surrender," Marci mourned.

Diana watched as Marci opened her Greek salad and frowned at it. *Surrender* was such a strange term for giving up a baby for adoption. Diana pictured the girls lined up, waving white flags. Strange that the adoption establishment would use a word that implied defeat, a throwing down of arms. A throwing up of arms. Giving up. What did one have left after one surrendered? Probably years of denial that anything had happened.

Howard Liebowitz returned to the unit just before one. "Bet you thought I forgot," he called as he disappeared into his office.

"Well . . ."

They walked three blocks to the Bum Steer. The businesses they passed—an appliance repair shop, a tuxedo rental, a real estate office with fading, curling color photographs—did not seem to have changed their displays for years. The restaurant, on the other hand, had been deliberately renovated into a fictitious past. Lit by gas lamps and filled with posters for *Birth of a Nation* and *Limelight,* it reminded Diana of restaurants in London that were deliberately trying to look "American." The same garishly painted wooden Indian that stood in the lobby here was posted out on a sidewalk in South Kensington.

They were shown to a high wooden booth in a corner. Today Howard had on a three-piece navy suit with a gold dress shirt and fat red tie, colors that were becoming to his ruddy skin and bright brown eyes. But his dark curly hair seemed as uncombed as usual, his fingers stained with the ink of the cheap black pens the agency issued.

Diana watched him shuck a peanut. *Clean him up and send him to my tent.*

A waitress, dressed in a Charlie Chaplin tuxedo and little mustache, appeared immediately. Diana ordered cold shrimp on red leaf lettuce and a glass of Chardonnay. Howard selected the diet burger platter and a Coke. The first time they had eaten there and she ordered white wine, he asked, "You *drink* during the day?"

43

"Just wine. I'm French."

"Really? I thought you were from upstate."

She might be part French-Canadian. She had seen a lot of people with her skin color in Provence. "I haven't lived upstate since I was eighteen."

After college she had left the country as soon as she could, traveling and writing a column, *The Eccentric Traveler*. It had eventually been syndicated in most large Sunday travel sections. Although she based herself in Paris, she traveled everywhere. Some of her adventures had been fun—piloting a hot-air balloon over the veldt, going places in Ladakh where tourists were forbidden, comparing public baths in Turkey. But there had been a lot of pressure to come up with a new oddity every week, and she had gotten tired of men who found her as much of a novelty as her adventures—but didn't love her. The black anxiety that enveloped her at odd moments had gotten more frequent. She came home, found a therapist, and cobbled together a freelance living. It didn't seem odd to her that she wrote for both *Women* and *Cosmopolitan*.

The possibility of what she and Howard might be to each other still hung in the air, though she had tried to settle it at their first lunch. Glancing at his left hand, still faintly tanned with a lighter white strip, she had declared, "You look married."

He looked where she was looking. "Well . . . more or less. Two kids."

More or less? She knew *that* type. Never again would she get involved with a married man. She had faced her own neediness in a therapist's office in Brooklyn, in an orange wool tweed chair whose arms had already been plucked to threads. She had relived the year thrown away on the TV correspondent she met in Paris who assured her that his wife would never be allowed to emigrate from Korea, the semester of the American Literature professor who gave her a C for spite.

In a particularly devastating session, Margaret had pointed out to Diana her pattern of trying out different lifestyles, looking for authenticity, then renouncing and abandoning each one. "The thing is, you're almost smart enough to pull it off. It's not as if you fail at anything. You just decide it's not really you, and move on."

"I haven't been a nun." But she had tried farmer's daughter, travel journalist, passionate feminist, and young professional with Erik. Now she was getting restless again; she just didn't know where she was headed.

But she didn't need to replay her pattern of being rejected by unavailable men. In her first conversation with Howard—feeling as if she were inflating a rubber doll—she had brought Erik to life, describing his adventures as a staff photographer for *Vogue*. She had not mentioned that his specialty was photographing hands and chic fingernails. *Get a life.* She had also been vague about the fact that they were now living apart.

They settled back to the tinny sound of "The Maple Leaf Rag," shelling peanuts and dropping the husks on the floor. "I shouldn't be eating these," he mumbled through a mouthful.

"So? Exercise more."

"I play tennis when the sun's out."

"When's that? Once a year?"

He glanced at his straining vest buttons ruefully. "That bad?"

"No." *Naw, Boss. Of course not, Boss.* "I'm just surprised that someone so obsessed with his health doesn't exercise."

"What makes you think I'm obsessed with my health?"

"Howard, how many people keep a portable blood pressure machine in their desk drawer?"

"That was a going-away gift from my old unit! They figured I'd need it with this job. And I do. Wait till you see them tomorrow."

"You mean Baby Day?"

"Thank God the *baby* won't be there. They'd be pulling her apart, trying to grab an arm or leg for their favorite couple. And don't quote that." He pushed the basket of peanuts away from him.

Howard was one of the few people she had ever interviewed who could make the connection between a casual remark and its ap-

45

pearance in print. Amazing, really, the way people assumed she would edit what they said to remove anything unflattering or indiscreet. Most of the time they just wanted a listener; they seemed to feel that telling her things gave legitimacy to their lives.

"How did you know about the blood pressure machine anyway?"

"I snoop."

"I believe it." But then he stroked his mustache, looking serious. "There's a lot of confidential stuff in adoption," he warned. "Things that you might hear about accidentally in the unit and not know not to use."

"But I'm not using real names or situations. You can check the final draft if you like." *What, are you crazy?* "I mean, for breaches of confidentiality in specific instances."

But he still looked dissatisfied. "It's just that our records are sealed. Their contents can't be divulged except by court order."

"Let's not make ourselves too self-important," she felt like saying. She hated it when people put themselves behind the barricades of Law and Order. "I wanted to talk to you about Crystal."

She paused as the androgynous Charlie gave Howard a plate with a naked hamburger and cottage cheese, and placed her shrimp in front of her. Then she told him about her morning. "Very strange the way Eileen wouldn't let Crystal out of her sight," she concluded.

"She was being protective of her?"

"Well . . . yes. You *could* look at it that way. But the fact that she was out of the hospital and walking around so easily a day after giving birth?"

"They release them very fast these days. But what are you trying to say?"

Stop salting that hamburger to death. "That maybe Crystal didn't just have the baby yesterday? But why would they lie about it?"

He spread his hands expressively. "Maybe Eileen Norris was even more derelict in not calling us than she wants to admit. You're right, she didn't call Dolly till the afternoon. But don't forget, when Heart's Retreat was private, the staff was right there on the premises.

46

Dolly will have to make clear to Eileen that she has to call the agency now."

"What about what she said about the birth weight? When everyone said she was overdue."

"You think she was *trying* to mislead you?" He fiddled with his straw. "In a crisis people tend to hear things wrong."

"That's true." The mystery seemed to be dwindling as they spoke. "What's Dr. Hazelton like?"

Howard laughed. "Sid's fine—if you like charming British types with egos the size of England. The expectant mothers of the island adore him. They must be starved for authority."

"Me too. I'm seeing him this afternoon."

"Good luck."

Sidney Hazelton's office was on the outskirts of Martinville in a Tudor-style brick house. Diana opened the door onto an Ellis Island of pregnant women. Some napped, heads thrown back, as if still on the voyage. Others chatted, braided one another's hair, and minded the children at their feet. The room felt close and smelled of chocolate, lemon air freshener, and dirty diapers. Diana stepped over a yellow plastic school bus, but slipped and nearly fell on an issue of *Woman's Day*.

She identified herself to a receptionist who seemed frazzled enough to be a mother herself.

"He's running very late—couldn't you come back?"

"I only have to talk to him a minute. I'm not a patient."

"Oh." She looked back at her book to make sure the name was written down. "Well . . . you can wait in his office, I guess."

She felt a multitude of resentful eyes watching her as she was led down the hall past the examining rooms. Dr. Hazelton's office was what she imagined Park Avenue offices to be like. There was an oriental rug on the wide-planked wooden floor, and an immense cherry desk. On one corner was an arrangement of red and orange tulips that appeared to have been sent by a grateful couple. At least, the card was signed, "Joan, Bill, and Clancy." Why did people give their children names better suited to blue collar workers and terriers?

She moved closer to look at the oil painting behind the desk, of two blond girls in velvet dresses, then chose a red leather wing chair and sat down to wait. Was this where he talked girls like Crystal out of abortions?

"Excuse me?" A lanky man wearing gray pants under a white lab coat was staring at her from the doorway. His hair was a blend of gray and brown, and he had a clipped Hitler mustache. Diana was reminded of the actors who played nondescript British officers in World War II movies, modestly saving the world for God and country.

"Oh. Hi." She hated to be put on the defensive.

"Who *are* you?"

"Diana Larsen. I know your wife. Dolly."

The sound of his wife's name did not create any conspicuous joy. Was this the man everyone else found so charming? "You pulled me out of a very busy schedule. May I ask why?"

So he knew who she was. "I had an appointment." *And I'm not spending four hours in your waiting room like your other fans.* But she stood up, annoyed.

He waved her back down and went to the matching red leather chair. He stood with one knee in the seat, resting his weight on it. "What do you want?"

"I need to know about Crystal Andresen."

A sigh. "What about her?"

"I still don't understand how her baby could have weighed only four pounds."

"Four pounds!" His voice was incredulous. "Who told you that?"

"That's what the housemother said. And the cord was wrapped around the baby's neck?"

"And who told you *that?*"

"Crystal," Diana admitted. "She said that the baby had been

dead inside her for weeks. But I'm sure I saw it kick more recently than that. So did Dolly."

"Of course you did! That young lady has some imagination." He shook his head. "Did she also tell you she gave herself a whopping dose of castor oil? It's an old wives' tale that it brings on labor. All it did was clean her out very thoroughly!"

Why hadn't Eileen mentioned that? It was the kind of detail that made stories interesting. "You don't think it hurt the baby?"

"No way it could do that. Hundreds of women have done the same thing."

"What day was Crystal's baby born?"

He blinked at the question, then shut his eyes as if consulting an interior calendar. "Monday morning, I think. Monday or Tuesday."

"You don't *remember?*"

"But I wasn't there! I was feeling poorly that day, I didn't do the delivery. I only heard about it later from Sol Maria Cruz. We cover for each other."

Eileen the Candid had never told her it was a different doctor, either. "But you'll deliver Roxanne and Shane?"

He moved his arm slightly to look at his watch. "I certainly plan to."

"Do you ever arrange private adoptions?"

"No."

The answer was so unequivocal that she let herself look surprised.

"I see women with fertility problems who eventually come to that point. I advise them any way I can. But do I procure babies for them? No."

"But you don't do abortions. Even though they're legal in the state of New York."

"Excuse me, Miss . . ."

"Larsen."

"Miss Larsen. How old are you?"

"Twenty-eight."

"Please don't take offense." *The usual prelude to giving it.* "But you

49

have a lot to learn about the differences between what's legal, what's moral, and what simply feels right. Until New York State holds a gun to my head and tells me I *have* to do such a procedure, then I'll continue fostering life—not ending it." He pulled himself up. "I don't have time to debate the issue now. Was there anything else?"

"I was hoping you could give me the names of some people who had adopted privately. I'm writing a story on the alternatives to abortion, like adoption. That's why I interviewed your wife." She said it mildly. She could play the game too.

"Well." He pulled at his ear lobe uncertainly. *Sounds like . . .* "They might not want to discuss it. But two of my infertility patients, Caroline Denecke and Belle Apolla, just adopted. It's common knowledge. They're in the phone book." He looked openly at his watch now.

She stood up. "Thanks. Thanks for your time."

"I doubt I told you anything useful." The self-deprecating officer again.

"Actually you did. Thanks."

FIVE

When Diana walked into the Adoption Unit the others were already gathered in Howard's office. She threw her jacket on her desk top and dragged in a green vinyl-upholstered chair.

"How's Diana today?" Hannah Connors shifted her chair over to make room. She was the adoption worker who fascinated Diana most. Though in her early sixties, Hannah had surprisingly girlish features—upturned nose, round green eyes, pouty lips. She wore her gray-blond hair in a skinny braid twisted up the back of her head. Marci had told Diana, awed, that Hannah was independently wealthy and spent time in fashionable resorts with one or another of her daughters. As it was, she only worked part-time. Acerbic in the mornings, by afternoon she was sociable and confiding. Diana assumed it was the result of a forty-proof lunch.

Thus relaxed, she would lecture Diana on the history of adoption, pausing so Diana could take notes. Her experience reached back to the 1950s, back to the days when babies were so plentiful that they had sent the surplus to the New York Foundling Home. "You know," she squinted at Diana, "the less desirable ones."

This was too much! "What made a baby 'less desirable'?"

"Well . . . situations where there had been no prenatal care. Or where the heredity was poor. Sometimes the girl just *looked* dull."

One afternoon Hannah had reminisced about taking infants whose paternity was questionable to the Museum of Natural History where an anthropologist would measure their heads and study their bone structure before certifying them Caucasian. "He was only wrong once."

"That's right," Pearl Kong spoke up unexpectedly. She was a small, golden-skinned woman whose features almost disappeared in profile. Perhaps because it was winter she wore a tan beret all day long. "They were wrong about Poor Teddy."

Poor Teddy, Hannah explained, had started out as a normal white baby. But his skin had gradually darkened until, when he was eight years old, his heartbroken parents had to return him to Heart's Retreat.

"What do you mean, return him?" He wasn't a microwave that had broken down.

"People were very prejudiced then, Diana. White parents couldn't raise a black child. It just wasn't done."

"So what happened to him?"

Pearl and Hannah frowned at each other. "New York Foundling?" Hannah asked, and Pearl nodded. "We were just lucky the family didn't *sue*. Fortunately, they were good people."

It was an interesting definition of good people.

"These days people will take anything," Pearl added disapprovingly, returning to her typewriter.

Diana, ever conscious of skin tones, stared at her. Didn't such prejudice bother her? Adoption was a rarefied world indeed.

"Look, Diana! How would you like to take *her* home?" Marci was handing her a Polaroid they had been passing around. Evidently it was the baby of the day, Nicole Something.

"She's not from Heart's Retreat?"

"No. Just placed in foster care by a caseworker."

"A caseworker who's *late*," Dolly announced.

"Looks that way," Howard agreed.

"There's not a chance the mother changed her mind, is there?" Dolly brushed at the skirt of her ample black cashmere suit. "I could place today's baby twenty times over!"

"That's good. Maybe one of your families is at the top of the list."

Dolly turned her round eyes on him, the same round blue eyes as Nicole possessed. "I certainly hope so, Howard. I'd hate to think that in some rush to fairness we're shortchanging a *child.*"

"There's nothing wrong with my couples," Marci protested, hurt.

When Heart's Retreat came under the county's auspices, Dolly and Hannah had brought their own waiting families with them. Howard, faced with that waiting list for newborns, as well as the county's own, had tried to blend them fairly. But even Diana had to admit that the couples on the Heart's Retreat list were more distinguished. Marci's Social Services couples all seemed interchangeable: both overweight as if to mimic pregnancy, working as McDonald's restaurant managers or dental assistants. Their pictures were taken in front of a ranch house or in a darkly paneled den in front of the Christmas tree. Of course, the county's emphasis, under the New York State mandate, was to place minority and handicapped children; these children were usually adopted by their foster parents.

"Hello?" A muscular black caseworker in a dark leather jacket appeared in the doorway, his face shining as if oiled. Poor Teddy grown up? Was *this* man married?

"Hi, Pete," said Howard, waving an arm in welcome. "Come in and meet the folks."

"Howdy." He dropped down onto a gray metal folding chair next to Howard, then looked around at the group, giving Diana a wink. It identified her as the other outsider.

Howard went around the circle, naming the adoption workers. Then he turned to Diana. "Pete works in Voluntary Services. Any foster care placements that don't go through Child Protective Services come through him."

"But where's the baby?" Hannah broke in. "Didn't you know you're supposed to bring the baby so we can see her?!"

Pete raised his eyebrows. "The hospital's not gonna let her out just to come *here*."

"She's still in the hospital? I thought she was six weeks old."

Howard put up his hands. "Let's give Pete a chance to tell us about Nicole."

"Well," said Pete, pressing his fingertips together and looking heavenward, "like the man said, her name is Nicole. She's a real cute kid." His *but* hung in the air for a moment, then landed. "The only thing is, she's got this condition, Apert's syndrome, where her esophagus and windpipe aren't separate. She has to take a swallow, *then* take a breath, take a swallow, take a breath. Otherwise she'll choke to death. But they can operate in a year or two."

Everyone stirred, bewildered. "But the operation will make her normal?" Dolly prompted.

"Normal? I don't know about *that*. They think she might be blind."

"Blind?" Marci gasped. "They think she's *blind?*"

Diana saw Dolly close her eyes. Hannah looked at Pete as if he had just unzipped his pants and brought out something ugly. He nodded several times, as if this was the reaction he had been expecting.

"What about her intelligence?" Diana asked.

"We don't know. No one knows about the Dad. The Mom fried *her* brain on drugs."

"Jesus Christ!" It was Hannah.

"Cute though. And she's not HIV-positive or anything."

54

"But we don't have homes for babies like that," Hannah reminded Howard.

"You're working for a new agency, Hannah. In this agency we find homes for children—not babies for couples."

Dolly leaned toward Marci with a smile. "How about one of your homes? Don't you have a family who likes Down's syndrome?"

Marci shook her head. "She already has *eight*. Aren't there any foster homes?" she asked Pete.

"They're scared of the medical thing."

"Okay, enough of this." Howard slapped the edge of the desk with a manila folder. He was flushed, slightly bulky, larger than life. "Dolly, since you said you had so many anxious couples, I'm putting you in charge of Nicole. Phone around and see if any of them are willing to take a risk."

"But, Howard, I've never done a special-needs adoption." She said it reasonably, objectively. "Marci—"

"This one's for you."

She shrugged and turned to Pete. "How much do they know for certain? Except for this trachea thing?"

Would she really pass the baby off as normal? Was that what had happened with Poor Teddy? Some social worker saw a hint of something, but decided to go with it anyway?

"Don't even think it, Dolly," Howard warned.

"Why? Doctors always give a worst-case scenario. Believe me, I should know!"

"We have to tell the family everything we suspect."

"Then none of my couples will be interested." She raised herself suddenly, like a family leaving church.

"I'm not participating in this charade either!" Hannah pushed to her feet, her skimpy gray-blond bangs trembling. But in her haste she banged her orange cup against the edge of Howard's desk; coffee sloshed over a stack of pale green case records. "Damnation!" She yanked a wad of tissue from under her sweater sleeve and dabbed at them, then stormed out of the alcove. Diana helped mop up. Could Hannah and Dolly do that, just get mad and walk out? If they didn't need the money, they probably could.

Howard was shaking his head. "Why does everybody hate kids who aren't perfect?" He turned apologetically to Marci. "Do you have anything?"

"No, no. If it's assigned to me, I'll *do* it." Dolly suddenly reappeared in the doorway. "Even if I have to take her home myself. But I can't believe we're letting the baby's parents off the hook this way. They should be made to face up to their responsibilities."

Howard glanced ruefully at Diana. "You might as well know the truth; they don't say that when the baby's fine."

After the conference Diana announced that she was going back to the maternity home. No one objected and she left, determined to find out the truth. Crystal, she would say, you're not telling me what really happened. She would point out what Dr. Hazelton said, and then find out why Crys had her own version. From there she could go see Caroline Denecke and Belle Apolla. Experience had taught her that it was better not to phone first.

Eileen was again waiting for her at the door. This time she was wearing a salmon pantsuit with a frilly white blouse. Her shiny black bangs were low over her eyes. "You certainly pick the right times to show up."

"Why? What happened?" If there been another stillbirth, a second tragedy . . .

But the lines around Eileen's mouth expressed grim amusement. "Crystal's gone. And I bet she's the one you've come to see."

"I can come back later."

"No, I mean she's gone. I was at the doctor's with the others and when we got back, Crys still wasn't up. I sent Roxanne up to tell her to rise and shine—there's a limit to even my tolerance for sloth—but she was gone."

"Where did she go?"

"Who knows? Come in." Diana followed her through the narrow hallway. On damp days like this one, the home smelled like a summer attic. The hall was papered in a dark brown design of emblems and shields and decorated with British engravings of African scenes. Diana's eye landed on the one that showed two giraffes dwarfing the foliage. She wished she'd seen that Africa.

"Maybe she just went out."

"With all her clothes?"

"I guess not." She had an odd image of Crystal bulked out in everything she owned, like a street person. "Was there anything she *didn't* take?"

"Just some stuffed animals. You want to see her room?"

It seemed a strange invitation—as if Eileen had to prove that Crystal was really gone. But she said, "Sure." She had never been on the second floor.

At the top of the landing the floor divided in two, with closed doors on each side of the worn dark red runner. The lack of hall tables, mirrors, or any decoration made Diana think of a seedy hotel.

Eileen turned left and stopped at a door halfway down. "It's a mess," she warned, her hand on the tarnished brass knob. "I try and make them clean on Saturdays. But last weekend she didn't do anything."

Even so, Diana was shocked that such disorder would belong to Crystal. There were empty soda cans, hairstyle magazines, and plastic wrappings from new clothes. She opened the closet and saw a few lonely maternity tops. The room had the feeling that everything of importance was gone.

She followed Eileen down the narrow servants' stairs at the back of the hall and into the kitchen. The housemother pointed at the table and Diana sat down. This time the coffee was waiting in a glass carafe decorated with daisies.

"The girls don't usually stay here long after giving birth," said Eileen. "But they don't just take off, either."

"Did she have a fight with anyone?"

Eileen considered it, plumping out her cheeks. "No. But she had something going with that modeling plan, I'm sure of it. She's been asking for a lot of change lately and going off to call someone."

"She doesn't call from here?"

"Of course not. I keep my phone locked up. I don't get paid enough to support the phone company."

The girls couldn't even call out? *Help, I'm a prisoner in a maternity home.* She glanced over at the white refrigerator with its stacks of Entenmann's bakery boxes on top.

"I *do* feed them once a day. If they ask nicely."

Caught, Diana laughed. "Some places restrict the food, I hear."

"Well, there's nothing like that here; they can eat all day long. And most of them do. I guess you haven't lived with teenagers. I have a walk-in freezer out back just in case we get caught in a blizzard. When this place was full, I kept it jammed." She settled herself across from Diana, the white wooden chair giving a frightened squeak. "When girls first come here, all they want to do all day is talk to the friends they just left. So I direct them out to the street, to the pay phone on the corner."

"Sounds okay to me. If you hear from Crystal, tell her I want to talk to her. Would she have told Shane or Roxanne where she was going?"

"I doubt it. Crystal's a funny kid. She only used them when she wanted something. And they didn't have much she wanted."

Time to get serious. "You told me Crystal's baby was four pounds."

"Did I say that? I said that it was small—given the fact of how pregnant she was. But I don't remember saying any weight."

"I thought you had." Their eyes locked. "And what about this idea that he—it was a he?—had been dead for weeks."

"I know I never said *that*," the housemother protested. "It might have been for a day or two—but Crystal misunderstood."

"Did she think that taking castor oil killed the baby?"

"You'd have to ask her that." But Eileen's pale blue eyes looked guilty.

"Do they do that often?"

"Often enough. Or beg me to take them on a bumpy ride." She shook her head, giving a rueful laugh. "Sometimes it actually works."

"Is low birth weight a problem at Heart's Retreat? Do you ever have girls here on drugs?"

"I hope not!"

"It seems fairly common." She told Eileen about Nicole—the baby nobody wanted. "Are most private adoption workers like Hannah?"

"Hannah's been in the field a long time. And don't forget, Diana, these couples have been waiting *years* for a child. Is it fair to give them one who will probably die soon?"

"Not when you put it like that."

"Did you want to speak to the other girls?"

Did she? They didn't fit the profile she needed. Roxanne was having the baby because she planned to keep it, and Shane's pregnancy had been discovered too late to do anything about it. Crystal, coerced by Dr. Hazelton, would have been perfect. But since she was disguising the girls anyway, she could always create a composite. "Sure."

Eileen returned to her routine of calling up the stairs. "Roxie? Roxie! Move it or lose it." And when the girl clumped sullenly down the wooden steps several minutes later, Eileen picked up her cup of coffee and retreated to the alcove to watch a talk show.

Roxanne, black hair teased high, was wearing a red-and-white-checked smock with a white pique collar and a big black bow, and black leggings. Her normal expression was that of a truck driver caught in traffic. But that was misleading. She had, Diana complained to Howard, the personality of a slug.

"We don't call it that," Howard pointed out. "You might say that she has a flat affect. Or a submerged personality. But slug is not a recognized diagnosis."

"But why does she hate me so much? She doesn't have to talk to me if she doesn't want to."

"She obviously wants *something* from you. Maybe to show an interest in her beyond her delicate condition? And no slug jokes!"

"Okay. But there's not much *beyond* her 'delicate condition.'"

"Ask her about her boyfriend. Tell her you like her hair."

"I hate her hair."

"Diana . . ."

"I'll do the boyfriend."

Roxanne plopped down at the table and looked Diana over. Diana winced as the baby Roxanne was carrying kicked so violently that her belly jolted the white wooden table. Like a flatulent passenger in an elevator, Roxanne pretended that nothing had happened.

"Must be a linebacker."

"Huh?"

"So how's Richard?"

"*Who?*"

"Richard? Your boyfriend?" Wasn't that his name?

"He's okay."

"Do you have a picture of him?"

"Richie? You want to *see?*"

"Sure."

Looking as if Diana had lost a few brain chips, the girl pressed herself up from the table with both hands and lumbered up the stairs. A moment later she was back, cradling a photograph in one palm. She dropped it in front of Diana, careful to avoid any accidental contact. Diana picked up the Polaroid snapshot. It was limp from constant handling, and showed a tall, skinny young man with pitted cheeks, wearing a blue-and-orange Mets jacket. His hair had been clipped close to the sides of his head, and left high on top, fifties style.

"He looks nice," Diana said. "How old is he?"

"Twenty-five."

"Hmm." No wonder he had been looking for more than a cute date. "What does he do?"

"Sometimes he works in his father's deli. Sometimes he goes to Skills Unlimited."

Diana studied the picture again. This time Richie's blue eyes seemed more vacant. "He lives at home?"

"Yeah. But my mother says she hasn't seen him around. She thinks they might of sent him *away.*" Her voice wavered with fury on the last word. "But he'll be back. He knows when the baby's due."

Diana nodded. Time enough for Roxanne to face reality after the baby was born. "What?" She saw that Roxanne was looking at her as if she had just discovered a new use for journalists.

"*You* could talk to Richie. Tell him the baby's almost born and that he better call me. He listens to adults." She made it into a personality defect. "You can tell him that I play our song every day."

"What's your song?"

A grotesquely coquettish smile. "I'm not telling *you.* Just ask them at Johnson's Deli where Richie is. They'll know."

"Okay." She should be talking to some unwed fathers anyway.

Roxanne pushed back from the table. "I gotta pee."

So much for bonding. "Ask Shane to come down, will you?"

Howard's technique had borne fruit. Strange fruit, but fruit.

Shane Norman clattered down the backstairs, sliding into the chair across from her with a grin—as if she knew some secret that Diana didn't. She was as slender as Roxanne was chunky, her stomach a round ball under her black Madonna T-shirt. Shane's brown eyes were large and innocent in her bony face, a face that made Diana think of Dorothea Lange's migrant photographs. Eileen had told her in a hushed voice how Shane's mother had run off to Florida with a trucker hauling shrimp, and how Shane's father had again taken advantage of her absence to visit his daughter's bed. But this time there had been consequences. Although Shane had not been enrolled in school, a neighbor in the trailer park finally noticed what had happened. By then Shane was more than six months pregnant.

"What's up, Shane?"

"Peckers."

"Been learning anything from your tutors?"

She leaned on one elbow and sucked a strand of hair. "It's real tough. They keep sending retards."

"*Retard's* a bad word, Shane." She sounded like a mother. But that was what the girl needed.

"They keep asking me all these stupid questions! Like why I'm here. And what my 'plans' are." After Mr. Norman's arrest, when his family from West Virginia had swooped down and claimed Shane's brothers, she had refused to go.

"What do you tell them?" Had any of them even tested her to see if she could read or write?

"That I'm waiting for my mother. She won't know where everybody's gone!"

"Any other reasons?"

"No."

"You saw Dr. Hazelton this morning?"

Shane pressed the limp chestnut-brown hair across her lips. "He thinks I might have this disease."

"*What disease?*" Was there a conspiracy to keep from telling her *anything*?

"Like this kid on TV? He swelled up all over and turned gray? Then his skin cracked. And he got to go to Disney World before he died."

"And Dr. Hazelton says you have this disease."

"Well, he said I *might*. When I asked him."

Oh. "And what did he say about the baby?"

"What baby?"

Diana pointed at Shane's stomach.

"That's not a baby. I'm only thirteen. How could I have a baby?" Her thin, high-cheekboned face looked reproachful, as if Diana were talking about something she should not even hear.

"Well, it happens, Shane. It can happen to any girl once she gets her period. It's nothing that anybody makes happen by *thinking* about it; it's just biological."

Shane scratched at the yellow raffia mat with her fingernail, attempting to dislodge a sticky ridge of debris.

"Sometimes people—fathers—do things that are wrong. But it's not the girls' fault."

"But some girls might like it," Shane objected.

Diana covered Shane's nervous fingers with her hand. "You think that makes the girls to blame?"

Shane shrugged.

"Fathers can find other ways to be close to their daughters."

Shane twisted in her chair. "I knew a girl in Ferguson, her *brother* gave her a baby."

"Do you think it was her fault?"

"I don't know—she always wanted everyone to do it with everyone after that."

"You think after girls have babies they get that way."

Shane pulled her hand away and looked over at the boxes on top of the refrigerator. "I need chocolate."

Diana watched her get up and examine the white boxes. Shane came back with a carton of devil's food cupcakes. Removing one, she offered the rest to Diana.

Diana shook her head. "I guess you miss your mom."

"I don't know why she doesn't come back!" Tears that seemed to come from nowhere streaked down her narrow face. "No one cares what's happening to me."

It seemed true. Diana held out her arms until Shane pushed herself onto her lap, her head pressed awkwardly into Diana's shoulder. Her tears ran thin and wet. "Why can't they just be like regular people?" she sobbed. "Why do they always have to pull shit like this?"

Diana stroked her back while Shane argued it out.

"But my father was fun! And she could be okay. Sometimes we'd have real good times together, all of us in the van. At night we'd snuggle up in the back and tell creepy stories, and then have jelly doughnuts for breakfast. We'd go where there was work." She raised her head, her expression stony. "It's *her* fault. She was always running around like she wasn't anyone's mother. If she'd been here this wouldn't have happened."

"Maybe not."

Shane shifted to Diana's other knee and wiped at her face. "I wish . . ." Then she stopped.

"What do you wish?"

"Nothing."

"You want your mother to come back."

"No, I don't!"

"You wish you weren't having this baby."

"*What* baby?"

"You wish you could go to Disney World."

"How did you know?" She pulled back and looked at Diana, then traced Diana's eyebrow with a playful finger. "You're so smart!"

Diana laughed.

"I bet I know what Roxie wants."

"What?"

"A man!"

Diana laughed again.

"It's so weird, she, like, talks to herself. Like there's some guy in her room. She goes, 'Oh, Richie, that's so *sweet!*' And then she goes, 'Ooh baby, Ooh, baby' in this deep voice."

"You'll get older too," Diana promised.

"Yuck."

Diana picked up a strand of greasy chestnut hair. "Eileen locking up the shampoo along with the phone?"

"Big Mama says we use too much hot water."

"She can't be talking about *you*."

"Are you coming next week?"

"Probably."

"Good. Bring chocolate."

SIX

They would have to find Susan. It came to her with the force of a revelation that if they found her they could find out her blood type. And then, if this baby's was something different they would *have* to look for Zach! The police didn't believe her about the diaper, they didn't believe her about the sleeper being new, but they'd have to believe scientific evidence.

But what if they found Susan and the blood types were identical? It was a risk she would have to take. Meanwhile she hoped Joe wouldn't blame her forever.

Her fear and the wine she had sipped for the rest of the evening dropped her immediately into a dark, dreamless place. She woke, shocked, by the alarm; at first she imagined that she was waking on a weekday and was late for school. Then she remembered what had happened the day before and was instantly, coldly, alert.

"Don't get up," Joe mumbled from the other side of the bed where he was pulling on his slippers.

"No, I'm awake."

He shrugged and moved in the direction of the bathroom. They had kissed good night, holding each other, but had not talked any more.

But they had to talk before he left for work. By the time he was downstairs, showered and dressed in immaculate gray wool slacks and a navy blazer, she had made coffee and poured orange juice. She watched him bring his bran flakes over to the table along with the handful of vitamins he swallowed daily.

"You didn't have to get up," he said.

"No, but I wanted to." She tried to smile, but couldn't. "I feel terrible about what's happened. I'm afraid everything is my fault."

"You know what? You need to go back to work. I know your job is filled, but they might make some arrangement. It's no good for you to mope around the house." He rubbed at the bridge of his nose, as if getting rid of the bone would solve their problems. "You're a very social person. And you love kids."

"But . . ." She slumped back in her metal chair, confused. Did this mean he wasn't taking Millar's threat of arrest seriously? Maybe it was just his way of minimizing his own fear. But how could she even think about working when she believed Zachary was alive somewhere—and maybe with people who were mistreating him? Terrible things happened to children sometimes. There were things like witchcraft. And the sickest kind of sex. Anyone capable of stealing a baby was capable of anything.

"Caro?" Joe was looking at her anxiously; she realized tears were slipping down her face again. "Are you okay?"

She nodded. "I was just . . . worrying. What if someone took Zach to *do* something to him?"

She saw his face close down. "Look," he said firmly. "You're just making yourself upset. No one took him. He died."

"Joe, I saw the crib when there was no baby in it! *You* remember."

He raised his cup, then put it down again. "You thought you dreamed it."

"But I didn't! Now I know I didn't. What about the brand-new

67

sleeper? And the different kind of diaper? And he looked older and different."

He put up his hand to halt the litany, then pushed back from the table.

"You didn't finish your coffee," she protested.

"I don't have time. Listen to me." He came around behind her and pressed her head backwards against his chest. "If the police come and start badgering you, call me. Call *Martin*. Don't talk to them at all!"

"Okay."

"Maybe you should go see Dr. Fisher. He can give you something to, you know, make you feel better."

Was she that bad? Joe did not believe in medicating problems. But she nodded.

"I'll call you on my break."

"Okay. Joe? I love you."

"I love *you*." And he hugged her warmly.

When he was gone, she reached for the coffee he had left and sipped it slowly.

She had to find Susan. But was she from Crane Island? She had known enough to suggest the Sunshine Diner as a place where they could talk—chances were good that she was local. Closing her eyes, Caroline tried to visualize Susan, and panicked when she could not. Black hair, thin features, she reminded herself. A little like Cher. She had last seen Susan in the hospital parking lot. Joe had handed her the envelope of money, and she went over and got into a car. Caroline remembered being surprised that the car was an expensive one. It had one of those slashes in front, she made herself recall; it must have been a Volvo. But then Joe handed her the baby and she stopped seeing anything else.

What color was the car? In memory it was pale, unwilling to be identified. White? Silver? She closed her eyes more tightly, but nothing came. The doctor had seen her, of course. But probably she knew Susan only as Caroline Denecke. Who else? Susan might have had a roommate in the hospital, someone she talked to about her future plans. People did talk in those situations. But would the hospital tell her? Then, remembering something, she went quickly up the stairs.

The nursery was still the place where she felt closest to Zach. But when she opened the door, the scent of dying flowers swelled out at her like a billowing sheet. She coughed, then reached inside and switched on the overhead light. Moving to the bookcase, she pulled out *My First Year*. It was a baby book with old-fashioned pictures from the Metropolitan Museum of Art, the first baby gift they had received. She turned to the clipping from the *Crane Island Advance,* which she had pasted near the beginning. She had thought it would be fun for Zach to see if he met any of the other babies in kindergarten:

NEWCOMERS

We welcome the following Crane Islanders born this week, and offer our heartiest congratulations to their parents:

Shannon Marie Brennan, 8 lbs. 5 oz. born February 15 at Jefferson Hospital.

Zachary Joseph Denecke, 7 lbs. 10 oz. born February 17 at Jefferson Hospital.

Tamika MacDonald, 6 lbs. 8 oz. born February 18 at Jefferson Hospital.

Ezra Paul Steinfeld, 9 lbs. 1 oz. born February 16 at North Shore Hospital.

She had met Kathie Brennan once, at a shower for her friend Beth. Given her position as the wife of a prosperous lawyer, she had probably had a single room. Ezra Paul Steinfeld had been born on Long Island. A high-risk baby? That left Tamika MacDonald.

Chances were, if Susan had had a roommate, Tamika MacDonald's mother was the one.

As she turned to go downstairs to call the hospital, she noticed a gap in the row of stuffed animals. She looked to the crib to see if one of them had been moved in there. But the crib was still empty. That dog-faced policeman must have moved them to check for whatever he was looking for, then put them back carelessly. Anger flared that he had been pushing around her precious things. Rapidly she did a roll call. There was Paddington Bear, the stuffed tiger right beside him, and King Babar. Raggedy Ann and the little gray mouse from the baby shower. But where was Tuggy? His lithographed face was so worn from the kisses she had given him, the food she had tried to feed him, that she had not even risked bringing him to her classroom. Besides, she had been saving him for her own child. She looked frantically in the closet and under the crib's quilt again. She looked everywhere. But Tuggy, her stuffed tugboat boy, was gone.

All she could think was that the police had taken him. But why?

She was sitting in the den, hours later, finishing a stack of thank-you notes for the funeral flowers and gifts of food, when she heard a car pull into the driveway. She looked at the banjo clock on the wall. Joe? It was way too early. But maybe they had dismissed school because of the threat of snow in the forecast.

But when someone knocked on the door, she felt herself freeze. What if it was the police, come to arrest her? For a moment she did not move. Then she got up slowly and walked into the foyer.

When she pulled back the door, to her great relief a young woman was standing on the stoop. "Hi. Mrs. Denecke?" She was olive-skinned, with dark hair tied back and a red hooded parka. Her gray eyes were unusual, a lighter color than her face. "I'm Diana Larsen, from *Women* magazine. Dr. Hazelton gave me your name."

She pulled the door back a little wider. How much was this bit of charity going to cost her? "I already have a lot of subscriptions," she began.

70

"Oh—you think I'm selling subscriptions?" She smiled, amused, showing pretty white teeth. "I'm a writer."

"You mean you write for the magazine?" That particular magazine, a cross between *Ms.* and *Vanity Fair,* had never appealed to her.

"That's right. Can I come in?"

"I guess." She was still no clearer on what the woman wanted. And what did Dr. Hazelton have to do with it?

When she brought Diana Larsen into the den, she saw how messy it was, spilling over with newspapers and magazines. But at least it was cozy. The deep blue wallpaper and white woodwork had come from an idea in *Better Homes and Gardens,* and Caroline had added the overstuffed red sofa and chairs. "I thought you might be my husband."

"No, I'm not married."

Caroline looked at her uncertainly, then realized it was a joke.

Diana sat down in one of the red chairs, neatly squashing a Baby Opus. Reaching behind her, she picked it up and looked it over. "Cute."

"Thanks. My students gave it to me for Christmas. I try to discourage them from buying me gifts, but they know I like penguins."

"You're a teacher?"

"Special Ed."

"Great." She looked around expectantly. "Where's the baby?"

Caroline felt herself freeze. Obviously she didn't know what had happened. "Unfortunately Zach—the baby—died Monday night. They . . . think it was a crib death."

"My God! Every time I go to write about a baby I find out it's dead." It didn't seem to occur to her to offer condolences. "What's going on here? Is it something in the water—or the air? Maybe it's me."

Caroline shifted in the matching wing chair. "How could it be you?" Her voice sounded testy to her.

"Oh, I don't know. It was just something to say. Maybe I have

71

bad karma. But everything on this story is going wrong."

What in God's name was she talking about?

"Have you noticed that around here? A lot of babies dying?"

"*No.*"

"If you had, it would be another kind of story. Nothing to do with adoption, though."

Caroline watched with a sinking heart as Diana unzipped her jacket. This . . . person was settling in to stay! "Tell me how you came to adopt. If you don't mind talking about it. We'd change your name if you wanted confidentiality, though it's always nice to use photos. But it would be up to you."

"But we don't have the baby. And it's a long story."

"I have time."

Caroline sighed. But why not talk? "He was a beautiful, beautiful baby," she began. She told Diana about the ad in the paper, the meeting in the diner, and bringing home Zach from the hospital. She left out the circumstances of his death. For all she knew Diana could be someone working undercover for the police, just waiting for Caroline to confess. Like Millar, Diana was writing in a small notebook.

"Did his birth mother come to the funeral?"

"No. I didn't know how to reach her."

"She doesn't know the baby's dead?" The nostrils in her pretty face flared, reminding Caroline of an angry pony. "But that's terrible! She could go through life imagining him alive when he isn't."

This was too much. "But if she has no contact with him, what does it matter? He's dead to her, no matter what."

Diana reached behind her and brought a long, dark braid next to her face. "That's a weird thing to say. How old is this girl?"

"I don't know," Caroline admitted.

"You don't know?"

"She wasn't *that* young. She talked about college."

"That's not young?"

"Well." Did they take advantage of Susan? She had seemed so

72

certain about what she wanted to do that Caroline hadn't even questioned it.

"She came to us, after all. Nobody was making her give him up."

"That you know."

"That we know," Caroline agreed.

Diana tilted her head to one side. "Maybe she thought she had to give him up because she didn't have the money. The system isn't exactly supportive of single mothers."

"That's ridiculous!" How do I get this woman out of here? "There's welfare and everything else."

"But day care's a mess if you want to work." She glanced around the den, at the twenty-seven-inch TV, as if to emphasize the gap between Caroline's affluence and an unwed teenage mother.

"Well, I don't make the rules."

"We all do."

She should have been warned when she heard *Women*. She held out her hands, palms up. "So what do you want me to do?"

"Oh, I don't know. Nothing, I guess. It's just weird that she would go through life thinking he was happy and safe when he was actually dead—you know?"

Caroline nodded. "It would be easier if I knew where she was. She wouldn't even give us a phone number or address. Or her last name. Just Susan!"

"Really? Did you try the hospital?"

"Yes. I did." But she couldn't admit to this woman that Susan had used her name. "I think she roomed with a Gloria MacDonald. But the hospital wouldn't give me her address."

"No kidding! I know Gloria. I interviewed her after she left Heart's Retreat. But I don't know if she's still at her aunt's or not. Her boyfriend's in the army, stationed in Georgia, and I don't know if she's gone to him yet. She could still be at her aunt's."

"You really know Gloria?" If this wasn't a sign, this woman coming to her house, what was? "Do you have her address?"

Diana thought. "I'm not sure I still have the address. But I can show you where the house is. I'm pretty sure she doesn't have a phone."

"I just need to ask her a few questions."

"Oh, she wouldn't talk to you."

"But I'm sure she'd talk to *you.*" All her resentment of Diana's pushiness came out on the last word—so much so that Diana laughed. But as she zipped up the red parka she added, "You're sure you want to do this? If we find your baby's birthmother it won't be easy telling her."

"No. But I will."

Little India was a mysterious community at the tip of the island that had originally been called Little Indian Point. But with the influx of blacks and even some gypsies, the ending had been dropped to imply a more exotic locale. Much of the area was still beach grass. But the winding streets and wooden houses crammed in crooked rows reminded Caroline of the tipsy block villages her classes built. She would have been hard-pressed to locate an address here. Of course, the way Diana Larsen drove, they might not live to find the house, either.

She was not just reckless, she was dangerous. Braking suddenly, Diana turned left through a dying yellow light. "It's easy to get lost around here. Shit!"

"*What?*" Caroline realized she was huddled in the corner beside the passenger door.

"There's a cop behind me. Was I doing anything wrong? I wasn't doing anything wrong!"

Caroline turned and saw the flashing red lights behind them. It's not you they're coming for, she wanted to say, it's me.

Diana sighed and pulled over to the curb.

Joe had repeatedly told her that if she were ever stopped she should jump out and go to the squad car, not make the policeman come to her. But Diana simply rolled down the window and waited.

"Don't you think you should get out?"

74

"In this neighborhood? No way."

After a minute a face was framed in the window. Caroline recognized the mournful, uneven eyes of the young policeman, Donald.

"You have a reason for being in this area?" he asked Diana. Then he peered beyond her to Caroline, surprised. "Oh—hi," he said. "How are you doing?" But his expression was puzzled, as if he were trying to pull her name out of his memory. He seemed to remember the tone of their meeting, but not who she was. Caroline prayed he would not recall who she was.

"We're going to visit someone on Shell Street," Diana said. She gave him her smile.

"The way you were weaving, I thought—"

"No, no, I'm not drunk. Just lost."

"Shell Street is the second right. Just go straight." He straightened up, then leaned back down. "When you park, be sure and lock your doors."

"I guess he thought we came here to buy drugs," Diana said after she rolled up the window.

"Did you just learn to drive?"

"Me? No. I learned at fifteen. Of course, I've been out of the country for a few years. And I didn't have a car in the city. The magazine is renting this one for me." She lowered her head and squinted at the row of houses. "I know it was around here somewhere."

By the time they reached the house on Shell Street it was completely dark. Diana turned another corner and stopped the car. "I think this is the house. I just hope Gloria's here. Her aunt hates white people."

"Oh, great. Why?"

"Gloria was taken away from her by CPS after she complained in school that her aunt tried to make her drink Lysol to abort. But Gloria was determined to have this child."

"My God! Was the baby *okay?*"

"Tamika? She's fine. Gloria's aunt finally came around. But she still hates CPS."

When Diana shut off the car lights the street was black as a cellar. They sat in the darkness for a minute, staring at the house, then Diana said, "Let's do it." They picked their way up the uneven cement walk and Diana banged on an old screen door.

A stocky black girl wearing maroon and white sweats finally opened it. "Miz Larsen," she said to Diana with an amazed smile. "What you doing here?"

"We wanted to see Tamika. I wanted my friend to meet her."

"O-kay. Tammy's got real big." She stepped back inside so they could come in, and pointed to an ancient woman sitting in a green vinyl recliner holding a baby. Waltzing over, Gloria scooped up the child. Then she gestured at them to sit down on a tan plaid couch whose yellow foam boiled up from beneath stretched threads. Jiggling the baby, she settled on the coffee table opposite them, her knees touching Diana's.

"She's adorable." Caroline felt her arms reach out to the tiny chestnut infant. The baby's shrewd brown eyes reminded her of the old woman's.

"Ain't she?" Gloria rubbed noses with the infant. "You wanna hold her?"

"Can I?"

"I wasn't sure you'd still be here," Diana interrupted.

"Oh, yeah . . . we're still waiting. He's s'posed to send for us."

Caroline held the baby close against her chest, breathing in a warm coconut smell. Tamika fit into her arms perfectly. She was exactly Zachary's age.

"You remember when you were in the hospital?" Diana asked.

"Sure. Uh-huh. That was the cutest little bathroom I ever saw!"

"And the girl you shared the room with?"

Gloria screwed up her face. "Nobody. I didn't share the room with nobody."

Caroline's heart dropped. Had she figured it wrong, after all? "Not a girl named Caroline?"

"Oh, her. She didn't hardly talk to me. And then she went home."

Evidently that did not qualify her as a roommate in Gloria's eyes. "Her boyfriend come to see her. And all these other people."

"What other kinds of people?" Caroline asked quickly. "Just friends?"

"Well . . . it was really like they come to see the baby. Like they were really excited about *him.*"

But she had never gone to the hospital! And who else . . .

"Did she ever say where she lived?" Diana asked.

Gloria closed her bright brown eyes as if this were a test she had little hope of passing. "Near the water. She talk about taking her boat to Long Island."

"Do you remember where? Comsewogue? Logan Point?"

"That one."

"Logan Point?"

"Uh-huh."

"Did she tell you where she worked?" Caroline asked.

Gloria's face brightened. "In a supermarket."

"Did she say which one?"

"Naw."

Caroline pressed her knees together. On top of everything, she felt unnerved; her period had been due yesterday. Gloria and Susan had spent several hours together. They had to have talked about something. "What did you talk about?" she asked finally.

"I dunno. We watched MTV."

Across the room the ancient woman in the recliner stirred.

Caroline wanted to ask Gloria if she had seen Zachary, if she thought he was cute. But she said, "Let me give you my phone number." She felt in her pocket and pulled out a grocery receipt. Reaching around Tamika on her lap, she wrote it awkwardly on the back. "In case you remember anything else, could you call me?"

Gloria laid it down carefully on the coffee table, smoothing out one bent corner.

It felt time to leave. Slowly she handed Tamika back to Gloria, rubbing her lips across the baby's head. There was a cold place against her chest where the baby had been.

Out in the car Diana looked at her for a long time. "I'm confused," she said finally. It was the tone of someone demanding an explanation.

"About what?" But it sounded feeble.

"For one thing, you asked her if she shared a room with 'Caroline.' That's your name. And I'm sure you told me her name was something else."

"I did?" She was just buying time.

"Yes. You did." She leaned back in the driver's seat. Caroline had the feeling she would not start up the car until she had an explanation.

"It's a long story."

"I bet."

"Can you drive and listen at the same time?" She was nervous about that.

Diana turned the key in the ignition. "If your story's that spectacular, I'll buy you a drink."

SEVEN

After Diana dropped Caroline off and got back to her apartment, she found one message on her machine:

"Hi, this is Jennifer! I'm calling for Erik. He said to tell you he has a late shoot, and if the snow starts he won't come out at all."

What a surprise. He had missed last weekend completely. She was the only attraction for him on Crane Island, and her signal seemed to be weakening fast. She wasn't sure how much she cared.

Still, he did come. She woke to find him standing beside the couch where she had fallen asleep reading. He was wearing an olive green cashmere overcoat she had never seen before; the color made his flushed cheeks and fair hair vivid. His gold-rimmed glasses were, as usual, halfway down his nose. What made people stare was his smile. His teeth were tiny but perfectly formed, a startling contrast to his sharply drawn features. When Diana first met him, his bright, dark eyes had reminded her of Pinnochio.

She struggled awake. "What time is it?" It felt as if they were meeting after years of being apart, as if he had already been consigned to her past.

He consulted a watch as new as his coat. A Rolex? A Rolex knockoff, anyway. They were sold from suitcases all over Manhattan. "One twenty-five. What's for dinner?"

"You're kidding."

"Why? I didn't eat. There's nothing here?"

She tried to think. "There's yogurt. And some carrots."

"*You're* kidding."

"Maybe some beer."

"Jesus Christ!" When they had lived together, he had done the shopping. Now he expected her to keep the larder stocked with expensive food that he didn't show up to eat. The Friday before, she had gone to Foods of the World and spent a fortune on smoked salmon, duck liver pate, and triple-creamed Brie—only to have to eat it for dinner for the next five nights herself.

"Isn't there any smoked trout left?"

"It ran away with the arugula."

"You're just pissed because I'm so late."

"It does shorten the weekend."

"You're blaming me for the weather?"

"No." She closed her eyes, sinking back into sleep.

"We'll make up for it tomorrow," he promised.

But in the morning he was still out of sorts. He wandered out at ten-twenty, toweling his golden hair dry. His face looked pinched in places, his mouth disagreeable.

Diana was finally ready to feed him. "Hi!" She went over and kissed him on the mouth, letting her tongue explore his teeth. "Want an omelet?"

Erik squinted. "No. Just toast. Dry. And black coffee."

"Orange juice?" She felt like a waitress.

"Is it real orange juice?"

"No, Erik, it's Tang. So you can be an astronaut when you grow up. Of *course* it's real orange juice. There's a little man in the kitchen straining the pulp out right now."

80

A shadow of a smile. "You mean you have men here when I'm not?"

"Relax. This one's only two feet tall. He sings and dances, and he'll be crushed that you don't want the cheese omelet he's preparing."

"What kind of cheese is he using?"

"Only the finest grated Swiss."

Erik sighed, and patted his stomach, flat in narrow jeans. "Okay. But I really have to watch it."

"What? Your waist must be all of twenty-eight inches!"

"Twenty-seven. But I'm getting a tummy."

"Where? In your ear?"

"I'm serious, Diana."

"Actually you could move it to your neck and have a goiter. No one would blame you for *that*."

He looked unamused.

"I think I hear a little man calling me."

They ate at the white Formica table that came with the apartment, under the imitation Tiffany tulip lamp. Diana had been lucky to find Mario's Vacation Apartments. She liked living in the white stucco complex with orange tile roofs and fake palm trees. The only rule at Mario's was "No Pets," and she wasn't even tempted to break it. The off-season monthly rent of $400 was more than reasonable by New York standards; in May it ballooned to $425 a week. But by May she wouldn't be here.

Like all the apartments, hers was furnished with an off-white quilted couch, two blue duck director's chairs, and framed travel posters of the Swiss Alps and Rio. (She had found Switzerland bland, loved Rio). A microwave, color TV, and VCR were included. In the living room only the neat stack of books on the coffee table were her own. A Macintosh computer and laser printer were set up on a card table in the bedroom for the travel writing she still did sometimes—drawing on her past experiences as if they were banked money she had saved from a flush time.

81

"So how was your week?" she asked, cutting into her omelet with a knife. Despite his good intentions, the little man in the kitchen was not a great cook.

"Quite wonderful." Erik relented just a little, relaxing into the canvas chair. "We had a Russian model with us on special loan; she was absolutely adorable. Her chaperone would have made three of her."

Diana considered asking why she hadn't, but stifled the joke and listened to his descriptions of picnics on location, forays to the Frick museum and the Bronx Zoo for backgrounds. Hands were photographed in a lot more places than she had realized.

After breakfast they discussed how to spend the day. A fine drizzle fogged the window, blotting out the cars in the parking lot below. Erik insisted it had been snowing the night before, but no traces of snow remained.

"We could go to the movies," Diana said, making cream cheese designs on a bagel.

"What movies? I can see the best movies in the world all week. Why bother with the dreck they have out here?"

"It's not *that* bad."

"A matinee with a bunch of screaming kids? No way!"

She sighed. Why hang out with someone who wasn't any fun? Fun had been the glue that kept them happy together. When they met it had felt like progress that Erik was single and available, though she sometimes found his affectations—the World War I bomber's jacket and white aviator's scarf, his personally blended cologne—a little ridiculous. They had never discussed any permanent commitment. Now it seemed, oddly, as if they were married and already bored with each other.

"Let's go back to the city," she said.

"And do what? I just *came* from there."

"So? We could stay in the apartment tonight."

He shook his head impatiently. "You know I share it."

"It's still yours." *And it was mine.*

82

"He pays his half. You know I can't manage the rent on my own. But I'm just as happy to get out of there weekends."

Then why don't you act it? Stop treating me like your hostess in the Hamptons.

Erik glanced out the window. "I need exercise."

She knew he meant a bike ride. "It's pouring!"

"So? Wear rain gear."

"Be my guest."

He pushed up from the couch. *"I have to get some exercise."* Going to the bedroom, he pulled on a yellow nylon rain suit; after several minutes he left. Diana watched out the window as he unlocked his bike from the rack on his battered Renault and rode away. His silver Peugeot was a part of his life, like a cowboy's beloved horse. Loaded down with cameras, tripod, and umbrella lights, he rode it everywhere in the city. She kept expecting to hear that he had been hit by a taxi or beaten and robbed. But so far he had been lucky.

It was a good day to organize her notes. She made a mug of almond tea, but when she opened her canvas bag she pulled out a copy of *The Counterlife* instead and settled down to read.

By two she was too restless for even Philip Roth. She was wasting *time*. They wouldn't let her hang around the Adoption Unit indefinitely. And Leslie, her editor, was expecting a first draft soon. Not just a first draft, but a statement of faith in everything the magazine stood for. When they had hired her, based on her freelance record, they had questioned her closely about her beliefs. It wasn't that she didn't have the same positions as *Women*; it was having to affirm it as a religion that was starting to annoy her.

She put the paperback down on the coffee table and thought about the aspect of adoption she liked least—her own. Karin Larsen seemed, in retrospect, to have been unable to decide whether she wanted Diana to know she was adopted or not. Diana remembered the time she had asked her, "But where was I *first?*"

"You were a little angel in Heaven. And one day God looked

83

down and said, 'Oh my, Mommy and Daddy Larsen are so lonely for a little baby now that Lydia and Janice are teenagers, I think I'll send them Diana.' And he did."

"Why didn't he just put me in *your* tummy then?"

"You ask too many questions." Karin turned away crossly. "It's not nice in a child."

Their relationship had teetered through her childhood like a tire losing air until that night in the kitchen. Karin had been making lunches for the next day. Already past fifty, she was as pinched and faded as the woman in *American Gothic*.

Diana pulled up a wooden kitchen chair and sat down backwards. "I think there's something wrong with me," she announced.

Karin, slicing turkey, sighed at the interruption. "There's always something wrong with you. You can't miss *another* day of school."

"But I haven't been getting my period." It had taken her a while to realize that. She had never been regular; every time her underpants turned red it was a surprise all over again.

Karin's eyes opened. "You mean you've been—" Abruptly she turned and opened the refrigerator without saying anything, then squatted there, forehead against a metal shelf as if praying.

Diana stared at the pattern of the yellow Formica table, the white and yellow chunks that looked uneven, like mountains, but underneath her finger were completely smooth. She hadn't done it *that* many times.

When Karin finally emerged with the mayonnaise, her face looked gray. "Go to bed," she muttered. "We'll see how you feel in the morning."

Was that a reprieve? The true reprieve came in the morning when her pajama bottoms were a sticky red mess. But before then she had crept into the hall to listen to her mother's conversation with Eimer. She found out things she could not have imagined.

Crouched there, ready to bolt if the door opened, she heard Karin say bitterly, "We're not spared one single thing. She'll have to go to that home in Albany where Lydia went." Lydia, Karin's own

84

daughter, had had a baby? She was married now and living outside Buffalo.

Diana was trying to figure out when it could have been when she heard something else, Karin hissing furiously, "I knew she'd grow up to be a tramp like Earline! I knew it when she used to take her panties off in front of people. Once it's in the blood, there's nothing you can do about it."

That was how she found out who her own mother was. *Earline was my mother. I knew her all the time.* But not any longer. Earline Jontra, her father's cousin, had drowned in Packer Lake when Diana was ten. Earline, never without a cigarette and a sharp barking laugh, had seemed exotic, though abrasive. After the drowning she had become a strange and sad family myth. She hadn't even been pretty, her teeth were too crooked and her nose was like Richard Nixon's.

Because Earline was Eimer's first cousin, she and Diana had been together sometimes at family parties. But Earline had never let on that there was any bond between them. Once Diana had seen her with several men in front of the Black Kitten Bar, laughing and smoking. Karin had put her arm firmly around Diana and turned her away from the scene.

But it was my mother! And that night she had wondered, *How could my mother be someone like that?*

Erik returned around six, cheerful again. On his way home he had stopped at Foods of the World and shopped for dinner. Humming, he prepared Hunan prawns with tree ears, cellophane noodles, dry-sautéed string beans, and fresh pineapple chunks with mango. For dessert he had bought custard eclairs. They sat down to eat about three hours later.

"You're a great cook," Diana said. It sounded grudging, though she didn't think she meant it to be.

"*You* could learn. I bought you those cast-iron pots."

"It's a waste of time for one person."

"What's your alternative? You aren't back in Paris. This is not Shangri-la."

"I'll hardly wither and die for lack of fresh pasta!"

He bit into a cube of pineapple with his perfect teeth. "How's the story going?"

"Slow. I'm not getting the stuff I need. You know how sometimes everything falls into place, how the whole thing gets a shape of its own? Well, it's not. But listen to this: A baby is stolen in the middle of the night from a crib and a dead one is left in his place. So the police are saying that the parents murdered him, and the parents are saying it's another baby."

"That's part of your story?" He tilted his head so he could see her through the glasses on his nose.

"No. Not yet. It's what someone who adopted a baby told me. I mean, do you think it sounds possible?"

"No."

"*I* do. Because all kinds of unbelievable things happen in life, things you wouldn't think to make up." And Caroline Denecke impressed her as a realist. Her lanky, boyish body and scraggly blond permanent, her background as a teacher, made her seem very real. There was something about her physically that reminded Diana of Crystal; maybe the wide green eyes or powdering of freckles. But Caroline seemed honest, whereas Crystal . . .

And if it *were* true, what a story that would be! She had promised Caroline she would try to find out if Susan had ever been at Heart's Retreat. In any case, she would stay involved.

Erik yawned.

"Christ! Don't die from the excitement." She jumped up and grabbed their dinner plates.

Because he had cooked, she did the cleaning up. When she finally came into the living room, he was absorbed in a movie. And by the time they were ready to go to bed, it was after one. Diana took a hot bath and brushed out her long dark hair. When she came into the darkened bedroom, Erik seemed to be asleep.

"Erik?" She climbed into bed and pushed at his shoulder gently. "Uhh."

"Wake up! Don't you want to *do* anything?"

"Uh." He turned onto his side facing her, but without opening his eyes. "Do you?"

Do I? An image of Howard, black hair tousled, cheeks flushed with feeling, jumped across her mind. His eyes were wise and— what? Patient? Amused? Shit! "My body does."

"Not good enough, Diana."

She started. Which one of them had said it?

Erik, light lashes unmoving beside his sharp nose, appeared to be sleeping.

Maybe he had a wealthy benefactress. Where else had he gotten a five thousand dollar watch? She didn't think he would wear an imitation. *Tell me again how you're sharing our apartment with a guy named Jim.*

 EIGHT

Friday night, by the time Diana dropped her off, Joe was home.

"Hi, it's me," she called from the hall.

There was no response. "Joe?"

She went into the den and found him sitting on the couch, the newspaper spread across his lap. She could tell by his face that he was furious.

"What?" she asked.

For a moment he looked too angry to answer. "Where have you *been?*"

"Just out. With . . ." How could she describe Diana? She didn't.

"My God, Caro! I come home, your car's here, but you've disappeared. No note, anything. I thought . . ." But he would not put what he thought into words.

"I'm sorry!" She came over and sat down next to him, stroking his arm. "I didn't think I'd be so long. I should have called."

Seeming partially mollified, he turned and kissed her cheek. "If your car had been gone too, I wouldn't have thought much about it."

She nodded. Of course it would have been frightening, on top of everything else. It would seem as if she had been taken away by someone or was lying dead somewhere. She leaned against him. "This woman, Diana Larsen, stopped by. She wanted to talk, so we decided to go out for something to eat."

"So you're not hungry either."

"You're not?"

She felt him shake his head. "I didn't want to bother you with it, but today was the bake sale for the Saint David's choir. They still need three thousand dollars for the Europe tour. So I was eating all day."

"Bring me anything?"

It was his turn to sound guilty. "Sorry."

"Thanks. Maybe I'll make some popcorn." After two glasses of chardonnay and a basket of peanuts she wasn't hungry for anything else.

While the kernels popped in the microwave, she looked up supermarkets in the Crane Island directory. There weren't that many places on the island where Susan could be working. She could hit them tomorrow morning.

When she came into the den, Joe was sitting on the couch, playing absently with the channel scanner. Caroline settled in beside him, the bowl of popcorn between their thighs. But the brief flashes of sports and comedy made her dizzy. "Can't you *find* anything?"

He shrugged. "Friday nights aren't that good. Is that all you're eating?"

"Um. My stomach's kind of weird. I haven't gotten my period yet."

He reached into the bowl and tossed a single kernel into his mouth. "You're just late because of everything that's happened."

It wasn't the response she had hoped for. "How do you know?"

"It's just the shock that's made you late." He reached out and tweaked a strand of her hair. "But I talked to Martin again. He says they need motive *and* evidence. Nobody is so perfect that they can't find something about them, of course. But we're pretty good."

"But we didn't do anything!"

He clicked the TV off altogether. "Anyway, there's no point in sitting around here worrying about it. Let's go cross-country skiing tomorrow."

"Skiing? Where? There's no snow."

"There is upstate. I already checked. We can go to Manchester, to the trails around Hildene. We'll leave early tomorrow morning and stay somewhere tomorrow night. Maybe in that bed and breakfast you like."

"But . . ." *I have to look for Susan!* Each day that went by made finding Zach more remote. "I thought we couldn't afford it."

"That's what credit cards are for."

And what if she was pregnant and skied and lost the baby?

"We won't spend a lot; we can have dinner at the Sirloin Saloon."

"It's kind of short notice."

"That's what makes things fun." Giving the back of her neck a squeeze, he stood up. "Come on, let's get our stuff together. If we get there early enough we'll get a whole day in! And Sunday morning."

This was the Joe she had met at Beth's house six years ago: enthusiastic, handsome, athletic, a man with no odd quirks. He was still all those things—and a few more. Sometimes grading everyone on their performance like the schoolteacher he was, inclined to withdraw when he was annoyed, nursing a gloomy superstitiousness that flared up at odd times. And someone she loved dearly and who loved her.

Only, what a terrible choice—between the baby who in the week she had had him had gripped her finger so tightly as if he were afraid he would lose her, and Joe, who was offering them a respite they badly needed.

Monday morning she had to admit how beneficial the weekend had been. There was something eternal about being in a pine forest in the winter, something in its green and white stillness that took her beyond what had happened and calmed her. Maybe years from now . . . But she didn't want to finish the thought.

Despite the special boot they had had made for her foot, she was only able to ski for an hour at a time. But even the time she spent in the shadow of Hildene, Robert Lincoln's former mansion, or in the warming shed, she felt at peace. They made certain accommodations, of course; one of them was to eat dinner at ten to avoid seeing people with babies. Sunday afternoon she fell asleep before they crossed the Vermont border, and slept for the whole trip home.

During the weekend, at odd moments, Diana Larsen had come into her mind. The more she thought of her, the more irritated Caroline became. She realized that Diana reminded her of her sister. Ruthie, after being in therapy the first time, had gloried in saying whatever she felt, not holding anything unpleasant back. Diana had the same blunt way. She remembered how Diana had criticized her attitude toward Susan. And she was the worst driver she had ever ridden with! She took her inability to explain to Joe who Diana was as a sign she should have nothing more to do with her. If she called, Caroline would just refuse to discuss anything else with her. Imagine her thinking that they would let her write a story about them!

At nine-thirty she left the house to visit the supermarkets of Crane Island. She worked her way through Comsewogue, Martinville, Stony Road Point, Dillon, and Coyne's Cove, convinced that she and Susan were about to come face to face across a black ribbon of conveyor belt. When she did not see Susan, she looked for the employee who seemed the most experienced and described her, mentioning her recent pregnancy and her resemblance to Cher. Several of the clerks knew Caroline by sight and were friendly. But no one appeared to know Susan.

Next she drove around Logan Point, looking for Volvos. By two she had seen seven or eight, and written down their license numbers. If they were parked in front of stores she simply waited until the owners of the cars came out and drove off. She had to admit that most of those people seemed unlikely candidates for a connection with Susan, but recorded the license numbers anyway.

It was almost three when she rounded Pocantico Lane to her house and saw a dark blue car parked in front of it. It was not a car that she recognized, certainly not Diana Larsen's rented Sentra. It was a plain, no-nonsense kind of vehicle, slightly dented, like that of an electric company employee. But it didn't have the CILCO emblem on its door. Then, as she pulled around the car into her driveway, she recognized Rafe Millar sitting inside.

He saluted as she walked across the front yard to the door. What should she do? Hands shaking, she unlocked the front door. *Run! Run through the house and out the back door. Hide in the woods.* But she couldn't do that. Anyway, would you arrest someone you had just waved at?

Instead she waited in the foyer. Its colors—the striped green-and-gold wallpaper and mingled greens of the braided rug—seemed vivid, as if she had never seen them before. The needlework cat doorstop her mother had made smiled its Cheshire grin. But the knock on the front door came like something out of Poe.

She moved the few steps and opened the door.

Rafe Millar was wearing a tan suede jacket with fringe and mirrored sunglasses. As he rocked back on his heels, she expected him to read her her rights. But he said instead, "I have the autopsy report."

"You *do?* When did you get it?"

"A couple days ago."

She felt betrayed by the system. This morning before leaving the house she had called the Medical Examiner's Office to try to get a copy of the autopsy and been told that she would have to put her request in writing.

"But I'm his mother," she had protested. She had hoped to pick the report up in person.

"You have to be next of kin to even request it by mail," the woman informed her. "Or have the permission of the person who is."

"How long does it take?"

"A month to six weeks."

"That *long?* Why?"

But there had been no negotiating with the voice. She had given up and written down the address the woman gave her.

"What does it say?" she asked him.

Millar stepped into the hall, an old black leather folder under his arm. "I have just a few more questions."

She panicked. "But—I can't talk to you without a lawyer!"

"Who says?"

"My lawyer." It sounded dim. "I mean, you can take what I say and twist it around."

"Not if you're telling me the truth. You don't need a lawyer until you've been charged with something, Mrs. Denecke. You haven't been charged with anything." He removed the sunglasses and let his pale blue eyes corroborate his goodwill. "If you want to pay someone a hundred and fifty dollars an hour to sit on his ass and listen, that's up to you. I can't tell you not to throw your money away."

She stared at him. Was *that* what lawyers cost now? A few hours with Martin would bankrupt them!

She thought. "Can't you send the report to him?"

"Naw. I'm not fooling around with that kind of thing." He took a step backward. "I just thought you might want a look."

"I do! But—"

"I didn't get a chance to look at the room the other day. There's something I want to check out." His skin glowed redly in the light from the cranberry glass wall sconces. *Like the devil. He's like the devil.* "I can get a search warrant, easy, and take this place apart. But I'm trying to avoid that with just another quick look." He eyed the stairs behind her. "You don't have to talk to me if you don't want to."

She shrugged and let him pass her, conscious of how much her foot was aching. After the weekend of skiing, the morning of driving and standing around in supermarkets had aggravated it further. At the top of the stairs he stopped and let her go down the hall ahead of him. When she got to the nursery she gripped the doorframe, suddenly dizzy. Was this a mistake, letting him in? Maybe she was making a terrible mistake.

"You okay?"

"Yes."

"Jesus H. Christ!"

She whirled around, but he was looking beyond her.

Belatedly she saw he was looking at the flowers. Shriveled and dried brown at the tips, they looked like a travesty of funeral arrangements. The scent had gone from overripe to decaying, the smell of rotting garbage. The crib, standing exactly in the center of the room, seemed like an altar in some horror movie.

She hadn't been in the room since Friday. She opened her mouth to explain and closed it again. What was there to say?

He was already poking around the display of ointments and powders on the dresser, peering into the crib. What could he be looking for? Finally he went over to the window and yanked back a gingham blue-checked curtain. The windows in the house slid open from the side instead of being raised vertically. Traces of blue fingerprint powder still decorated the frame. He pushed the window open and stuck his head through, then drew back and measured it with his eyes.

Caroline, leaning against the doorjamb, lifted her sore leg and shook her foot gently.

"The other second-floor windows? Are they the same size?"

She nodded.

"You said you heard a noise like this." He pushed the window back and forth along the track.

"Yes." It was impossible not to answer him.

"But nothing else. Not the front door opening or closing. Not anybody on the stairs."

Was that a trick question? "Just those other sounds I told you about. Like opening the dresser, or walking on the floor."

"But *in* the room."

"Yes."

Millar rolled his eyes with exaggerated exasperation. "Give it up, Mrs. Denecke." He ran his hand around the inside of the window, outlining the shape. "You think anyone on earth could fit through here?"

"But—*I* could."

"I doubt that very much."

"Of course I could!"

He pulled a tape measure from his tan pants pocket and moved it expertly across the opening. "Fourteen inches. You weigh how much?"

"About one hundred and ten." She moved toward the open window. "I'll show you!"

He caught her wrist, as if he thought she might jump. "You have the same window downstairs anywhere?"

"In the den."

"How come you don't lock your windows?"

"We do! But upstairs we leave them open a little at night. For ventilation." Did he know how much she regretted it now? If only Zach's window had been locked that night none of this would have happened.

In the den Millar measured the end window with his tape. She opened it and they went outside.

The window was on the south side of the house, four feet off the ground. Caroline stared at it. "We don't have a ladder." But she grasped the metal frame of the window and attempted to pull herself up. Her forearms weren't strong enough. Next she tried to crouch and jump to get height. Finally she just held on and crawled up the side of the house with her knees. She started to twist her way inside. But once her head was inside the window she was blocked by her shoulders. She tried turning sideways and sliding in vertically, but could not support herself at that height and dropped back awkwardly to the ground. Quickly she righted herself. "I

95

would have fit if I'd had a ladder. If I'd had a ladder, I could have slipped in sideways, feet first."

"Up on the second floor?"

"Yes!"

"Come here, Mrs. Denecke." He beckoned to her, and they moved around to the rear of the house. Seen from that perspective it looked huge to Caroline, a distorted rhomboid in a photograph. Looking up at the miles of clapboard, she had a sudden cold doubt. Who would be brave enough to attempt it with a ladder, especially in the dark?

Millar voiced her doubts. "You think anyone would even try to wriggle into a window way up there?" He squatted several feet from the foundation of the house, brushing away snow as if to show her the undisturbed ground. Caroline knelt down beside him. He stopped suddenly.

"Look!" she cried.

There was a grid pattern, where the ground looked as if it had been deliberately stamped on by a running shoe. Why would some-one try on purpose to leave a print? You did that only if you were trying to get someone in trouble—or to hide something else. But what? There were also two rectangular indentations that could have only come from the legs of a ladder.

"Anybody been working out here?"

"No! The windows upstairs are Thermopane, we don't have to put up storms. We haven't been out here for *weeks.*" She shivered, feeling the frozen ground through the knees of her jeans.

"You said you don't have a ladder."

"No."

"What kind of running shoes does your husband wear?"

"Oh, come on! If he were going to do anything to Zachary, he wouldn't have to go through the *window* to do it."

"But he might try to make it look like someone had been out here."

"But we don't even have a ladder! Anyway, Joe doesn't believe that that's what happened."

Millar looked over, trapping her reflection in his silver glasses. "What does he think happened?"

Good, Caroline. That's why you're supposed to keep your mouth shut. Now he knows that even your husband doesn't believe that crazy story. "I just mean, he wouldn't fake it. You've got the evidence that someone's been here right here!"

He motioned for her to get up, and they walked around the house and back inside.

As she opened the front door, Millar said to her, "You got any enemies?"

"Enemies?" Limping over to the black wooden deacon's bench, she sat down, brushing at her soaked knees. He pulled off his sunglasses and crunched himself in beside her, the smell of pine aftershave warring with tobacco.

"Someone who doesn't like you, who might do something like this."

He did believe her! The trouble was, they didn't have any enemies. She searched her memory for any children's parents she or Joe might have offended, other people they might have had disputes with. There just weren't any. Finally she said, "Lorraine, Joe's ex-wife, doesn't like us very much. It was before I knew him, but the divorce was pretty bad. But his daughter, Connie, wouldn't come to the wedding; we haven't heard from her since."

Millar whistled and raised his eyes to the ceiling. "It's the perfect revenge. To take your ex's new baby and leave a dead one in its place. He doesn't have a kid anymore, and he's charged with murder."

While she tried to decide if that was possible, he turned to her. "But not this time, Carol, not this time. The idea that *anybody* would take a baby from a second-story bedroom with a window that nobody could get in or out of insults my intelligence. It's a cockamamy story, Carol."

Can't you even get my name right?

He placed his hand on her jacket sleeve and brought his face very close. "I had a talk with a shrink. He said a woman can go into shock when a kid dies. Sometimes not believe it for hours. Or days. Look at me." His blue eyes had a webby bloodshot pattern. The pores on his reddish nose seemed large. "They can even get amnesia about what happened; they may not remember *how* the baby died. Or even that they did it. That sound familiar?"

Did it? She almost remembered holding Zach and pretending to feed him because Joe was there. The milk running out of his mouth, all over his clothes. *No, that was the time that Zach and I both fell asleep.* She tried to push up from the bench to get away. *Call Martin.*

But Millar held on to her. "A case like this, you'd probably get a finding of diminished responsibility. Your conscience would be clear, we'd wrap the whole thing up." His voice was almost a whisper. "Accidents can happen—we all know that."

Caroline pulled away and stumbled backward off the braided rug as he suddenly released her. "I'm calling my lawyer!"

"Suit yourself." He unzipped the leather folder. Standing up, he handed her a white paper. "See what your lawyer makes of *this.*" Then he was out the door.

The autopsy was short and badly typed, a poor photocopy on a kind of chalky, shiny paper, stamped "Preliminary" at the top. She rested her forearm on her knee, to stop her hand from shaking long enough so she could read it.

It began by talking about "normal extremities" and "unremarkable organs." The baby's length was 28 inches. His heart was described as having an enlarged opening of the foramen ovale. And there was a puncture in the upper right arm consistent with an IV. What was that all about?

The next paragraph listed Zachary's blood type as O-positive. The sentence that came after that chilled her: "Decedent's stomach was empty at time of death; time of death at discovery is placed between 24 and 36 hours, due to morbidity and the presence of potassium in the vitreous humor." If it was Zach, then she had let him starve. But this baby was four inches longer than Zach was at birth. How could he have grown four inches in ten days?

She skimmed the rest. Death was due to acute pulmonary edema, most likely caused by asphyxiation. Tiny hemorrhages in the lungs and thymus were consistent with this diagnosis.

"Preparation of final report awaiting background records from the delivery doctor, Sol Maria Cruz."

Call Joe.

Later she would feel that calling her husband had been a terrible mistake, that she should have waited until he was safely home. But she was too upset not to tell him what had happened. His classes were just ending, and his afternoon coaching had not yet begun.

He was on the phone sooner than she expected. "Caro?"

"Hi! I'm okay." She answered the question in his voice. "But I got a copy of the autopsy."

"So soon?"

"Well . . . Rafe Millar brought it by."

"The police? Did you call Martin?"

"Not yet."

"Caroline, you didn't let him in!"

She crossed her fingers. As she did she realized she couldn't tell him about the conversation, how Millar had terrified her. "Well, only for a minute. But listen! We walked around to the back and found *footprints*. And marks that looked like a ladder had been placed against the wall. I told him *we* hadn't been out there for weeks. So it must have been whoever took Zach! It had to be."

The silence on Joe's end went on for so long that Caroline thought they had been disconnected. "Hello?"

"I'm here." He sounded weary, a preview of the tired, worn-out man she wanted to keep him from ever becoming. "What made you go in back at all? And why did you say anything to him?"

"I just told him *we* hadn't been out there."

"Caro, I have. I walked around back there the day after to see if it could possibly have happened like you said. It didn't seem possible—frankly."

"But *you* didn't leave ladder marks!"

"That's not the point! If my prints are around the backyard, they can just say I faked the other thing."

"But you didn't!" *Tell me you didn't.* "Didn't you see the ladder marks when you went out there?"

"No. But I wasn't looking for anything like that. Listen, I've got to go."

"Wait!" But she was not sure what she wanted to say. Something warned her not to discuss the autopsy report with him. "Okay. I love you."

"I love *you.*" But it sounded more like a burden he had been given to bear.

Caroline decided next to try the obstetrician, Sol Maria Cruz. Maybe she could explain what it meant about a heart abnormality and a mark that looked like an IV. The phone listing was for a medical building on Comsewogue Road, but she learned, dismayed, that the doctor was out, recovering from an operation. Her home number was unpublished. Why didn't anything ever work out? When she called back the service, saying that she'd like to send flowers to her home, the friendly receptionist told her that Dr. Cruz lived in that big orange house on Main Street in Martinville, but she wasn't sure of the number. But certainly the florist would know.

Caroline thanked her and hung up.

The ache in her foot was insistent now, flaring into starbursts of pain. She limped upstairs; she would have to lie down.

She didn't plan to sleep. But when she woke, after a strange dream in which she was attacking the side of the house with an ax, she found herself in total darkness. Alarmed, she checked the digital readout. It was after seven! Joe would already be home; nothing was started for dinner. She knew he didn't approve of her sleeping this way. Pushing the comforter aside, she swung her feet to the floor and tested the right one. It was better, but still sore. She would have to take better care of herself.

"Hi!" she called at the bottom of the stairs.

She expected to find him in the den watching the news, but the first floor was also dark, just as she had left it. Had swimming practice run late? At least this would give her some time in the kitchen. And there was plenty of food; in each supermarket she had gone into to ask about Susan she had purchased three or four items. Tonight's dinner was Cajun catfish with wild rice and asparagus.

When Joe was not home by eight and had not called, she took up watch in the living room. Now she was frightened. What if there had been an accident at school, one of the boys hurt in swimming practice? Didn't bad things happen in threes? She didn't really want to believe it, but sometimes when she counted up, it was true.

When the police car pulled into the driveway, lights on but not flashing, she knew that the next bad thing was happening. They had intercepted Joe on his way home and were coming to get her. What had she said to Millar that convinced him to arrest them? Or maybe he planned to do so all along, but had been hoping for a confession to save him some work. Her body feeling like running water, she leaned against the front window. *I don't even know what to take!*

But Joe was climbing out of the backseat of the car. As he approached the front door, the cruiser began retreating down the driveway.

She managed to get to the door and pull it open.

Joe gestured at the gauze taped across his forehead. "Listen, I'm okay."

"What happened?"

"The car. I had an accident."

"But the police!"

"They were nice enough to drive me to the hospital, then bring me home. It was that policeman who was here that night. The young one, Donald."

Donald certainly got around. "Was anyone *hurt?*" She moved closer but did not hug him, afraid that she would aggravate some wound she could not see.

But he put out his arms and held her tightly against his tan jacket. "There were no other cars. I must have dozed off; I hit an embankment on the side of the road."

"My God!"

"Fortunately, I wasn't going too fast. The car's a disaster, of course."

"But you're okay?" She didn't feel as if she could take any more. What if she had lost him, too?

"Just bruised, really. I was lucky. I guess."

Something about his last comment sounded so ominous that she drew back and read his face anxiously. Weren't one-car accidents considered suspicious? Then she moved in and hugged him again. "You were lucky," she repeated as if it were a litany. "Only to be bruised a little. It doesn't matter about the car." She pressed her cheek against him. "Are you hungry? Can you eat anything?"

"I can always eat something."

As they sat across from each other finishing the catfish, Joe said, "In a way, it's a good thing you're not working. I'll have to take your car for a few days. They can fix mine, but it'll take time."

"My car?" She put down her fork, dismayed. How would she look for Susan?

Joe lifted his face inquiringly. "You don't need it during the day."

"I do sometimes." She thought. "Maybe one day I can drop you off at school and pick you up again."

"Maybe." But his face pulled together, displeased.

"I don't need the car most of the time. But I do have errands and things."

"Whatever."

He still did not look happy. But Caroline would not yield any further.

A moment later, when the phone rang, she signaled to Joe to let the machine pick it up. Sitting in the greenhouse, she could tell only that it was a woman. But when she played the message later she was dismayed to hear Diana's voice telling her that she had some news and would stop by Tuesday afternoon.

After dinner Joe changed from his rumpled suit to the red plaid flannel shirt and old gray pants he liked to wear, and settled into the den. Caroline watched him lean his silvery head back against the sofa and sip a tumbler of whiskey and water. "Ah-hh."

"You're sure you're okay?" The gauze taped to his forehead frightened her. What if there was internal bleeding? What if he had a concussion they had missed diagnosing?

He smiled up at her. "I'm okay."

"If anything happened to you . . ."

"Nothing will. I just get tougher with age." He patted the sofa next to him in invitation. She went over and sat down, letting him stroke her hair. *I do love you.*

They stayed that way for several minutes, moving against each other, making little loving sounds, while Caroline wrestled with how to ask him about Connie and Lorraine. Talking about Connie only made him unhappy. But if there was any chance, *any* chance, that they had Zach, she had to know. "Joe?"

"Umm."

"Do you know where Lorraine is these days?"

"Lorraine? My ex-wife Lorraine?" His tone was meant to point up the curiousness of her question, especially when they were holding each other with such affection. "Still in the nursing home, I guess. Why?"

It was a dive into icy water she didn't want to make. "Well . . . Rafe Millar asked if we had any enemies." She said it meekly. "Someone who might have taken Zach."

"And you mentioned Lorraine?" He pulled away from her. "Way to go, Caroline. She'll tell him anything. That I killed the family dog and beat the girls. Anything to get me in trouble!"

"But what if they're involved?"

"Involved in *what?* Lorraine? Living in a nursing home? Come on!"

"Connie."

"Caroline, I'm warning you. You can't seem to keep your mouth shut. If you talk to him again and get arrested because of what you tell him, I can't be responsible." His hand, holding the drink, was shaking.

"What do you mean?"

"I'm trying to get it through your head to stop giving the police information! Everything you tell them they can use against us. They'll lie if they have to; they'll do anything. They aren't accountable to anyone."

She looked down at her lap. "They wouldn't *lie.*"

"No? You're an expert now? All they're looking to do is close cases. They don't care about *you.*"

"Do you want to see the autopsy?" she whispered.

"I guess. But promise me, Caroline, promise me that you won't talk to the police again. Don't even answer the door!"

She promised.

NINE

Monday Diana went into the Adoption Unit at noon. She spent the morning on a travel essay about the phrases tourists *really* needed to know—"Does that ring mean you're married?" and "Is that white stuff poisonous?"—phrases that weren't in most guidebooks. Her cash was running low. If there wasn't a book on adoption here she would need to finish the article and move on to something else.

When she came in, Dolly was unloading a brown leather tote bag branded with initials onto her desk, pulling out a container of fruit salad and a bottle of Perrier. Dolly's desk was a work of art. Daffodils and irises were arranged in a smoked black glass vase to the left of a blotter with a classical architectural print in black and white. Pictures of her daughters, adorable in matching straw hats and holding Easter baskets, stood in a designer frame to its right. Dolly's white tape dispenser, pencil cup, and letter opener were not agency issue, either.

Howard was leaning on his doorjamb, watching Dolly. He was wearing a shaggy blue plaid sweater and morning shadow. "So what's the verdict?"

"On the Senaks?" Dolly smiled. "They're wonderful. You should see the house they live in!"

"Want to tell me about *them?*"

"I think they'll do just fine. Fleur is warm and loving, a real earth mother. And they live right on the water!"

"That should make Nicole happy. We think we have a home for Nicole Quinter," he said to Diana. "These people called Friday afternoon. They have one child, they're anxious to adopt another. And they're willing to take a handicapped baby."

Dolly was nodding vigorously. "Fleur said she thought she could handle the medical problems. They went to the hospital this morning to see Nicole. If they want her, we can place her tomorrow."

"That soon?" Diana said.

"Not soon enough for Infants Hospital!" She fluffed her golden helmet with practiced fingers. "Really, that place is impossible. When I told them Friday we were still looking for a home, this nurse started *screaming* at me! She kept saying how Nicole's taking up a bed and costing hundreds of dollars a day because we won't get off our duffs."

"Really? Didn't she know you were Dr. Hazelton's wife?"

But Dolly only laughed.

"What's Michael Senak like?" Howard asked.

Dolly opened her mouth, then stopped to choose the right words. "Interesting! I mean, he's fine. He even had on a suit for the interview. But he says he'd *really* like to be a jazz musician." Her smile was indulgent.

"Can he make a living doing that?"

"No, of course not. I mean, he doesn't. He owns a landscaping business. But it does show a nice range of interests."

"He show you pay stubs?"

"How could he? He's self-employed." She unscrewed the top on her water bottle. "But they're certainly solvent."

Howard scratched his neck. "I don't know, Dolly. A wanna-

106

be musician . . . no demonstrable income . . . a kid named Starry Night . . ."

"Who happens to be adorable and well behaved! Come on, Howard. First you demand I find a home, then when I do you get suspicious. They live in the nicest part of Comsewogue!"

"After all, it's the mother who's the primary caregiver," said Hannah, moving to Dolly's defense on her way back from Mr. Coffee.

"And Fleur's absolutely warm and wonderful. Just what this baby *needs*. In any case, they'll be a foster home first. That'll give us time to work out any . . . wrinkles."

Hannah stepped nearer. "Honestly, Howard, Dolly's right. You have a suspicious mind."

"I don't have good reason to?" But he raised a hand in surrender. "Okay. If they visit the hospital and feel they can handle it, we'll try the placement. But, Dolly, please get their documentation ASAP. Get this home study done!" He turned to Diana. "Maybe you'd like to go along tomorrow? It's a good chance to see what's involved in a home study. There's references, medicals, subsequent interviews. Certain things you have to look for, things that weren't said but should have been."

"Sounds like being a writer."

"I'd like a second opinion, anyway. We *never* move this fast. If you think they're wild and crazy, or underestimating the problems involved, just to get a child . . ."

Dolly's blue eyes turned rounder. "You don't trust me?"

Howard laughed. "I don't trust anyone."

Diana followed him into his office and waited for him to sit down. He looked up and gave her a warm smile.

Let me brush your hair. No, no, Diana, that's what his wife is for. "A girl named Susan."

" 'A Boy Named Sue.' Johnny Cash, 1969."

"No, a real girl named Sue. Susan. At the maternity home."

He shook his head slowly.

"She was at Heart's Retreat about a month ago," Diana prompted.

"I don't know who that could be. Sometimes Suffolk County will place girls there if they know we have a vacancy. The housemother would know."

"Okay, I'll ask Eileen."

But she forgot about it until that night, when her phone at home rang. It was Eileen calling to say that Roxanne's water had broken and she couldn't fix it. "It's a joke," she explained unnecessarily, and paused as if waiting for Diana to write it down. "You said you wanted to know when we left for the hospital."

"Yes, thanks! Can you call me as soon as the baby is born? I'll stop by then. By the way: Do you remember a girl you had recently named Susan?"

"Susan?" Her voice was a shade less welcoming.

"I don't know her last name. It would have been last month."

"Diana." The tone was disapproving. It was the voice of someone who had suffered incursions good-naturedly and kept quiet, but now was being pushed too far. "You know I can't give out information like that! A girl who has been here, had a baby, and left is entitled to confidentiality. No one told me I had to give you that."

This was Eileen "You can use my real name" Norris? "But she was from Long Island?"

"I'm taking the Fifth on that." A chuckle. "Listen, I have to go. Roxie's moaning in the living room and scaring Shane."

Roxie could scare anybody. And so could you.

She'd have to call Caroline and give her the bad news.

Infants Hospital for Catastrophic Illnesses was located at the eastern end of Crane Island. Its spectacular grounds had belonged to I. P. Henderson, a shipping magnate, who, charmed by its sea views, moved his entourage to the island in 1925. After the stock market crash he moved his family out West to start over again, simply abandoning the immense fieldstone mansion. It stood empty for years, then was made into a convalescent home for children with TB before being purchased and enlarged by the hospital board in 1974. The gardens had since been pruned to reveal ornamental trees, topiary animals, and small mazes with benches at their centers; the angled hedge had been clipped to read INFANTS HOSPITAL.

Diana was charmed. She parked next to the newer white clapboard wing on the right side of the mansion to wait for Dolly. She assumed she was early. But as time passed and Dolly did not appear, she decided to go inside.

On one wall of the lobby there were large cardboard cutouts of Snow White, Winnie the Pooh, and Big Bird. On another hung a large brass plaque with engraved names. It was called "Our Honor Roll." Diana expected it to contain the names of the hospital's donors, but as she got closer she saw, chilled, that the names were of children who had died there: George "Buster" Bigelow 1976–1978. Monique Murlo 1983–1988. For many names the years of birth and death were the same.

Quickly she turned away and faced the staircase. As she did, she saw the receptionist gesturing to her.

"Are you Diana Larsen?"

"Yes?"

"Your office called. A Marci Potamkin. She said to call her right away."

"Oh, okay. Thank you." There must have been a delay of some kind.

She found a pay phone in an alcove next to the gift shop.

Marci answered. "Diana, hi! I'm so glad you called. Listen, we've got a problem. Dolly was supposed to meet you? But she forgot she doesn't work Tuesdays? And Hannah's out in the field somewhere. Howard's in training, and I'm here by myself. Do you think you could just bring Nicole to her foster home? I mean, you're already there."

"Me?"

"I can fax a copy of the Permanent Surrender—I already asked if they have a machine. I'll call them and give you authorization."

"But shouldn't she travel by ambulette?" What if she died on the way there? "I don't even have a car seat!"

"I'm sure the *hospital* can lend you something. You'll bring it right back."

"But what do I do?"

"Just wait in the lobby until someone comes down. I'll call and make the arrangements. Do you need directions to the house?"

"Yes!" *This is crazy. This is weird. Howard will hate it. I don't know anything about babies.* But she wrote down the information, then went back into the lobby and waited against the wall. Finally she saw a tall, very thin woman with lavender hair and rimless glasses coming down the stairs. Her steely eyes hit everywhere, with the emphasis of a blind person tapping a cane. She moved unerringly toward Diana.

"Miss Larsen? I'm Trudy Blocksma."

"Hi. Glad to meet you."

She felt the woman sizing her up, weighing her frivolous red parka and pile-lined boots against the weather reports for sleet.

"So your agency is finally taking responsibility for Nicole."

There were several responses, from a simple "Yes, Ma'am" to "It's not *my* agency," and "How dare you insinuate . . ." But none seemed worth the trouble. Diana just nodded.

"Did you know her new foster parents never came to the hospital to discuss her care with us?"

"Really? I thought they came yesterday."

"That was the *old* couple."

What old couple? Were there grandparents involved? *I'm missing something.*

"The couple who came here," Miss Blocksma amended. "I interviewed them myself, and I can tell you I was not impressed. After they came I called that woman, Mrs. Hazelton, from your office, and she promised me the baby would *not* go to them."

110

You're dead meat, Dolly.

"Nicole is a seriously handicapped child."

"I know. But—is there something beside the swallowing-breathing problem?"

The gray-blue eyes pinned Diana to the wall next to Dumbo. "You don't think that's enough? Nicole is able to regulate her breathing herself right now. But if future problems arise, people have to be very alert."

"Mrs. Hazelton said—"

"It's not that they aren't enthusiastic. But this isn't a puppy they're buying. And there's something about that young man, something slippery—I think he must be on drugs."

The standard insult of the times. Before she could offer to leave Nicole there, Miss Blocksma said quickly, "I've signed the discharge papers. It's on your heads now."

This woman did not leave you a lot to say. As she turned back toward the stairs, she added, "Tell them they must bring her here for checkups." And she was gone.

Diana returned to the pay phone. She expected Pearl to answer, but it was Marci again.

"Look, the hospital doesn't want her to go to the Senaks."

"They're refusing to discharge her?" Marci sounded wide-eyed.

"No, they've discharged her. They just don't want her to go there."

"Listen, Diana, it's *our* baby. We have guardianship and custody. They have nothing to say about it."

"But what if something happens to her on the way there?"

"She's that fragile?" Marci sounded shaken.

"I guess not." Even Trudy Blocksma had said she was fine, for now. "It's just, a lot of things seem to be happening to babies these days."

"Listen, Diana, no one will blame you if . . . But she'll be fine."

"Okay." She saw that two young nurses had appeared in the lobby, carrying a car bed. "See you later."

111

Nicole was beautiful. Even if you weren't attracted to babies, you couldn't help grazing your knuckles over her perfect rosy skin. Her blue eyes had a slightly milky quality, but they seemed to be tracking whatever was around her. Diana talked to her all the way to the car, reassuring Nicole while she strapped the car bed into the front seat. There was barely room for her to drive, but she wanted the baby where she could watch her.

Nicole fell asleep instantly with a snore that bounced off the far corners of the Sentra. When they were nearly to Comsewogue, she woke up but did not fuss. It was as if she sensed that with all her handicaps she could not risk alienating people further.

Dolly certainly had been right to rave about the house. It stood on a rise of grass that was very green for winter, and seemed all glass and silvery wood. The back of the house, which you saw first from the road, was beautifully landscaped. But of course, that was his job. The white pickup parked to one side had a green logo of a tree and two bushes on its door. Diana shifted Nicole to her other arm and walked along a path of tree slices set in white grit to the front door. To one side an Arcosanti wind chime with a weathered bronze pelican clanged faintly. A large cedar deck went right to the water.

As soon as she knocked, there was a stampede of feet. A tall, slender child with a head of golden curls yanked back the door dramatically. Her mother was right behind her, her smooth brown hair pulled back in a short French braid. Both were wearing madras muu-muus showing chains of jungle animals. Their faces did not lose their grins as Fleur reached for Nicole and took her from Diana.

"Come sweetheart, come sweetheart, come to Mommy!" she crooned, reaching down with her finger and smoothing the baby's face. When Nicole lunged for the finger, Fleur laughed delightedly and let her suck on it. It seemed to be an instant connection. "Here, let's get you undressed," she said, sitting down on a buttery beige sofa in the high-ceilinged living room. Starry Night perched on the wide leather arm for a moment, then disappeared.

Settling on a matching couch opposite, Diana looked around the room. Oriental rugs accented a quarry tile floor, matching the kilim pillows scattered on the furniture. Instead of a coffee table, three granite squares held several art books, a bowl of paper whites, and a primitive iron sculpture of a creation scene that Diana recognized as Haitian art. *I think they'll be able to feed her.*

Fleur unzipped the bunting and shook it away, then reached inside a yellow stretchie to feel the diaper. "Dry!" she exclaimed, as if Nicole had performed a feat of exceptional intelligence. "You're just a little cuddle bunny, aren't you? *Look* at that tummy. I can see they've been spoiling you in the hospital." But she didn't sound at all annoyed. "I always wanted to be a pediatrician myself," she confessed to Diana. "I actually majored in chemistry. But then I got married. After Starry was born, I stayed home to have a big family. And guess what? I never got pregnant again!"

It was not hard to imagine Fleur in the center of a flock of children, doling out juice and fancy Band-Aids. Or in a white jacket, charming her little patients. Why hadn't *she* gotten an adoptive mother like that instead of the stiff-faced Karin Larsen? *I could have been very happy in waterfront property.*

"Are you from Crane Island?" Diana asked.

"Not originally. But we've gotten to love it. Especially Starry." Fleur frowned. "Where *is* she? Starry?"

The child came out of the hallway slowly, giving Nicole a quick, murderous glance.

"Sweetheart, why don't you bring the Pound Puppy we picked out for Baby? You can give it to her." She smiled at her daughter. "Remember how much you wanted a new baby?"

Yes, but not a little cuddle bunny.

Starry rolled her eyes. "I changed my mind."

Fleur gave Diana a conspirator's smile. "Well . . . why don't you bring her the puppy anyway?"

But Starry stalked off as a man sauntered in. He was dressed in jeans, a brown print jersey shirt open to the navel, and a tangle of gold chains. Hazel eyes a little too small, a little too close-set, a mocking twist to his mouth. No wonder Miss Blocksma hadn't wanted to take him home. "Where's the other lady?"

"She doesn't work today. She'll probably stop by tomorrow."

"You want to see the room, too?"

"Okay."

She got up and followed him, noticing they were close to the same height. Starry's bedroom was large enough for seven or eight little girls. There were a lot of ornate wicker rockers and toy shelves, white against the pale peach walls. Starry's white wooden bed had a cutout heart at the head and the foot, and was delicately painted with Beatrix Potter scenes. Across the hall in a slightly smaller room, Nicole's narrow-spindle crib had a fluffy canopy with brass filials and was filled with soft white lamps and lacy pillows.

"Fleur wants to keep her in with us for a few days."

When they returned to the living room, Fleur was still engrossed in Nicole. "Look at this, she's grabbing my finger! She found it; I didn't give it to her." She glanced up, her face shining. "I bet she's not as bad off as they say."

"She does seem aware of things," Diana admitted. Then, unable to quash her curiosity, she asked, "What happened when you went to Infants Hospital?"

Fleur sighed; Michael made a face. "That bitch needs a kick in the ass!"

"I don't think they thought we were serious enough," Fleur said, bringing her face down to Nicole's stomach, then tickling it with her nose to try to make her laugh.

"We *know* how to handle her breathing," Michael put in. "Any moron would." He turned to his wife. "How about some tea for the lady?"

Fleur looked at Diana doubtfully. "We only have herbal."

Of course. "Country Apple's fine. Or cranberry."

"Great! Here, you hold Baby." Fleur nestled Nicole in Michael's arms, and went into the kitchenette. Starry Night entered immediately from the opposite hall, holding a small tan stuffed animal.

114

With a grim smile she went over and held it just above Nicole's face, poised to smash it down.

"Don't!" Diana cried.

Michael looked. "Not *in* her face, kiddo. Just put it next to her."

Starry balanced the puppy on Nicole's stomach and scowled at her father.

"Don't worry," Michael said to Diana. "Starry will be okay."

"This baby gets hurt easily," Diana said to her. "You can't really play with her."

Starry's wide features looked interested. "Is she gonna die?"

"I hope not. But you have to be very careful with her." Fleur would need to keep an eye on *this* one. "I thought maybe you'd be in school today." As she said it, Diana recognized it as a wish. *I guess I just don't like kids. Dolly loved her.*

"I don't *go* to school," Starry announced, curls bouncing as she did a split on the floor. "Only to ballet and gymnastics."

"We've been home-schooling her so far," said Fleur, coming in with the cups on a tray. "Of course that could change any time. Anyway, this is a big day!"

They toasted Nicole's coming with cranberry tea, then Diana asked Michael, "Where can I see you play?"

"Well, not around here." He squinted, amused. "We don't do weddings. We've had a few gigs in clubs around the Village. And sometimes we do open mike nights."

"But they're very good," Fleur protested.

"It doesn't exactly pay the rent," he pointed out. "So what happens now?"

"I guess Dolly Hazelton will be out to see you tomorrow. She'll bring papers for you to sign." She knew that Dolly had already put their names through the Child Abuse Registry in Albany, and they had come out clean. "She said you have to be fingerprinted."

Michael snorted. "Sure they don't want a sperm sample? And my hat size?"

"Mike, stop!" Fleur reached over and swatted at his hand. "They

115

have their regulations that are important to them." She turned to Diana. "He can't stand bureaucracy."

"Who can?" She stood up to pull on her jacket.

"Thanks so much for bringing us this little doll!" Fleur had Nicole back in her arms. "It would have been terrible to leave her in the hospital any longer."

Feeling satisfied, Diana drove to Caroline Denecke's house.

TEN

Let's go back to the beginning. Tell me everyone you ever showed Zach's room to."

"I told you. Just my friends." Caroline looked over her shoulder from where she knelt beside the fireplace, poking a log into place. Diana, in jeans and a bright red sweater, was reclining on the den couch, her feet tucked under one of the seat cushions. It looked as though she would never leave. At her elbow, on the magazine table, was her third cup of coffee.

"Tell me again. Because if someone came in the window and took him, they would have had to know where his room was. Right?"

"Right." Diana had fastened onto the story like a cat with a bird in its mouth, and would not let go. She made Caroline show her the layout of the house, then had settled in the den to ask more questions. "Any workmen? Who put up the wallpaper and painted?"

"We did."

"Any meter readers? No, I guess they wouldn't go upstairs."

Caroline, satisfied the new log would catch, went back to the wing chair. The thing about Diana Larsen was that when you were with her she kind of caught you up and swept you along. It was afterward, thinking about the things she said, that made you annoyed.

"Could they tell anything about the rooms from outside? By special curtains? Do you have a mobile or anything in the window? One of those bright orange stickers that tell the fire department there's a child in there?"

"No. I was going to get one, I just hadn't had a chance." Why was she apologizing to this woman? "And the curtains are all the same on that side."

"That doesn't exactly make it easy. Or, it makes it too easy. Anyway, let's go back to last week. Your friends came to see him. What about any of them?"

Caroline shifted against the armrest with shock. "None of my friends would do anything like that! I'd trust them with . . . my life."

"Really? I don't have *any* friends like that. I guess you get them if you stay in one place long enough. Or maybe it's me." She moved her eyes around the room as if considering that, then back to Caroline. "Okay: Any delivery men? UPS, you said. Anybody send flowers?"

"Only . . . after." This morning, first thing, she had gone to the nursery and trashed them. That is, she had thrown away the dead flowers and put the containers and bows down in the basement along with the furniture her parents had left behind when they moved south. The area was already crowded with all the antiques she planned to refinish someday.

"You didn't have a nurse or anyone come in to help you?"

"No. There was that woman from the hospital, but she didn't . . . oh Lord, yes she did!"

"What? *What?*"

But Caroline put up her hand for silence so she could try to remember it more clearly.

The woman had come to the door on Zachary's third day home, holding out a wicker basket with a handle.

"You didn't take your goodies," she scolded. "From the hospital. It's got some *lovely* things in it." The woman was round and black-haired. "Jefferson Hospital is good to new moms."

"Oh! Come in."

The woman stepped quickly over the threshold. She was wearing a navy wool car coat with a limp plaid scarf dangling, untied, and white polyester slacks. An off-duty nurse? "And how are you getting on with your wee one?"

"Good! He's sleeping right now." Impulsively, she added, "Would you like to see him?"

"Could I? Seeing the babies is the nicest part of my job."

And Caroline had led her through the hallway, up the stairs and right to where Zachary's room was.

"Oh! This nursery is *cunning.*" The woman came up heavily behind her, head swiveling at everything.

"Thank you."

"And there's the tiny man!"

They moved together to the crib. Zach was cuddled in a little ball, rump up, looking adorable. Impulsively Caroline scooped him into her arms and brought him back downstairs to see their visitor out. When the woman was gone, she settled with him on the couch. "Let's see just what kind of goodies we have here." She peered into the basket, and pulled out a vial of baby lotion, diaper rash ointment, and blue baby shampoo.

"Look, Zach!" She showed him a yellow sponge duck, a bath toy, tickling his chin with it gently. His dark eyes tracked everything, his tiny red fists opening and closing. She couldn't wait until he started to talk. "And here's a frame to put *you* in." She had already taken photos of Joe and Beth holding him. The small porcelain frame was hand-painted with tiny blue flowers.

Caroline had laid Zachary on the couch next to her as she pulled out the last item from the basket. It was still in plastic—a heavy blue blanket sleeper with a white teddy bear appliquéd on one side. It had seemed a pretty classy gift for a hospital to be handing out.

She left the blanket sleeper in the hope that he would be wearing it when they came, to make the exchange of babies quicker. Even if I hadn't put it on him, in the shock and confusion I might have thought I had.

She opened her eyes and looked at Diana. "Someone did come. A woman who said she was from the hospital. And, yes, I showed her Zachary's room."

Diana flipped her legs to the floor and sat up. "Did she give you her name?"

Caroline thought. "I don't think so," she said finally.

"Just said she was from Jefferson Hospital?"

"Uh-huh."

"Well, it's easy enough to find out. Just call the hospital and ask."

"Ask what? If they have a short, fat woman with a black bowl cut who gives out presents?" She giggled, despite herself, at the counterpoint to Santa Claus.

Diana laughed too. "No. Just ask who distributes the complimentary gifts."

"Good idea." She burrowed under a stack of newspapers and came up with the directory and a portable phone in the shape of a cat.

Diana rolled her eyes.

She dialed the hospital.

"Switchboard."

"Hi. May I have the gift department please?"

"The *what* department?"

"Whoever distributes the sample gifts for new mothers?"

"Hold on." There was ringing and then a voice barked, "Public Relations."

"Hello? I'm calling about the gift baskets you distribute for new babies."

A pause then, slightly mystified, "What *about* them?"

"I'm trying to reach the woman who brought mine to the house."

"To your house?"

"She said I had forgotten to get it when I left," Caroline pressed.

"We don't have anyone who *delivers* the samples. The nurses are supposed to hand them out when the women leave. Half the time they forget."

"Oh. What's in the baskets?"

"The usual. Samples of toiletries mainly. They're not baskets though—the things are in plastic bags."

"Not . . . toys or clothes or anything?" She was embarrassed to even ask.

"No. Nothing like that."

"Thanks."

She pressed the off button and turned back to Diana. "They don't have anyone like that."

Diana brought her legs, narrow in jeans, back up to the couch and rested her chin on her knees. Her loose dark hair flowed to one side. "That makes it even more likely that Zach was taken," she mused, "since somebody came to your house on false pretenses. If there really had been a person who brings gifts, then it might only be coincidence that she was here. But this way, you *know.*"

"Know what?"

"You know that someone pretended to bring you gifts just to get in here and see the baby's room."

"So what do we do now?"

"Find out who."

"How?"

"You could go look around the hospital and see if you saw her again. I mean, she had to be someone who knew about the hospital giving stuff out." She lifted her head. "Tell me again what she looked like."

"Short, kind of roly-poly. With black hair."

Diana was staring at her. "You said a bowl cut?"

"Did I? I guess I did." Caroline wiped at her forehead, surprised to find it was sweaty.

Diana reached back and gathered her hair into a bundle. "Because it sounds like someone I know! Eileen, the housemother at Heart's Retreat. The maternity home. She would know about complimentary gifts. But—wow! I can't imagine Eileen would have the nerve to do something like that. I mean, she's an ex-nun and all!"

Caroline shifted away from the fire. The woman had seemed so genuine, so full of goodwill toward them. "Maybe she didn't know what she was doing it for. Maybe someone just asked her to deliver it."

"Maybe. But she's the one who got all coy when I asked her if Susan was ever there. Suddenly everything was 'confidential.' But what would Eileen be doing mixed up with stealing a baby?"

"Maybe she was trying to help Susan get him back."

They settled into silence to consider it. With the daylight waning, the fire was starting to stretch shadowy fingers on the walls.

"If Eileen *was* trying to help her, maybe that's why she didn't want to give you information," Caroline added.

"It makes sense," Diana admitted. "She's very protective of the girls."

Caroline burrowed into the chair. She was suddenly chilled again. "So maybe you don't really want to help me get him back. I mean, the other day you thought Susan should have him. That we had 'victimized' her." She couldn't keep the edge out of her voice.

"But you can't—you shouldn't take what I say that seriously." She stretched, dropping her legs to the floor. It seemed a prelude to leaving. "If she wanted him back, it was not the way to do it. Leaving a dead baby in his place. That's gross! Would you recognize Eileen again if you saw her?"

"I think so."

"I'll try to get a picture of her or something. Meanwhile, Crystal would tell me about Susan. I'll keep looking for her. Plus, I have one other place to try to get Susan's address. I'll call you about it tomorrow."

Caroline felt breathless with thanks.

ELEVEN

The Mother and Child Pavilion in the new wing of Jefferson Hospital had been created to take advantage of the trend toward older parenthood. An artist from East Hampton had been commissioned to fill the walls with swirling pastel shapes of mothers and children. There were complimentary appointments with a hairdresser and a nutritionist, and the night before discharge the hospital provided a candlelight dinner of lobster and wine for the new parents.

Diana wondered what single mothers or women in for late abortions were given. If there even were any of the latter. Was it possible that there was a whole island in the shadow of New York City with a pre-1970s stance? It would make an interesting sidebar.

But Crane Island was a strange place anyway—a kind of storage dump for what people wanted out of sight. Infants Hospital had many more terminally ill children than could ever have been born on Crane Island. Heart's Retreat had traditionally hidden away pregnant girls from everywhere else. There was a psychiatric hospital in Coyne's Cove that housed patients from Manhattan. She

124

would not be surprised to find an AIDS hospice as well.

So why *not* a theme maternity ward? She found Roxanne in a blue-and-white room with a gold anchor on the door. In the green hospital gown, her hair slicked back severely from her sallow face, the teenager looked much older. A TV talk show about Wall Street cocaine use echoed off the paintings of sailboats.

Diana reached up and turned the sound down, then pulled a red canvas director's chair close to the bed. "Hi, Roxanne. How *are* you?"

Roxanne turned her head away.

Diana sat holding the small box of Godiva chocolates she had brought. It was her all-occasion gift. "Earth to Roxanne."

A grunt.

"Roxie, are you okay?"

The girl jerked her head around, looking persecuted. "Yes! But I need my blow-dryer. Miss Norris keeps forgetting to bring my blow-dryer!"

"How are you feeling?"

Roxanne, looking straight ahead, muttered something Diana could not hear.

"What?"

"I *said*, like I got my period."

"You mean because of the bleeding—are you wearing a pad?"

"The way it felt yesterday!" She eyed Diana balefully, as if it were *her* fault.

"Here." Diana held out the beautifully wrapped package.

"What's that?"

"Candy. For you."

"Oh. Thanks."

"I stopped and saw the baby. He's adorable."

Roxanne closed her eyes.

"Do you have a name picked out?"

"Yes, and they better not change it! He's Richard Karl Johnson. Junior."

Who would change it? Marci had told her that although a father's name could not be put on the birth certificate without his written consent, there was no law against giving a baby the alleged father's name. Or any other name the mother chose.

As if reading her thoughts, Roxanne said, "I called up Richie. I told him he had a son."

"Really? What did he say?"

"Good."

"Good? He said good?"

"Whadja think he'd say?"

It was not a question to which she had given much thought. "Is he coming down?"

"Maybe."

"Have you talked to your mother?"

"I just had a baby," Roxanne whined. *Get off my back.*

"Did the doctor say when you can leave?"

"Yeah." She sank back on her pillows. "Tomorrow."

"Really? You seem . . . exhausted."

"I'm fine. I just need my fucking blow-dryer!" She pushed at her lank hair with a fretful hand.

"Where are you taking the baby?" Diana knew she could not bring him back to Heart's Retreat. It seemed a bit of final coercion, left over from the days when it was thought dangerous to let the still-pregnant girls in the home see someone actually keep her baby. Faced with no place to bring a child, there were always girls who capitulated and surrendered at that point.

"Where do you think I'm taking him? He's mine, isn't he?"

"That he is."

"You never believed that Richie and me were getting married." *Guess what? I still don't.* "Well—good luck."

On the way out she stopped for another look at baby Richard. He was adorable, red-faced, with a shock of black hair and a look of perpetual surprise. In the sixties, given his heritage, he might have been sent as surplus to New York Foundling. Now, of course, any number of couples would have snapped him up. As she turned away from the observation window, one of the nurses she had gotten to know, a cheerful young woman with bright red hair and three babies of her own, stopped her.

"Diana! You're visiting the girl in Anchors Aweigh?"

It sounded more like a musical comedy than a room. "Yes. Why?"

Jocelyn dropped her voice. "I have to tell you, she's very strange with that baby. I mean, she just won't acknowledge him! When the nurse brought him in yesterday to feed, she sent him right back—like an airplane meal that needed to be reheated. She said to bring him back after *Geraldo.*"

Diana smiled at the image. "Did she ever feed him?"

"No! After that, the nurses didn't even try. But she's never even gotten out of bed and gone to look at him."

Still, it had been less than twenty-four hours, Diana thought in Roxanne's defense. Low-energy types didn't bounce right back and run the halls. "Did anyone talk to her about him—what to do, what to expect?"

"That's Social Services' job. I would assume she's surrendering him for adoption. But still—poor little tyke!"

Diana, looking down the bright hall, thought of something else. "You don't do abortions here?"

Jocelyn blinked. "Of course we do."

"But Dr. Hazelton said he didn't."

"Sidney? He does sometimes. He doesn't like to, but if somebody's amnio comes back bad, the fetus is damaged, he will if they want to. He's good that way."

"Hmm." Maybe it was only healthy teenagers he tried to force into having babies that could be adopted.

"Diana, *nobody* likes to see abortion as a form of birth control."

As long as you don't legislate that. Belatedly she remembered something else. "When Gloria MacDonald was here she became friendly with another girl. They wanted to stay in touch, but Gloria lost her address. Is there any way I can get her mailing address?"

"Do you know her name?"

This was the sticky part. "It was either Susan or Caroline. She told me, but I forget."

Jocelyn frowned. "I think somebody called a few days ago trying to reach *Gloria*. Maybe it's the same girl trying to reach her. I'll have Admitting look it up. Call me tomorrow."

"I will."

Next she stopped in at the Adoption Unit, hoping she and Howard could have lunch together. But there was nobody there but Pearl, eating what looked like a green-tinged hot dog from the machine in the cafeteria. She was bent over the scrambled-word puzzle. Today her beret was sky blue.

Diana nodded to her and sat down at her borrowed desk, closing her eyes. A few minutes later she heard a phone ring. And then Pearl was calling her name.

"Can you get that please?" She gestured at Marci's phone.

"But I don't work here."

"I'm on my lunch hour! They're not supposed to all go out at once. Just take a message," she added more calmly.

Diana shrugged, and went over to Marci's desk and took the receiver. She was eye level with a saucy coiled cobra, wearing a plaid tam and a wink. "Diana Larsen."

"Are you in Adoption?"

"Yes." *I am now.*

"Good. I want to give back a child."

"Give *back* a child? Was he adopted?"

"She. She came over when they brought all those kids from Viet Nam. Five years old, and as cute as a bug's ear. Tiny. *That* didn't last. She's fourteen now—going on twenty-five." He took Diana's snort for amusement. "It's not that funny. She's fresh, she's defiant,

128

and she ran away twice. We gave her a gorgeous home, Nintendo, everything. And you know how she repays us? By hanging out with blacks and Puerto Ricans! A lot of Orientals are very smart; they get scholarships and everything. This one? Dumb as a post. You say something to her, she just looks at you."

Diana raised her eyes to heaven. "You should get back in touch with the Open Door Society or whoever you adopted her from. They might have some ideas." *Like having you eliminated.*

"Huh! They were the ones who talked us into this in the first place. What my wife really wanted was a Korean orphan. A baby."

"Talk to them anyway. I'll give you the number." She riffled through the card file on Marci's desk until she found it.

"Wait a minute. Someone told us we could sign papers with you people to have her unadopted!"

"Well, you can't. You're her parents now. Especially since she comes from a foreign country."

Diana looked up and saw Howard standing by the desk, stroking his mustache with concern.

"Listen, miss, I won't be responsible for what we do if she *stays* here. You guys may end up with a dead gook on your hands."

"I can't believe you said that! If that's the way you talk when she's around, no wonder you're having problems with her! You can't—"

Howard reached down and slid the receiver out of her hand. "This is Howard Liebowitz. How can I help you?"

Diana didn't stay to hear the rest of the conversation. She returned to her desk. *Try to help out, and that's what happens.*

When he got off the phone he came over. "Come in and talk to me." His tone was grim. He started for his office, pulling off his leather bomber jacket.

You can't order me around. First I'll get a cup of coffee. On her way to the machine, Hannah, back from lunch, waved her over. "That man's insufferable," she hissed, closing a Bloomingdale's catalog. "I

129

wish you'd done your story when we were still a private agency. He just doesn't realize what adoption's all about. This idea that every child is suitable for placement, and that every couple deserves a baby! Just because they can fill out an application does *not* mean they'll be good parents. We're not doing these little ones any favors by being democratic." She looked up at Diana earnestly. "With Maida Foreman running Heart's Retreat we did a far better job. And we got a lot more babies, too!"

Diana smiled sympathetically. "I'd better face the music."

Howard was on the phone, talking too low for her to hear. As she sat in his office, she looked at his posters again. One was a giant cartoon of a smashed Humpty Dumpty surrounded by soldiers; a man was pushing his way through the crowd shouting, "Let me through, let me through, I'm a chef!" Another, an adoption recruitment poster, showed a defiant-looking ten-year-old girl with the caption "Make my life."

He hung up. They stared at each other.

"Well?" he demanded finally.

"Well, what? Pearl insisted I answer the phone. There was no one else here." But it sounded ludicrous, blaming the secretary.

"I'll speak to Pearl about taking messages."

"Do you always grab the phone away from people?"

"Only when I see they're about to lose it. You were really going at it hot and heavy."

"Well—that idiot shouldn't be allowed to just give her up!"

"You think she's better off living with a bigot?"

"No . . ."

"But you think he should be punished forever," Howard prompted. He didn't quite smile.

"Okay. I was overreacting." She looked at the case records stacked high on his desk. "*I* was adopted. It was private, within my own family, but it was not happy. My mother would have dumped *me* as a teenager, if someone had told her she could."

"Wow." The corners of his mouth softened. "I didn't know that. Who adopted you?"

"My real mother's cousin."

"Your birth mother's," he corrected.

"Whatever." Now that she had told him, she didn't want to talk about it anymore. But she saw from his expression that she would have to. "They were too old, their own children were almost grown. Karen saw me as a way of feeling like a young mother again. But it didn't quite work out that way."

"Did you talk about it?"

"Talk about it? Not with them. Only with my therapist. Country people don't *talk.*"

"Diana, Diana." He looked as if he wanted to hug her.

Howard, Howard, Howard.

They looked at each other for a long moment before he doubled back. "You were in therapy?"

"Is that bad?"

"No! It's good. It helped you work out your feelings about adoption." He considered that. "Some of them, anyway."

"Listen, before I forget, Roxanne had her baby yesterday. She is now the proud Mammy of a little boy." She smiled as Howard put his hands out, Jolsonlike, and started to kneel beside his desk. "But there's something weird about it."

"About the baby?"

"No, no, he's fine. I mean, she's keeping him and all, but she won't take care of him in the hospital. On the other hand, they only brought him to her once. They're not being supportive, either."

"I'll send Dolly out there tomorrow to work it out."

"Speaking of Dolly, Infants Hospital is still on the warpath."

Howard rubbed his forehead where his eyebrows met. "Why?"

"They hate the Senaks. They told Dolly how they felt and she promised the hospital that Nicole wouldn't go there. So she just didn't show up yesterday. I think she was hoping that I could just spirit Nicole away."

"Jesus!" Howard looked appalled. "I'm in training one lousy day and the whole place falls apart. Just what was the hospital objecting to?"

She hesitated. "Mostly their lack of medical background. But Fleur's great."

"You think the kid's okay there?"

"Absolutely. Instant bonding. I really think she'll be fine. And I can see why Dolly didn't want to face the hospital; the administrator was a real gorgon."

He still looked unhappy.

"Are you upset?" She wanted to comfort him.

But he wouldn't let her. "Upset? Me? Just because I can't control my workers? Just because Infants Hospital wants to wipe us out? Diana, how you do go on!" He winked at her and picked up his phone, ending the conversation.

Brooding, she left his office. Maybe he didn't see her as serious, someone with whom he would consider getting involved, much less feel tormented about. Diana the Lightweight. She reminded herself that *she* had ruled out any involvement. Yet she wanted it to be a possibility; something to play with. Was that part of her neurosis, that the whole world had to love her?

A few minutes later Dolly returned from lunch. Diana watched her strip off brown leather driving gloves and set her mink hat carefully on her blotter. "I'm sorry about yesterday," Dolly apologized. "Did everything go okay?"

"No."

"No? You're kidding! What happened?"

Diana tapped her pen. "The hospital had this funny idea that you were getting *another* foster home for Nicole. The charming Ms. Blocksma said you had assured her that Nicole would not go to the Senaks."

"Oh, Lord." Dolly closed her eyes dramatically. "That hospital

132

is impossible! I was hoping you could avoid her and just *take* Nicole."

"You don't think you could have warned me?"

Dolly gave her an appealing look. *She must practice it on Sidney.* "I thought about it, when I realized I couldn't make it. But then I thought, if you didn't know, you wouldn't feel you were being deceitful."

"Really? You thought that all out?"

"Of course. Anyway," Dolly gathered strength, "she *is* our baby. We have the final say on where she goes."

Howard, his jacket off to reveal a red plaid shirt, emerged. "Dolly." He jerked his head back toward his cubicle. "Now."

"Howard, I just got here!"

"This can't wait."

He turned and went abruptly back inside. Dolly raised her eyebrows at Diana. Diana shrugged, hoping it would convey that it was none of her doing. Maybe he was only going to tell Dolly about Roxanne. *Fat chance.*

She went back to her desk, planning to escape, but her phone rang. It was Crystal Andresen.

"I tried calling you yesterday," the girl said breathlessly. "But you weren't there."

But why hadn't Pearl taken a message? Pearl's attitude toward answering phones was beginning to annoy her.

"No." She had been with Caroline. "How *are* you?"

"I don't know. I have to tell you something. Something important."

"What?"

"I'll come see you." She was whispering now.

"Do you know where the office is?"

"Yes."

"I'm on the third floor. Come right now."

"Okay."

"Crystal, what's wrong?"

"They didn't do what they said! Hey!" It sounded as if she had turned her head away from the receiver. There was a banging noise, as if the receiver had dropped on the floor. And before Diana could say anything, someone had softly hung up.

She listened to the dial tone for a moment, then hung up herself, waiting to see if Crystal would call back. But when the phone didn't ring, she moved quickly to Howard's office. Dolly was sitting across from him, her cheeks glowing like red globes.

"Sorry to interrupt," Diana said.

Howard leaned back in his chair. "We're done."

Dolly left quickly. She would not meet Diana's eye.

"I just had this strange call from Crystal. She said something was wrong, but wouldn't tell me what. Then someone grabbed the phone away from her and hung it up."

He considered that. "She didn't say what was wrong?"

"No, but she's coming to see me. If she *gets* here."

"Why wouldn't she?"

"Howard, someone grabbed the phone away from her!"

"Maybe she's worn out her welcome where she is. That would explain why she wants to see you, and why they might break the connection if they found her on the phone *again*. Is that possible?"

"Anything's possible. But—"

"It's easy to imagine the worst."

What had happened to the soft-eyed man who had called her "Diana, Diana"? "It's also easy to be oppositional, too, just for the sake of being contrary. How come you always have a different interpretation?"

He tilted his head in surprise. "Do I?"

Give me a break. "Howard, you know you do! Sometimes when I'm trying to explain something, I can see you watching me, anticipating what I'm going to say, just waiting to contradict it."

He laughed then. "But you take things very, very seriously. Maybe it's because you're a writer—but you look for melodrama everywhere."

134

Was it true? Conflict was what sold magazines. Hell, it was what interested her. Getting to the bottom of things. Still, he had such plausible counterexplanations. "I'll let you know the next time you do it," she said.

"You do that."

Leaving Howard's office she looked around for Hannah—she could count on Hannah's taking everything as seriously as she did—but she was not at her desk.

For the rest of the afternoon she waited for Crystal to come in. At two she went back downstairs and reminded the receptionist where to send the girl.

At three-thirty Diana called Crystal's mother on the chance that she might know where her daughter was staying, but all she got was an answering machine with a message from Zeus Electricians. Diana hesitated, then left her own message and phone number. "Hi, Crystal, this is Diana Larsen. I missed seeing you today and want to hear from you. Call me if you're there."

It was an afternoon of answering machines. She next tried Caroline's number. After the beep she gave her name and started a message, but was interrupted by a click.

"Hello?" The voice was low and exhausted.

"Caroline?"

"Yes. Hi."

She sounded like a different person. Was she some kind of split personality that did things—like smothering babies—that she couldn't remember afterward? "Are you okay?"

"Yes. It's just . . . it's just . . ." But she couldn't go on.

"Talk to me."

"I'm—I guess I'm just scared. The police came back. No, first, this morning my principal called me. I thought he just wanted to see how I was doing, you know, after what happened. And he did talk about that. But then he said . . . first he asked if I was applying for a job anywhere, and I said of course not, I was planning on coming back in September. Then he told me that some man had come

135

to the school asking if there had ever been any *incidents* when I was there, any problems with me hurting kids!"

"My God! What did he tell him?"

"He said of course not. There's never been anything! But the way Ted sounded, as if thinking I would apply somewhere else, and he didn't even sound that upset about it!" Diana could tell she was starting to cry. "After thirteen years! I love my job; I love the kids. I got up every morning excited about what would happen that day. If they find out about this police thing, they might never let me teach there again." Now she was frantic.

"Maybe they already know." Diana tried to say it as gently as she could. "I mean, why would the school give out information about you without your permission? Unless it was for the police, someone they knew they had to talk to? It sounds as if he was just hedging his bets, in case—but you have lots of civil rights."

Caroline gave a long sigh. "You know how *that* goes."

"Listen, I talked to—"

"There's more! After that, the police came back." At least she had stopped crying. "And I didn't let them in. My car isn't here, Joe took it, so I pretended I wasn't home. That's why I'm not answering the phone. What if they're going to arrest me? It's all such a nightmare. I'm hiding out in my own house!"

"But what can they arrest you for? I mean, what proof do they have?"

"The autopsy? But that's all wrong, too." She sounded more matter-of-fact, more like herself. "The physical description is so different than Zach. That's why I wanted to talk to Dr. Cruz."

"The obstetrician?" She heard voices in the hall and craned to see if it was Crystal. It wasn't. "Why didn't you?"

"Because I called her office and she was out recuperating from some damn operation. And now I don't have a car. Joe had an accident with his."

"Do you know where she lives?"

"An orange house on Main Street. In Martinville. But—"

"So tomorrow morning we'll go there. I'll pick you up first thing. Meanwhile, don't answer the door. Do you want to come to my place and hang out? They won't find you there."

Caroline laughed shakily. "I'll be okay."

TWELVE

As soon as Joe left for school the next morning, Caroline dressed in her dark green suit. It had been over a year since she had put it on, and she couldn't remember what blouse to wear. Finally she took out one of Joe's white button-down shirts. It looked big and businesslike on her, but she had never liked frills anyway. Her black leather heels were scuffed in back, and her light hair stood out in twists. Brushing the scraggles back, she fastened them into a rubber band. A few pieces escaped, but even so it made her look more adult, more like someone who deserved serious answers.

She was surprised to open the car door and find that Diana was dressed up too. Instead of her red parka and jeans, she was wearing a black wool coat and a silk scarf of gold and royal blue; her hair was coiled at the back of her neck. *I hope she doesn't think she's going in with me.*

"Could we stop at the ATM?" Caroline asked. "It's early yet, and I need some money."

"Sure. No more from the police?"

"No." She winced as Diana considered a Yield sign into Irving

Drive, then decided to make a run for it. "Listen, I think it's better if I see Dr. Cruz by myself."

"Okay."

She leaned back against the headrest. *That was easy enough.*

But Diana wasn't through. "Just don't be so damned polite. *Make her give you the information.* Some of these doctors have a real attitude."

"What kind of attitude?" She disliked generalizations of any kind.

"Oh, that they aren't answerable to anyone. Listen, it's your right to *know.* If you can anticipate what people's attitudes will be, you're ahead of the game."

"Yes, but your own attitude comes into it," Caroline objected. "If you expect people to be negative toward you, they probably will be. I get the best results from my kids when I let them know I think they can do it."

"Yeah, but that's something different. What I mean is, you have to understand that people aren't just reacting to you, they're reacting to things in their lives as well. Is this the best way to Martinville?"

"Uh-huh. The Comsewogue Road is a little faster. But it has more lights." *And you're not that good with lights.*

They settled into silence. Caroline had noticed that Diana's driving seemed to improve when she wasn't talking, and kept quiet. There were still a few school buses on the road and some commuters, but it felt like the island had settled down to another business day. What was Rafe Millar doing right now? Was he at her door again, wondering why nobody was home?

The house in Martinville was not difficult to find, though it was coral with white scallop trim rather than the Halloween orange she had imagined. It stood on a Main Street of similar large houses and some shops, inside a black iron fence topped with pineapple finials. Pineapple meant welcome, a good sign, Caroline was sure. She imagined Dr. Cruz as an older woman, definite in her opinions but motherly and wise. The person she probably should have gone to in the first place.

"This must be it," Diana said unnecessarily. There was no name or number, but a silhouette of a stork carrying a bundle dangled from the arm of the lamppost.

Caroline looked up at the fairyland turret. Did Dr. Cruz live here all alone in this huge house?

Diana was staring at her. "You okay?"

"Yes. Just . . . nervous. I'm not scared of talking to her, I'm more afraid of what I'll find out."

"I'll be right here."

"Thanks."

Caroline climbed out of the car, walked to the porch, and knocked once at the door. Almost immediately there was the fierce yipping of a dog, frantic and high-pitched. She thought she heard someone call, "Come in!" but she hesitated. They might have been calling, "Coming!" And small dogs could bite, too. She touched her purse with the autopsy report inside.

The front door was a heavy carved oak with an oval window in the top half, so Caroline saw the woman before she opened the door. She looked young, with dark hair streaming down her back— and very heavy in a pink quilted bathrobe. The woman ducked out of sight, then appeared again several seconds later, holding a small white poodle. The dog was wearing a diaper and tiny plastic pants.

The door opened. "Yes?"

"I'm looking for Dr. Cruz."

"I'm Dr. Cruz." It was hard to read the woman's expression.

"Hi." She smiled reassuringly, establishing eye contact. *Remember attitude.* It was what she did with the children the first day of school. "I'm Caroline Denecke. I need to talk to you about something."

"What are you selling?"

"Nothing. It's—medical."

"You could have called first." But it seemed more a comment than a rebuke.

"I know. I'm sorry. I didn't have your home phone."

"My office does."

"They wouldn't give it out." As the woman nodded at that, Caroline continued. "Look, I know you're recovering. I'm sorry to bother you. But it's important."

"So come in."

Caroline followed her into a heavily furnished parlor. There seemed to be a lot of brocade- and silk-covered furniture, small marble-topped tables, and gold-leaf framed paintings. Off to one side stood a huge oak curved glass cabinet, filled with antique dolls. As she sat down on a royal blue-and-gold-striped settee she saw that bisque dolls in small chairs and tiny carriages had been placed all around the room. It was like stepping into a toy museum.

Dr. Cruz sat opposite her in a gold brocade chair and looked down at the dog she was holding. "Can I trust you, Pepi?" She looked at Caroline. "He won't hurt you."

"That's okay."

But Pepi had no interest in leaving Sol Maria Cruz's lap. He nestled into her pink satin as if relaxing on a bedspread. She tugged gently at the curls on his head.

"How are you feeling?" Caroline asked.

"Better. I didn't want people to know about the operation." She shrugged. "I guess it's all over town."

"No. I didn't know until I called. What was it for?"

"Ovarian tumor."

A hysterectomy? She wasn't going to ask *that*. The fear that she had already been indiscreet propelled her into the reason she had come. "Do you remember delivering a baby three weeks ago—a Zachary Denecke?"

Sol Maria Cruz put her hand to her face, sheltering her expression from Caroline. Then she looked up, her dark face wiped clean. "I got a call from the coroner. The baby died."

Caroline nodded.

141

"He wanted my records, but I didn't send them. With everybody suing everybody these days, I'm not giving anyone any ammunition. If he needs anything he can get a subpoena."

"I had Zachary with me."

Sol Maria Cruz nodded without surprise. "I figured some deal was going down. These girls can't take care of these babies, no way. But I don't ask any questions."

"Look, I'm not here to sue anybody. It's just, the police are blaming me for his death and I'm trying to stay out of jail!" If that didn't get information, what else could she do?

A flicker—was it shock?—in the round dark eyes. "What do they say you did?"

"Smothered him. With a pillow."

"Mother of God!"

"Listen, I *didn't*. It's complicated, but—I got a copy of the autopsy from the police, and it doesn't even sound like Zach. I mean, it talks about him having an abnormal heart condition. Nobody said there was anything wrong with his heart!"

Dr. Cruz shifted warily, and Pepi jumped down from her lap. As he came over and sniffed Caroline's black pumps, she saw that the plastic pants were covered with fire engines. This was too much! If Zachary *had* had a heart condition, would this woman have been able to spot it?

"You have this autopsy?"

"Yes. Here." She opened her purse and unfolded the paper. As she got up to hand it to Dr. Cruz, Pepi chirped nervously.

The doctor took the nearly illegible copy and squinted at it, then read it painstakingly, as if it were in another language. "That's *it?*"

"That's what they gave me."

"Why are they saying you smothered him?"

"I—I guess because it says asphyxiation."

"But that could mean any number of things! Mother of God, you get the same hemorrhaging in SIDS. It's in Sudden Infant Death about half the time. And this 'cause of death,' acute pulmonary

142

edema, only means that the lungs were congested—which happens with a lot of things. It's a *condition,* not a cause of death." She let the autopsy drop to her lap. "If they're trying to prove anything, this is worthless."

"What do you mean?"

"I mean, it looks like a natural death to me."

"But the police checked our pillows! They said they were looking for matching fibers. Or something."

"They're just trying to scare you." She looked accusing. "Unless—what did you *tell* them?"

"Nothing! There was nothing to tell. I fed him around midnight, went in an hour later, and he was freezing." She still had trouble saying dead. "That's another thing. This report says he had been—dead for a day. That's why I know it's a different baby, that someone substituted another one for Zachary."

"Wait a minute!" She held up a hand as if to stop the action. "Whoa. You just jumped off the cliff without telling me it was there."

So Caroline explained to her everything that had happened.

But before she finished, Sol Maria Cruz was shaking her head. "Things like that don't happen. People don't substitute babies. It's just a grief reaction to think that." She seemed alarmed that Caroline would express such an idea.

"But what about the time difference? And the difference in size? Could he really have grown four inches in a week and a half?"

Dr. Cruz glanced down at the autopsy again. "The coroner—for all his faults—measures accurately. He *has* to. Jefferson Hospital does it on the run. If the baby was curled up, they wouldn't straighten him out."

That was a blow. "But what about this heart condition? Is it common?"

Dr. Cruz hesitated, pulling a hank of dark hair over her shoulder and twisting it into a curl. "No. I interned at Bellevue—big hospital—and saw a few there. Enough to recognize it in any baby," she added defiantly. "I had one like this a couple of months ago! I had no difficulty recognizing it in *him.*"

"What happened to him?"

"He died in the hospital, waiting for the operation."

Caroline felt the air in the room change; it seemed to be thickening and buzzing around her ears. She looked across at Sol Maria Cruz and saw that she felt it too. Pepi jumped back into the doctor's lap, and she clutched at him. "Holy Jesus," she whispered. Then she straightened. "But it couldn't be. Seth died six weeks before Zachary was born. It's just a crazy coincidence."

"But you said you could diagnose that heart condition in *any* baby. And you didn't in Zach."

"Listen, the sound is very distinctive. And the baby's color. But I don't—you want a drink?"

"Uh . . ."

"You look white."

"I'm okay. Just water would be fine. But don't get up!"

"I have to get up." She grimaced, pressing down on the armrests. "I'm supposed to be walking these days, to get back in shape. I *never* walk."

"I'll have what you're having." That seemed safe.

Dr. Cruz moved by her laboriously, and over to a sideboard in the adjoining dining room. She came back carrying two glasses of golden brown liquid. "Brandy," she announced, handing one to Caroline. "I never drink in the morning, but . . . my stitches are hurting."

"Thanks."

Caroline rarely drank liquor, let alone at nine in the morning. But she sipped it anyway.

It was time to talk again. "This other baby . . ." Caroline began.

"I'm telling you, I saw him buried before I delivered your son!"

"Maybe they mixed up the autopsy reports." *Please, God, don't let that have happened.*

But Sol Maria Cruz shook her head. "Seth wasn't autopsied. His

144

parents wouldn't allow it; the cause of death was evident. He wasn't even embalmed."

"But he was buried?"

She sighed, raising her eyes to heaven as if Caroline was a saleswoman she wanted to be rid of. Then she tilted her head back and took a long drink. She was in no hurry to move the empty glass away from her lips. "I'm sure he's buried *now,*" she said finally.

Caroline waited.

"Greenhill couldn't do it in January. The ground was frozen. Or something."

Caroline propped up her head with her right arm, her elbow making a deep dent in the satin arm of the settee. Either the brandy—or what she was hearing—was making her dizzy. *I can't drink on an empty stomach.* "What did they—do with him?"

"They have a holding vault they use. Refrigerated."

"Where?"

"Don't even think it," Dr. Cruz warned. "This family does not need any more grief. They put it behind them at the funeral, and haven't looked back."

Caroline lifted her head. "But what about Zachary? It proves that something happened to him!"

"What do you need to prove? You keep your mouth shut, nobody can touch you."

"But I need to *find* him! I want him! If I can prove what really happened, the police will look for him, too."

"Whoa there." That word again. "I thought this was about your not being arrested for murder, that's why I— With all the babies in the world, you think you could even recognize him now? There's no way. Children change too fast. You're better off finding *another* pregnant girl who needs the money."

"That's a terrible thing to say!" This was her warm and motherly woman! She looked at Pepi in his diaper, lying quietly at Sol Maria's pink-slippered feet. "Could you just replace *him* with another dog?" She looked around the room. "It's not like buying another doll!"

The doctor sat back against the couch and pressed her fingers together, staring at Caroline. "You think I don't know anything about loss? I had two children, very small; I left them with my mother when I came up here to school. They aren't mine anymore; they're almost grown, and they don't even write." She looked away. "I stopped sending my mother money, and they got bitter. She stole them from me."

"Can't you go down and visit?"

"What's the point? Some situations are better left at rest. Like yours."

"No! You're just saying that because— What's the other baby's name?"

She saw Dr. Cruz was not going to answer.

"Please."

"How can I tell you something like that? It violates all confidentiality. I could get sued. And they would be right!" She shook her head. "I shouldn't have talked to you about it at all."

"But you did." It was Diana speaking through her. "I'm sure the death notice was in the paper. I could have seen it then. In fact, I probably did."

Sol Maria Cruz was shaking her head. "It's a crazy idea. This conversation never happened. Now, go!" She held out the autopsy report. "I should never have opened the door. When am I going to learn?"

"Thank you."

Sol Maria Cruz was more afraid of lawsuits than any doctor Caroline had ever met. But, given the fact that everyone was being sued these days, it was probably a reasonable fear.

While she waited in the car, Diana kept the heat on and made notes—not on the adoption story, but on Caroline herself. It was too easy to forget the details later on. Twice she looked at her watch.

The longer Caroline was in there, the better her chances of finding something out.

Finally the front door opened and Caroline came down the porch steps. She opened the door and got into the car.

"What happened?"

But Caroline, with a dazed look, didn't say anything for a moment. Then her voice was disbelieving. "I found out who the baby was who was left in the crib. The one with the heart condition."

Diana grabbed her arm and peered into her face. "What? You're kidding."

"No!"

And then they were laughing. Diana held up her palm, and they slapped each other high fives. "Tell me!"

"I will!" Caroline recounted the conversation as fast as she could.

"So somebody took this baby's body from a cemetery vault? My God, grave robbers! It's like something out of Robert Louis Stevenson."

"But you know what it means?" Caroline gasped. "It means I won't go to *jail*. This baby, the one they autopsied, died of natural causes. I guess Millar didn't understand what asphyxiate meant either."

What an innocent. "Don't bet the farm on that. If he's an experienced cop, he knew exactly what it meant. He was just trying to manipulate you. He saw that the baby had been dead for a long time and was trying to make you pay." She shook her head. "He figured you had to be guilty of *something*. Or maybe he just doesn't like teachers who live in big houses."

"I'm sure he thought he was just doing his job," Caroline argued. Over the years she had taught her classes always to obey a policeman.

"Yeah, right. Threats and insinuation. What a *creep*. I don't even know him and I hate him! Do you know where the cemetery is?"

"Greenhill?" Caroline pulled back a little. "You think *we* should go to the cemetery?"

"Who else?" She released the hand brake. "If they open the coffin in the refrigerator and it's empty, that's all the proof we need. Then your police pal will have to get off his ass and do something constructive for a change."

Caroline swallowed. "What if it isn't? Empty."

"For an optimist, you sure are a pessimist. Let's not worry about that now."

"But how are we going to make them open it?"

"We'll think of something once we're there."

They had to stop at a gas station and ask directions to Greenhill Cemetery. It was between Comsewogue and Martinville, far off the main road. The name, Greenhill, reminded Diana of a hymn she remembered from Sunday school. " 'There is a green hill far away, with'out the city wall,' " she sang. " 'Where our dear Lord was crucified, He died to save us all.' "

Caroline joined her on the chorus. " 'He died that we might be forgiven, He died to make us good. That we might go at last to Heaven, saved by his precious blood.' "

They looked at each other, then laughed giddily. "We shouldn't quit our day jobs," Diana said.

The entrance to the cemetery was brick, with GREENHILL arched across the top, the letters entwined with black wrought-iron ivy and morning glory vines. Driving through the gates, Diana's attention was caught by the monument directly ahead of her. It was a larger-than-life marble sculpture of a man and a woman lying side by side under a canopy. Two small children in late-Victorian dress sat forlornly on the three steps below, looking up at them, one stroking a stone collie. The name on the base was CUDLEIGH. "Look at that," she enthused. "This place is incredible."

Caroline nodded, but seemed to be looking more at the stalks of forsythia that would bloom in another month. "I can't believe it's almost spring. I don't know where I've been."

They parked outside an office disguised as an English brick cottage; perhaps at one time a caretaker's family had actually lived in it. Inside, a long wooden counter separated the waiting area from several desks. Diana stepped up to it, Caroline hovering cautiously behind her.

"Miss Lambert, is that you?" A tiny red-haired woman in an emerald green sweatsuit behind one of the desks recognized Caroline from the days before she was married. "How have you been?"

"Fine! How's . . . Jodi?"

"Good. She loves school now—her teachers still can't shut her up."

"Well, give her a big hug for me. If she remembers me."

"Of course she does! She talked about you and those puppets you had for years. But I hope nothing's—"

"No, no, everything's fine. I just have a question."

"I'll tell Ernie you're here."

A minute later she was back. "He's on the phone, but I signaled I was bringing people in."

They followed the secretary down a tan carpeted hall, past a bathroom that smelled like a pine forest, to a room on the right. There was a soft brown leather couch and paintings of sunsets over mountains on the walls. A large box of tissues angled on the desk corner reminded you of where you were. This must be where families sat and made decisions about buying plots.

Diana perched on the couch, Caroline right beside her.

The man in the matching brown easy chair opposite them stopped talking and replaced the dark red phone on a small table next to him. He was a compact, balding man in a houndstooth jacket, with rings denoting fraternal organizations covering his fingers. "Ernest Shockley here. How are you?"

"Diana Larsen and Caroline Denecke. We're fine."

"Diana. Caroline." He crooned it as if they were already old friends, although Diana could see he was trying to figure out why the two of them were there together. *We're HIV-positive lesbians, Mr. Shockley, and we want a family plot.*

But he labored on. "Have you seen our cemetery today? It's the

149

first thing on the island that turns green. In another month, with the bulbs up, it will be *spectacular*. We've got gardeners working year-round to keep it nice."

"That's an interesting monument when you first drive in," Diana said.

"The Cudleigh? Uh-huh. Uh-huh. It's a lot of history books, books about art. The parents died in a carriage accident. Had a lot of you-know-what though." He rubbed his fingers together to show money. "You know the Brown estate in Bayhead? That was originally their home."

"Really. Actually, we're here on a police matter."

"A police matter? You should have said so! Here, I'm giving you the grand tour. And I thought I knew everyone on the force." He looked very serious. "I hope we're not talking exhumation here."

Caroline came to life. "Oh, we're not—"

"We're not talking exhumation." Diana talked over her. "It's someone in your refrigerated vault."

"Oh, dear." He raised a glittering hand to his furrowed forehead. "Why couldn't you have come last *week?* We've started burying again!"

"A baby?"

"A baby?" He searched his memory. "The Greenspan child. He was interred five days ago. We had a couple of warm days last week, we decided to go for it. We figured it wouldn't break a back-hoe, and we had them piling up."

"Did you check the coffin? Open it, I mean?"

"Naw." He looked shocked at her question, then patted his sportscoat pockets nervously as if searching for cigarettes. Finally he dropped his hand. "It's not like we have another service or anything. No need to go through *that* again. We do them one, two, three. Bang-bang-bang." Diana felt Caroline fading at that. But as long as she kept quiet . . . "They can visit them beforehand in the vault. A few do. Not many."

150

"Do you keep a record of who comes?"

"No records. But Omar could probably tell you if anyone's been. He works over there, checking 'em in. And out. I'll call over." He reached for the red phone again, punched three numbers, then listened. "Omar! Ya keeping them quiet?" He winked at them. "I've got two police ladies here, want to know if you've had any visitors lately. Live ones, I mean." He listened. "Any for Greenspan? Small pine box? No, not *white*. Pine. Stained. Uh-huh . . . uh-huh." He covered the receiver with his hand. "No one he remembers."

"Hmm."

It was disappointing, but as he hung up he said, "You can't put too much stock in what Omar remembers. His alphabet's a little bit scrambled. Poor guy. He's okay for that job, the rest of the year he helps the gardeners, but his memory don't hold much."

"So this baby is actually buried."

"In the ground. Look, I don't even want to *know* what's going on."

His lack of interest sounded genuine—not a backhanded invitation for them to explain.

"Do you do a lot of exhumations?" Diana asked.

He played with a large ruby ring. "No. Bodies get moved sometimes, but caskets don't get opened. We don't have the rule here of having to bury in concrete yet. So opening one would be— messy." It sounded like a warning. "Police exhumations are a bitch, anyway. They have to take soil samples, have the whole thing videotaped, *then* take the coffin to the medical examiner's office to actually open it."

"It sounds complicated," Caroline finally spoke up.

"Think you'll be back for that?"

"We don't know," Diana jumped in. "We'll let you know."

"Why did you tell him we were from the police?!"

Diana had managed to keep her quiet until they were back in the car, but as soon as the doors closed, Caroline exploded.

"I didn't. That was his idea." She backed across the gravel with a screech.

"But you let him think that! Now what are we going to do?"

"Get an exhumation order."

"How? In case you don't realize it, we're *not* the police."

"So? Get your policeman to get one. He owes you big time." She paused at the road, though no cars were coming. "Look, Caroline, if he's the police he'll want to find out what happened."

"Maybe." But she sounded dispirited.

"Okay. What?" Diana turned off the engine and they sat in the shadow of the Greenhill gates.

"You can be arrested for impersonating an officer!"

"I think you have to be in uniform. Or trying to arrest someone else. Look, Caroline, who's going to know it? Even if Omar—*not* Omar, Ernie—says something, we can say it was just a misunderstanding. We were dressed up, he thought we were someone official. But all you have to do is tell your policeman you know it's a different child, and why. Then leave it up to him. You can call when we get back to the house."

Silence.

"Jesus, Caroline, I thought you'd be happy!"

"I *am*. It's just . . ." But she didn't say what it was.

Diana started up the car. "Do you really think Omar's such a lost cause? I mean, somebody had to go in to take the body from the vault. On the other hand, if he's that dim, slipping out a baby would be easy enough."

"Umm."

Back at the house, Caroline spoke again. "You want to come in?"

"I *could*. For a minute. I'm on the way to the city to stop in at the magazine, that's why I'm dressed up. Half the women who work there wear work boots and torn jeans; the other half Dress for Success. I wear what I please, that's why I don't fit in. One reason anyway." She turned the engine off and thought about it. "The other reason is, I'm so tired of rhetoric. It's not that I disagree with the

152

positions, I just don't like to have to pledge allegiance to them every morning. I suppose it's the same at *Cat Fancier,* too."

Caroline laughed. "The house is a mess," she warned suddenly. "I didn't even make the bed yet."

Well, I don't plan to sleep over. Why did some women still worry about a few dirty dishes offending people? What was worse to her, in Caroline's house, was the sheer volume of things. She guessed that Caroline was a collector—of antiques, of stuffed animals, of penguinabilia.

They settled in the den to use the phone there. "I'll call Jocelyn at the hospital after you call, to get Susan's address."

"You can call first."

"No, you go ahead."

"I think I have his number in the kitchen." She didn't move. "The thing is, Joe told me not to talk to the police again."

Diana looked up from *Architectural Digest.* "This is different. But be tough. Be aggressive. Pretend he's Sol Maria."

"Maybe he won't even be there. Maybe I can speak to Donald. You want me to put it on speakerphone, so you can hear?"

"Sure."

"Okay. It's in the kitchen."

Diana followed her down the hall and waited while Caroline retrieved a business card from the top of the refrigerator and went to the wall phone. Looking nervous, she dialed.

"Precinct. Millar speaking."

"Uh . . . this is Caroline Denecke. You remember?"

"Yes, Caroline." His voice sweetened. "You have something to tell me?"

"Yes. I know who the baby was who was left in Zach's crib that night."

"Wait: This is your story about your 'real' baby being stolen and a strange one left there? Way up on the second floor?" His voice crackled impatiently.

"Uh-huh. But it really happened! Another baby with the heart condition that they described in the autopsy—a condition Zach *didn't* have—died in January. And was kept in a refrigerated vault at the cemetery. That's why he was so cold that night. And you couldn't understand it. Remember?"

Way to go, Caroline! Diana thrust up her fist in encouragement.

"I think they expected him to be—thawed by the time we went in there in the morning," she went on, looking a little sick.

Silence. "How did you happen to find all this out?"

"It wasn't easy. Someone told me. But if you exhumed the coffin, I bet you'd find that this baby—the Greenspan baby—wasn't in it."

An amplified grunt. "Do you know what it takes to get an exhumation order?"

"You have to go to court?"

"If it's not for good cause, the family can sue. For disturbing the grave on a whim."

Caroline didn't say anything. Diana tried transmitting strength to her.

"It's not a whim," she managed finally.

"What if we do it and find he's just where he should be?"

"If that happens, I'll take a lie detector test. Or any test you want. And I'll forget that you made me think he was smothered when the autopsy doesn't say that at all."

"It doesn't?" But there was no force behind his words. "You'll have to give me some information about this child."

She told him the baby's name again and how he had died in the hospital.

"If we do this, it'll take time to get a court order and set it up," he warned.

"How much time?"

"Probably a week."

"A *week?* That's too long. This means Zach's alive somewhere, maybe in danger. You've got to treat it like a kidnapping now!"

"Come on, Mrs. Denecke. You haven't given me anything but some new theory you have."

"But it's true!" She sounded desperate.

Diana pressed her hands against the countertop, stifling the urge to grab the phone and threaten the bastard.

"Won't be before Monday, anyway." He still made it sound like a defeat.

"Thank you. Will you let me know when?"

"Why—you want to be there?"

"Absolutely." Unable to speak anymore, she pressed the button to cut him off.

"You did great. Absolutely great," Diana reassured her. "You kept him on the defensive the whole time."

"But it's true about Zach!"

"I know. Let me call Jocelyn."

She looked up the number of the Mother and Child Pavilion on her pocket directory, then dialed and asked for the nurse. They kept it on speakerphone.

"Hi, Diana."

"You asked me to call you to get the address of Susan? Or Caroline?"

"Oh, right. I've got it right here. It's Caroline Denecke, 10 Pocantico Drive, Dillon." She sounded pleased that she had been able to provide the information.

Caroline, shaking her head at Diana, did not write it down. It was her own address.

"But you know that other girl you were visiting? That Roxanne? I was glad to see that the man from Social Services came for the baby today."

"What man from Social Services?" *Howard?* "What did he look like?"

"Oh, I don't know. I'm sure you know him. Brown-haired, clean-shaven. Average height. A little below, maybe."

155

"Did he seem slow?"

"Slow? No. Just the opposite!"

"Any mustache—no, you said clean-shaven. Skinny?"

"No. Pretty well-nourished, I'd say."

"Then I don't know who it was. Roxanne told me they were going home with her boyfriend."

"Diana, it couldn't have been! This guy was wearing a suit and was very businesslike with her. And he said he was from DSS! I *did* think it was strange that he would take them both at the same time. Does this mean she walked out of here with that baby she's been ignoring?" Jocelyn's wail was as amplified as Millar's grunt. "And we *let* her?"

"You couldn't have stopped her."

"We could have called Child Protective Services!"

"But—she hadn't actually *done* anything."

"Not yet." Jocelyn gave it an ominous inflection.

"You can still make a referral to the eight hundred number."

"I'll talk to my supervisor about it."

When she got off the phone, Caroline said, "What was *that* all about?"

Diana told her, giving the background on Crystal as well. "But I'm still hoping to hear from Crys," she ended. "She'll have the real information on Susan. Listen, I've got to go." She wanted to get away from Crane Island to try to sort things out.

THIRTEEN

When Diana came into the Adoption Unit on Monday morning she saw that something had been left on her desk. Someone had carefully centered a newspaper clipping on the otherwise bare expanse of gray metal. That was not unusual—Howard often passed around social work stories from professional journals or the *New York Times*—but this had no routing slip attached to it. And the story was from a local paper, the *Crane Island Advance*.

She slid into her chair and looked first at the headline, MYSTERY GIRL FOUND ON TRACKS, then at the blurry photo. It looked like a canvas body bag in the woods. *Crystal?* Pressing her hand over her mouth, she started to read the story, but stopped when she got to the description. This girl's hair was black. It wasn't Crystal, after all.

But how about Roxanne?

"Who put this here?" she demanded.

No one answered.

She looked around. Marci, a huge red butterfly clip announcing her black curls, was staring at her like an apprehensive rooster.

Hannah and Pearl were also watching her. Even Howard had come out of his office. "Bad news?" he asked.

"Bad news for somebody."

"You don't think it's Crystal?" Howard rubbed his finger along his upper lip. "She never got here, did she?"

"No. But it's not her. It could be Roxanne." What would she think about Roxanne dead? She hadn't liked her that much alive; but no one deserved to die at eighteen. But why would Roxanne, of all people, throw herself in front of a train? *She doesn't have that much imagination.*

"Why don't you call the investigating officer?" Howard asked. "It gives a number, I think."

"You seem to know all about it."

He exhaled with sad amusement. "Diana, we all saw the story lying there and read it. It was there when I walked in."

She looked at the end of the column of newsprint and dialed the number given there. She had meant to spend the morning in an all-out assault to find Crystal. But that would have to wait.

"Coroner's Office. Magne here."

"Hi. My name is Diana Larsen. I'm calling about the girl in the paper."

"You think it's someone you might know?"

"I don't know. There are a couple of girls from the maternity home, we don't know where they are—but I guess it could be anybody, couldn't it? I mean, someone I don't even know." She gulped to swallow the saliva rushing into her mouth.

He waited.

"It's just that one of them had black hair. So . . . I thought . . . I'd call."

"Yeah, well the thing about the hair's a little misleading. It looks like it could have been dyed."

"Oh. Well." It let out those girls then. Roxanne's was naturally dark, and Crystal would *never* dye her hair.

"Could you stop by and make an ID? Sounds like you could eliminate two possibilities anyway. We're three miles out on the Bay Road from Martinville. You can't miss the signs."

"I—guess so."

"Ask for me at the desk. Terence Magne."

She replaced the phone as if in a dream, as if the receiver weighed nothing. "They want me to go make an identification," she said slowly.

"Of the girl on the tracks?" somebody asked.

"Well, you're not going over there by yourself," Hannah announced. "You don't even work here! Someone from the agency should be with you." She went over to the closet and reached for her green wool coat, flipping her gray-blond braid out from her white sweater collar.

"I'll go," chirped Marci.

Get a life. You think this is a trip to the Liz Claiborne outlet?

She looked at Howard, willing him to come with her.

He rubbed the back of his neck.

"No, it's okay." She picked up her red jacket from the back of her chair. "Dolly and I are the only ones who know what the girls look like. I don't need anyone. I'll be fine."

"Will you at least let me get my coat?" Howard demanded. He turned to Hannah. "I'll go."

She looked to Diana, unable to believe she would prefer his company to her own.

Diana smiled and shrugged, trying to convey that Howard was the supervisor and could make any overrides he chose. It felt feeble.

"I've never been to the morgue," Marci pouted.

"That's okay," Howard said, pulling on a black wool overcoat and giving her a wink. "You can go next time."

"That woman is unbelievable," Diana complained when they got out in the hall. "Talk about burnout."

159

"She's had a hard life."

"Who hasn't?"

Howard only smiled.

The Coroner's Office was a flat tan brick building surrounded by sand and choppy green growth. It had the desolate look of a desert prison. "I'm not very good at this," Howard warned, turning his station wagon slowly from Bay Road into the parking lot.

"Good at what?"

"Bodies. Morgues."

"That's okay. You don't have to look. But you've seen bodies at wakes."

He shut the engine off. "Diana, Jews don't *have* wakes. We slip them in fast so we don't have to look. Then we sit shiva to make up for it."

Diana sighed. "I've seen dead people. But never as young as this."

They got out of his gold station wagon and walked toward the building. She could see through the glass doors that someone was waiting for them.

"Miss Larsen?" Detective Magne was portly and balding, the genial kind of islander who spent weekends working on his boat. It was not hard to imagine the top of his head becoming freckled in the summer sun. Even now it had a healthy glow.

"Yes. Hi." She took his proffered hand. "This is Howard Liebowitz. From Social Services." Now it seemed silly to have brought an escort, but Howard and the detective shook hands solemnly.

"Do you know why you're here?" he asked.

"To look at a body to see if it's anyone I recognize."

He peered into her face. "Were you close to these girls?"

"One of them I was."

"This won't be pleasant."

Now you tell me? "I guess not."

"The stairs are over here."

160

The morgue was in the basement, in a room at the end of the hall. Taped just outside the door was a flyer advertising a fried chicken dinner sponsored by the Mercy AME church in Little India, and a poster illustrating the Heimlich maneuver. The room inside had green spatter linoleum and bars across the windows. Bars—to keep unauthorized out? Or the dead from leaving?

The far wall of the room was silver refrigerated drawers, but the rest of the space held desks and typewriters. There was even a coffee machine on a rickety white table. Certainly Crane Island could not have many unidentified dead; but was it possible that people actually worked here in the midst of the bodies? That they made jokes about their silent companions, and evacuated the room discreetly when an identification had to be made?

As Detective Magne brought them to the silver wall, Diana realized that she had been holding her breath and released it, gulping in a lungful of Pine-Sol and formaldehyde. Howard was somewhere behind her.

"This is going to be upsetting," the detective warned. "She's already been autopsied."

"They do autopsies *here?*" Diana asked. She didn't really care. But she needed to hear her own voice in this room.

"Across the hall. Makes for easy transport." He checked the numbers on a card in his hand, then pulled open the drawer that had 363 in heavy black marker on a card in the slot. Cautiously he lifted the canvas back inch by inch as if afraid of a sudden movement.

Diana heard someone behind her gasp, "Oh, my God!"

She felt a bitter stream shoot up through her throat and into her mouth. Closing her eyes, she managed to swallow.

You didn't tell me it would be Crystal. But it *was* Crystal. She looked again. The spiky, dyed black hair made her look as if she were wearing a fright wig. Her open green eyes gazed stonily at the ceiling. And—her head was attached to nothing. It was connected to *nothing.* It lay several inches from the blackened stub of her neck, like an adult Halloween mask. Her freckles had darkened into pits; on the cheek nearer Diana there was a slightly flattened gray-blue area.

She gripped the edge of the drawer with both hands to keep from falling. *If I fall down I'll lie there and never get up again.*

"For an autopsy they cut her *head* off?" she croaked.

"No. No." Terence Magne sounded offended. But as if to check for himself, he whipped the soft canvas covering back for a moment. And in that instant Diana had a glimpse of Crystal's chest sliced opened and explored, the flaps of skin put back crooked, skewing one breast higher than the other. She had been chopped off again at mid-thigh, her loose legs turning outward in a ducklike walk. Just as horrible were the faint stretch marks, branching delicately across her lower abdomen like flowery stems.

She felt the detective trying to pry her fingers off the drawer so he could close it. "The rain did it."

She held on.

"Come *on*, Diana." Howard was pulling softly at her shoulder. "Honestly, I never thought—I wouldn't have . . ." She let him put his arm around her tightly and move her away.

"Are you okay?" he whispered, his hand now resting on the back of her neck.

"I don't think so. Are you?"

"I've been better."

In silence they followed the detective up the stairs.

He didn't speak to them until he had brought them into an office and made them sit down on two folding chairs opposite him. "That could make you lose your lunch," he said. He seemed relieved that they hadn't.

Diana nodded, conscious of moving her head up and down. It felt fragile, a stem that could be easily broken.

"Did you recognize her?"

"Yes," she whispered. "That's Crystal."

She felt Howard jerk.

"See what I mean about the hair?"

"But I don't get that at all. She had beautiful hair! Why would she do something like that that would ruin it? And chop it off that way—she would *never* have cut her hair. She planned to model!"

He looked wise. "It was probably just a temporary rinse. If she was a runaway, she might not have wanted to be recognized."

"But her hair was *long.*" She stopped and covered her mouth; she could not push away the image of the train decapitating Crystal and shearing off her hair at the same time. The bile in her throat that had surged up at her first sight of Crystal could not be stopped now. Pressing her hand harder against her mouth, she flailed around, then caught sight of a metal wastebasket. She reached it just in time. Detective Magne held her shoulders to steady her.

"Ladies Room, first door on your right."

"Thanks."

When she got back the wastebasket was gone.

Diana sat back down.

"Pretty girl. Too bad she killed herself."

"What?" Diana stared at him. "Crystal would never have killed herself!"

"A lot of times it's a surprise to everyone."

"But she had everything to live for!" The old cliché. "She had her whole life planned. And when she called me, somebody grabbed the phone away."

"When was that?"

"Wednesday afternoon."

He relaxed again. "Well, they say she was alive when she lay down on the tracks."

"She *lay down?*" There was perhaps a way of accepting the fact that Crystal, giddy and maybe high, might have tried to walk the tracks as a game, and accidentally gotten caught. Maybe was even daring the train to hit her. But Crystal lying down on the metal bars like a human sacrifice implied more despair than Diana could accept. "Maybe she passed out first and didn't know where she was."

"Maybe." Opening the top drawer of a metal desk, he said, "There's a statement I need you to sign."

"Okay." She leaned shakily against the metal rim of the desk and completed a form giving her name, address, age, and other information, and swearing that, to the best of her knowledge, the body she had seen had been Crystal Andresen's.

"Wait! Don't sign it," Detective Magne cried when she got close to the end. "I'll need someone in here to notarize it. We'll also need identification that shows that you're who you say you are."

"Okay." She took out her lapsed driver's license. Since coming back from Europe she had never taken the time to renew it. Living in Brooklyn she had rarely used a car.

But it didn't do for the small woman in the violet pantsuit who entered the office, frowning, as if she had just been pulled away from important work. She stood over Diana as she signed, but shook her head after studying the license.

"This isn't current."

"Really?" *It got past the car rental people.*

"I'll verify she's who she says she is," Howard offered. But he turned to Diana. "What else do you have?"

"Credit cards?"

The woman looked disgusted and left the room.

"You mean all this was for nothing?"

"No, no, no." Detective Magne soothed her. "Now that we know who it is, we can contact the family."

"I have her mother's phone number at the office. It's also listed under Zeus Electricians." *Thank God I don't have to be the one to call her.*

"Somebody will be in touch to interview you. To get some background."

"Okay." She and Howard stood up.

"You're sure that was Crystal?" he asked as they walked out to the car.

She just sighed. But as he opened the car door for her, she said,

"I didn't really think it *would* be Crystal! It doesn't make any sense about her hair. She was so proud of her looks—oh, *God,*" she couldn't shut out the image of the mangled, severed body. Could Crystal have lived without legs? Without a head? "Crystal would never have killed herself! She had so many *plans.*"

"You said she was depressed about losing the baby," he reminded her. "And that she was upset when she called you."

"That was different. You don't lie down on the train tracks when something goes wrong. *She* wouldn't have." *Why couldn't it have been Roxanne?*

But that was mean. She didn't want Roxanne dead—just Crystal alive. Where was Roxanne, anyway? What if Roxie had actually been forced by the man who came to the hospital to leave, then was abducted and murdered?

I have to find her, find out if she's all right.

On the way back she could not stop talking about Crystal. Howard listened, making sympathetic comments. But she was sure that he was glad to get back to the office. In the parking lot she said good-bye to him and walked over to her car.

Roxanne Fierro's parents lived in a community of converted summer cottages. Their house was actually two bungalows that had been pushed together. An American flag angled out from the roof. As one of the cottages was considerably taller than the other, it looked like a mother and child standing upright, watching a parade. The yard was cluttered with porcelain toilets and washing machines, skeletal white lawn furniture, and long tables covered over by vinyl. A "Yard Sale Today!" sign was propped against the house. Diana could not imagine anyone wanting to buy anything they had.

Camelia Fierro came to the door, dressed in a white nightgown with a frilly neck—a huge, dour angel. "We're not open today."

"Hi. I'm Diana Larsen. I know your daughter from Heart's Retreat."

"You know Roxie?"

"Can I come in? I tried calling."

"Yeah, the phone's turned off again. Winter, you know? We use the neighbor's."

Inside the house, chairs and end tables were stacked along both sides of the room, leaving a narrow trail. Camelia evidently rescued the plaster statues out of the merchandise they bought and touched them up. In the living room, Diana noticed Casper the Friendly Ghost, Elvis Presley, Christ with a bleeding heart, and Snow White with two of the seven dwarfs. Michelangelo's David, painted gold, looked down from a doily on the television.

She chose a mahogany chair with an oak leaf design, an escapee from a Duncan Phyfe dining room, and sat down. "Is Roxanne here?" she asked, trying not to breathe in the odors of enamel paint, mildew, and cat feces. It was the second time in several hours she'd had to protect her nose.

"Roxie? No. She's at my sister's."

Are you sure? "I thought she might be with her boyfriend."

"Richie? Get out! Listen, he doesn't want to know her. A simple boy, anyhow. It's his mother I blame. His father. I think they were *glad* when the baby passed on." She crossed herself. "That way they don't have to pay nothing toward child support."

"The baby—Roxanne told you that the baby had died." She was careful not to make it a question.

"If you can say that about a little one that never drew a breath on this earth. That she didn't let us make a wake, that I feel bad about. Family is family—am I right? But my sister says she has to handle it in her own way."

Diana nodded. "That's true. But I'd like to talk to her about it."

"You want to *see* Roxie? She's at my sister's. She said she didn't want to see no one—but still." She recited the address from memory, then shifted in the red beanbag chair. "My sister, she always liked Roxie from when she was a little girl. Roxie was the first, and Marie liked to take her places." Her wide, sallow face was thoughtful. "When Roxie was seven, eight, I forget, the school thought

166

she was backwards. Marie wanted to take her in and get her tutors. I guess I should have let her."

Diana smiled.

"You know what Roxie's problem is? She's got a grudge against the world. She's mad because she wasn't born beautiful. Or rich. That we're not the Rockefellers. The girl doesn't see that it's up to *her* to make something of herself. At least, my sister has her on a diet." She replanted her thick legs. "I could call that you're coming, but the phone's off again."

"Don't worry about it. I'm not even sure when I'll get there." She would have to move fast to get to Bayhead before Roxanne was warned away.

Roxanne's Aunt Marie lived in a large California-style ranch. It was stained russet and sported several skylights and an atrium. The impeccable evergreens were bedded down by white stones. Diana felt her nose relax, and took an experimental sniff. It was safe to breathe at this stop.

No cars were parked in the driveway in front of the double garage, but as she got closer she could hear a television set on inside the house. She knocked and waited, knocked and waited, until someone finally pulled open the door.

Roxanne was looking better already. Her black hair had been permed in curls around her face, and she was wearing pink lipstick; her white sweatsuit bulged only slightly around her stomach and thighs. Recognizing Diana, she tried to slam the door.

Diana pushed against textured wood. Abruptly the pressure stopped, and she half fell inside.

"Hi, Roxanne." *Thank God you're alive.*

"What are *you* doing here?"

"I wanted to talk to you. You're looking good. Really good."

"My aunt said not to let anyone in!"

"I won't come in." But Diana moved farther into the quarry-tiled hall. A grouping of cacti and other succulents stood in one corner. Through a doorway to her left she could make out a Haitian cotton sectional couch and a black lacquered grand piano. "How are you?"

Roxanne shrugged.

There was no point in playing games. "Look, Roxanne. I know you lied to your mother about the baby. That's between you and your mother. But when I found out Crystal was dead I had to make sure you were all right."

"Crystal's dead?" Roxanne's eyes flew open, a flash of white in her olive face.

"Did you hear about the girl on the train tracks?"

"That was *Crystal?*"

"Yes."

Roxanne attempted to process the information. "But it didn't say so on TV," she objected.

"It will. I just identified her body today."

"You saw Crystal dead? That's *gross*. What did she look like?"

Diana sighed. It was a world of ghouls. "Terrible. I don't want to talk about it. And I don't want the same thing to happen to you."

"Why would it happen to *me?*"

"Because of what you did with your baby. Those are dangerous people, Roxanne."

"They are not! The doctor said—" She stopped suddenly, pressing up against the grass wallpaper.

I knew Sidney Hazelton was involved. I knew it! "Are they the same people who took Crystal's baby?"

"How should I know?"

"Well, I hope they gave you plenty of money."

By Roxanne's startled expression, Diana knew that they had not.

And, she realized, it had been the worst thing she could say. These were dangerous people. Shit! Suppose Roxanne went back to them and demanded more money? Is that what Crystal had done? "Who told you about these people?"

"My—" She stopped and compressed her lips.

My what? My aunt? My mother? My doctor?

"Your what?"

She twisted away. "Stop asking me these questions!"

"Just one more. Do you know where Susan is now?"

"No."

"Susan? From the maternity home?"

"I said no! I didn't even know her."

"Do you know where Richard was placed—the baby?"

Roxanne closed her eyes and shook her head.

"Would you like to get him back?"

She came to life. "Why? So Heart's Retreat can get him? So I can give him to welfare? *You* just want to write about it."

It made it sound like she was exploiting the girls, too. *But I didn't create the situation.* "All I want is for you to be safe. I don't know what you're mixed up in, but don't call anybody about what I said about more money. Okay? And make sure your mother doesn't tell anyone you're here."

"She told you," Roxanne objected illogically, as if that gave equal rights to anyone else who asked.

"But she knew *I* wasn't going to cut off your head." She waited until she saw Roxanne's eyes flash in comprehension, then reached for the knob. "Really, don't contact anyone. Just be glad it's over. What happened to Crystal—I still can't believe it! If you ever want to talk to me about anything, I'll give you my number."

"Okay." Roxanne waited.

Diana blinked and pulled a card out of her wallet with her Crane Island phone number scribbled in. Would she ever understand this girl?

Back in the car Diana shivered and started the engine quickly to get some heat. She had to call Caroline.

The first time she tried the line was busy. But she reached her on the second attempt.

"Caroline, hi. Diana. Listen, I have a lot to tell you."

"Really? Joe's home."

She was sorting through the implications of that when Caroline added, "Why don't you come over tomorrow morning? Or come for lunch. I'm going crazy here with no car, and I still haven't heard anything from Rafe Millar."

"That's right. It's Monday, isn't it. So call him tomorrow." She didn't want to tell Caroline about Crystal over the phone. Or Sidney Hazelton, for that matter. "What time do you want me to stop by?"

"Come around eleven. We'll start lunch early."

FOURTEEN

God, I love this room," Diana said, settling back and looking around the gazebo. "It almost makes me want to have my own place. If I could have this room to work in, I'd never be unhappy again."

"It was what sold me on the house," Caroline agreed. She pulled the cork out of the bottle of white wine and poured two glasses. "Is this okay for you? I have some red."

Diana looked over. "No, it's fine to start. But I mean, when you're in here with the plants and all, the warm, perfumy smell, you feel like nothing bad could ever happen."

Caroline sighed. "If only that were true." But she was shocked at what had just occurred. Talking to Diana, she had forgotten about Zach. That was not unusual, but when she did remember him her feelings were muted, without the knifepoint of shock. Was this the way it happened, the way things receded into memory? *I don't want that to happen!*

Diana took a long sip of wine and waited until Caroline was

seated across from her. Then she said, "I've got bad news about Crystal."

"She's the girl on the train tracks—isn't she?" When Diana looked startled, she added, "I figured it had to be when you called yesterday. The way you sounded."

"I sounded that bad?"

"You sounded awful."

"I guess I did. They made me go identify the body, but I didn't think it was going to be her. Of all the girls—listen, she was really beautiful. She wanted to be a model, and she could have been, too! That's why the idea of suicide is so absurd. She would no more have laid down on the tracks to die than—I don't know what."

"Sometimes, though, it's an accident. When people get hit by trains. Or maybe she was pushed."

"But then she would have been *hit* by the train." She got up and started wandering among the plants as if piecing it out. "She would have landed in the woods, instead of"—she shuddered, pressing her elbows into her sides—"all sliced up. I mean, she was decapitated! Even if people held her down, the engineer would have seen them running away after. The newspaper story said he saw her there but couldn't stop."

Caroline thought. "Maybe you could talk to him."

"Oh, I'm sure the police already have." Diana stopped by a red amaryllis in last bloom. She stared at it, then reached behind her and fingered her dark ponytail, as if reassuring herself her own hair was still there.

"If it was Rafe Millar, he'd see only what he wanted to see."

Diana sat down again. "That's true."

"But why would anyone want to do that to her?" A year ago, if anyone had told her that a kidnapping and a murder could happen on Crane Island, she would have told them how wrong they were. This was still a place where people never locked their doors.

"It's a long story." Diana took another sip of wine.

"Want some lunch first?"

Caroline had made potato cheese soup with bacon, and orange scones.

"Great. I didn't eat breakfast."

Caroline got up and went to the stove. As she did, a cramp knotted her stomach. *Go away.* She was starting to really believe that she was pregnant. In the past when she had been even a day or two late, she had stopped at the drugstore and bought a pregnancy test kit. But she had always felt crushed when the circle didn't turn blue, twisting it this way and that under the light to make sure. This time she would wait it out.

While they ate, Diana told her about the two girls, Crystal and Roxanne. "Both of them told people their babies were stillborn, and made private financial arrangements. Then, when they didn't pay Crystal or something, she was on her way to tell me. And she never made it. But Sidney Hazelton is involved. That's the really unbelievable part!"

"I *don't* believe it."

"But Roxanne said that the doctor said . . ." She stopped and took a bite of scone. Part of it crumbled in her hand and dropped to the table. "He was the one who was taking care of her."

"Said what?"

"Well, I don't remember exactly. Told her to do something. But he definitely was involved."

"But I *know* Dr. Hazelton. He would never do anything like that!"

"Listen, that would explain why Eileen Norris is involved. She's working along with him."

Caroline pressed her hands against her stomach. "You can't tell me that he would be involved in kidnapping and murder!"

"Well, he's at least involved in baby selling." She finished her wine stubbornly.

"Diana, no one on Crane Island will believe that."

She twisted the stem of the empty glass and looked challenging. "I'd think you would have had some experience with that— people not believing something that turns out to be true. I mean, who'd believe that someone would take a live baby and leave a dead one in its place?"

Caroline almost laughed. Diana reminded her of some of her former students. "That doesn't mean I have to believe every *other* improbable thing that I hear. I'm just telling you what people will think." *And that I don't have to believe what you're saying myself.*

"Pregnant teenagers can be influenced very easily. Believe me, I know." She emptied the rest of the bottle into her glass.

"I know, too." Caroline felt she was standing on the edge of a cliff over a blue sea. Her feet teetered on the edge, looking for safety. She dove in. "What would you say if I told you I got pregnant in college and had an abortion?"

The luminous eyes widened.

"I've never told anyone," Caroline whispered. She felt as if she was shaking all over, though when she looked down her body seemed still.

"Ironic, isn't it? When you're so anxious to have a child now."

"I wasn't then. I mean, I didn't even think of it as a child."

"It wasn't."

"Oh, I don't know about that." She got up and went back into the kitchen. *What have I done, mentioning it?* Opening the refrigerator, she brought out a half-filled bottle of chardonnay.

Diana laughed when she saw it. "I won't be able to leave here."

Without answering, Caroline uncorked the bottle and poured some into her own glass. Then she waited—waited for Diana to say something like, "Well, it's no big deal."

The sun still poured into the greenhouse. But there was no sound at all. Finally Caroline said, "You'd better forget I told you."

"Why? I'm really pleased. That you'd tell me, I mean." She

reached out and touched Caroline's wrist lightly with her fingers. "I know it's not because you're that crazy about me. But—I think you had to tell me, so we could be friends."

"It happened with this boy I was dating, Rob. We were really in love with each other. We really were. But he wasn't ready to get married. And I couldn't let my parents know."

"How old were you?"

"Twenty. Almost twenty-one."

Diana relaxed her fingers. "You were that afraid of your parents?"

"No. I wasn't afraid of them at all. But I didn't want to hurt them. They were so wonderful." As she said it she pictured her gentle, refined father, her warm and wise mother. "I knew it would kill them. They had this idea of what a family *should* be, and having a baby out of wedlock wasn't it. They'd had so much trouble with my sister that I couldn't hurt them, too. I was their only hope. It's hard to explain," she ended lamely.

"But *you* wanted the abortion too?" It was between a question and a statement.

"I didn't know what I wanted! What I wanted didn't matter. If I wanted anything, it was probably to keep the baby. But I knew I couldn't."

"So you just shut down emotionally," Diana suggested.

Was that what had happened? "Maybe."

"Tell me something. What did your parents think about this whole thing? With the baby and the police?"

"I didn't tell them. My father's heart—"

"But when it's all over, you'll tell them?" Diana interrupted.

"Probably not." Once Rafe Millar had accused her, she hadn't imagined ever telling them. "I mean, if we find Zach, I'll have to tell them what happened. But they'll be thrilled, then."

Diana leaned toward her, still questioning. "Then what good are they?"

"What?"

"Why even *have* parents if you can't share things with them? You mean that something as crucial to you as this, they would never know about? Did you ever complain about things when you were growing up, things that made you mad?"

She tried to remember. All she could think of were the times when there was cause for rejoicing.

"I think the price of keeping quiet is too high, Caroline," Diana was saying seriously. "For you, I mean. Do you think they wouldn't love you if they found out you weren't perfect?"

She didn't know what to say. "Of course they'd love me. But it would make them unhappy, it would make them anxious."

"Not that I should talk. I don't even see my parents—my *adopted* parents—anymore." She pushed back from the table and Caroline was afraid she was leaving. But she said, "Do you have a bathroom somewhere around here?"

"We have bathrooms everywhere. Just open a door."

"Good. Then you can tell me the other terrible things you've done."

By the time Diana left Caroline's house and reached Martinville, it was almost five-thirty. As she drove home, thoughts of Crystal played across her mind. Diana tried to remember her lively beauty and the funny things she had said, but kept seeing morgue images instead—the delicate whispers of stretch marks around Crystal's flat belly, the severed neck edges a gruesome black as if someone had charred creamy paper against a flame. Crystal, who had made up a story about a dying love, had herself passed into that mysterious land of the young dead.

She was glad to get to Mario's Vacation Apartments, to see its orange tile roofs standing out against the inky sky. Reaching into her mailbox she pulled out a credit card bill and an introductory offer to a new health spa. At the top of the stairs she unlocked her door and reached inside to flip the light switch. It turned on the hall light and the imitation Tiffany lamp. Putting down her canvas bag and purse, she pulled her jacket off. She wanted . . . she didn't know what she wanted.

There was a chilled bottle of Riesling in the refrigerator, but she bypassed it for lime-flavored seltzer. She had to get some work done tonight. She was headed for the sofa with the water and her poor imitation of mail when she noticed that her message light was blinking. Setting down her glass on the dinette table, she reached inside her bag for a pen in case there was a number she needed to write down. Then she punched the Messages button.

There was a sound like a train whistle, a long mournful wail. Then a voice whispered, "Like trains, Diana?" and the caller clicked off.

She stood there, frozen, trying to figure out what she had heard. When she finally lunged at the Save button it was already too late. Had it been a *threat?* No, probably a wrong number. She was just upset from the trip to the morgue. *But they used my name.*

Picking up her red down jacket and her purse, she moved out the door, pressing in the button to lock it behind her. Once outside she found that she was running, running in the direction of the stucco clubhouse. She took the three clubhouse steps in a rush, and collapsed against the rough-textured wall.

Mario's Vacation Clubhouse had been decorated to look like a tropical bar, with stuffed parrots in brass cages, palm trees in wooden tubs, and floral-cushioned rattan furniture. Fans overhead moved slowly back and forth like crocodile heads. But the other person in the lobby was not from *Casablanca.* She was a dwarfish woman with bulbous features and a crossed eye whom Diana knew by sight. She was arguing vehemently into the pay phone.

Diana leaned against the opposite lobby wall and waited for her heartbeat to return to normal.

The other woman was engaged in a litany. "I didn't say that. No. I didn't *say* that. Of course I didn't say that. Why do you say I said that?"

Finally aware of Diana, she wheeled around to look. "I gotta go," she said into the phone, and hung up.

"I'll only be a second." *Don't leave me alone in paradise.*

"It doesn't matter. It was getting retrograde."

The front door swung closed behind her.

Diana moved to the phone and dialed her New York number. For a moment she did not understand the recorded voice. "We're sorry, but 692-9341 has been changed to a nonpublished number."

Nonpublished? It sounded like a bad novel.

She thought about calling the operator, but what could she say? *It's my boyfriend's apartment? How dare he change the number and not tell me?* He could have forgotten, she thought, as anger crept up the back of her neck and threatened to explode across her head. Maybe the roommate did it and Erik didn't know. Of course. And in a minute the stuffed parrots would come to life and hum "As Time Goes By."

Damn him to hell! Her hands shaking, she reached under the shelf for the directory. She found Howard Liebowitz's number and dialed.

What do I say if his wife answers? I'm not that good with wives. But when the machine went on it was Howard's voice. "Hello. This is Howie Liebowitz. I'm unable to talk to you right now. But if you leave your name and number at the electronic beep, I'll get back to you as soon as I can."

"Howard? This is Diana. If you can call me in the next few minutes I'm at 478-1382. Otherwise don't—"

"Diana? Hi."

"Howard?"

"I'm here. I've just been getting some weird calls lately."

She laughed shakily. "Me too."

"I doubt they're the same people."

"Probably not. But I just had one now."

"Are you *okay?* You sound terrible."

"Well . . ."

"What happened?"

"I just got a message on my machine asking me if I liked trains—as in being hit by one?"

"You want me to come over? I'll come over. Just tell me where you live."

She gave him directions. "I'm in the clubhouse at the back."

"Okay. I'll see you in a few minutes."

"Thanks."

She hung up and went into the lounge, making sure to sit on a couch away from the window and from which she could see the hallway. She reached for a *New Yorker* on the glass-topped table, then put it back down. If Crystal had killed herself, why would someone be threatening *her?* But of course she didn't really believe Crystal had. Maybe Roxanne had called whomever she was involved with to demand more money, and said that Diana had told her she should. *That would make them real happy.*

She heard the front door open, then close softly. For a moment there was no other sound. It couldn't be Howard already! She froze against the sofa. The colors of the room swam together, then flattened out. *Get a grip. It's probably only that woman come back to finish her phone call.*

"Diana?" Howard came around the corner and into view, moving more rapidly when he saw her. He was dressed in another of his odd combinations: leather bomber jacket, narrow black sweat pants, fluorescent orange socks, and worn Nikes. His disheveled curls and mustache made him look as if he had dressed in a hurry.

"Thank God it's you!"

"It's me." He moved across the room and put an arm around her, giving her a hug as he sat down. She let her face rest against his wind-chilled cheek for a moment.

"Are you *okay?*"

"How did you get here so fast?"

"Fast? It's been twenty minutes. I kept picturing you dead."

"Me too!"

179

"What happened? Where's Erik?"

The question implied several different things, but Diana responded to only two of them. "He's in New York. He's okay."

"That's good. I guess." He grinned but drew back from her slightly, resting his arm along the rattan back. "What *happened?*"

Diana sighed. "I can't decide if it means anything or not. There was just this sound like a long train whistle. Then someone said, 'Like trains, Diana?' or something like that. And hung up."

He looked confused.

"I think it has to do with what happened to Crystal. That it will happen to me next."

"You'll kill yourself?"

"No! But I don't think she did, either. I don't know how they did it, but she never would have. You didn't know her, but she wasn't suicidal."

He kneaded her shoulder with his hand. "But why would someone threaten *you?*"

"Well—I did something they might not like."

"Meaning?"

"I'll tell you about it. But not *here.*"

They drove into Coyne's Cove, a seaport village that had been renovated for tourists. For an hour they walked around, moving out onto the pier and past closed frozen yogurt shops before settling into the lounge of the Phoenix Hotel. The hotel was shabby, dating back to the days when most of its customers were traveling salesmen. They picked a dark green velvet booth missing most of its nap. Above the table was a photograph of Main Street in 1883.

Diana described her visit to Roxanne, omitting Roxanne's current location as she had promised herself she would. Through several vodka collinses and a huge platter of steamed clams, she sat with her hand loosely on the table, Howard's resting over it. As her terror faded, she began to feel silly. Had she turned the message into a major event just to spend time with him? If he found her insubstantial as it was, in the cold light of day she would seem histrionic. She pulled her hand away, ready to confess. "I probably imagined the whole thing. It was probably a ploy to get you into my clutches."

"Right. A woman who marches through morgues, and hang-glides over Africa, is terrified by an imaginary phone call. I doubt that very much."

"I never went hang gliding. I only wrote about it like I did." Full confession time. "I would only go up in hot-air balloons."

"Oh, is that all? Diana, let me tell you the places *I* go. To the office. And then home. On weekends to the video store. For a big treat I'll go to a professional conference once in a while." He pulled at his mustache morosely. "Sometimes I think I'm agoraphobic as well as hypochondriacal. I barely want to leave the island."

"That's different. You have *roots*. I don't."

"Roots. If you're not careful, they can hold you in one spot forever." He said it darkly. *The married man's lament.*

"Do you feel trapped?"

"Sometimes."

" 'A palace and a prison.' "

"You got that right."

"Not me. Byron. What time is it?"

"A little before twelve."

"We'd better go." She reached for the small green check, but Howard slapped at the fingers he had been caressing. "For God's sake, Diana!"

"What? You came over as a favor to me."

"Give me a break, okay?"

Shrugging, she let him pull out a battered wallet to pay.

But in the car, his good humor was restored. He entertained her with stories of his early days in the Adoption Unit, when Marci secretly left cookies and cards in his desk.

"But she's too old for you."

"She's divorced. And young at heart."

"What kind of cards?"

"Friendship cards. Once she pasted her head on top of the Venus de Milo and wrote, 'But I have arms.' "

"That's cute. They must have suggested it in *Cosmo.*"

"Ah, Diana. Ever the cynic." He reached over and tugged her dark ponytail.

"What finally made her stop?"

He laughed. "What makes you think she has?"

She brushed his arm. "Will you ever succumb?"

"Not to her."

Going up the apartment stairs, Diana, though mellow, had a sudden prickling of wariness like the shock of pain felt even under Novocain.

"You want me to check around?" Howard asked when they were inside.

"Sure."

Too late she remembered her wildly unmade bed, the peaks of the comforter like ocean swells. Her clothes were piled up on chairs, creating strange animal shapes. Suppose he was compulsively neat like Erik? Suppose he viewed her messiness as a character disorder? *No man likes to crawl into a messy bed.* She heard closets being opened and shut, and winced at the jumble of boots on the floor.

But Howard came back with a different agenda. "No one there. But your friend is a man of few belongings. None I could find."

Diana laughed. "He commutes to the city."

"What, in a moving van? Tell me the truth, Diana." He gripped her arm through her down jacket. "Does he live here or not?"

She felt her face grow hot, as if caught in a lie. "He stays in our apartment in the city. But he's here on weekends." Oh, what the hell. "*Some* weekends. I don't even know how many more there'll be. You know what? He changed the New York number to a non-published one and didn't even tell me!"

"When did you find out?"

"Tonight."

"You called *him* first." It wasn't a question.

"Well—I tried." It sounded damning. "I didn't want to bother you."

Howard smiled.

"Look, I'm glad it was you! I'd much rather have you here than him."

"And I have arms." But his dark eyes looked vulnerable.

She moved closer and pressed against him. "I loved it when you held me in the morgue." But the way the words sounded made her laugh.

"Did you? I can't ever tell with you. You blow in here like some exotic butterfly, stirring people up. Stirring *me* up. But there's no telling what you're thinking or where else you'll touch down. Next week, Istanbul?"

Now she put her arms around him. They were immediately kissing, moving their mouths against each other's lips, Howard's tongue all over hers, heads twisting. *Writhing like sea monsters.* She reached up and ran her free hand through his dark curly hair, something she had wanted to do from the first day. It was as soft as silk strands. *Baby. Baby.* She felt him pressing his arms against the sides of her breasts, forcing them against his chest. *I want him, I want him, I really love him.*

Moving her tongue away from his, she explored his teeth. He slid his hand down inside the front of her jeans and began to rub softly. *Oh God oh God.* Together they moved toward the couch. She cupped the stiffness under his sweat pants.

And then she pulled away. "Shit!"

He looked down, surprised, but continued pulling gently at her nipple.

"Howard, we can't do this!" She caught at his hands and held them.

"Why?"

"Because you're married."

183

"Diana, I told you! We're separated; I'm getting divorced."

Oh, right. You think I haven't heard that a thousand times? It's new to you, of course. But once, just once, I'd like someone to say to me, "Yeah, I'm happily married, but I want you anyway." He might not get her, but at least it would be honest.

"You've got to understand this." She squeezed his fingers tighter. "I can't be casual about it with you. It has to be—different." *If we slept together now and it didn't work out, I wouldn't be able to trust myself—or anyone else—ever again.* How could she face seeing him again, listening to his jokes, knowing he would never love her back? There would be the phone calls he didn't return, the pained smile when he decided she wasn't worth the aggravation. *My wife and I decided to go for counseling.*

He stepped back, offended. "You only want to believe what you want to believe."

"Believe me, this is progress—for me."

He was shaking his head.

"Look: We'll have to see what happens."

He nodded, then asked belatedly, "Will you be okay here?"

"Sure."

"I could sleep on the couch."

"I've heard *that* one before."

"I mean it!" He sounded angry. "You *are* cynical, you know?"

"Just experienced. I mean, I know myself. This has been too long coming."

"Why can't we let it?"

She shook her head. *Remember his dark-eyed children.* "I'll see you in a few hours."

"If anything else happens, call me. Okay?"

"Okay."

They kissed again on the lips, but lightly, then Howard moved away. "Chain-lock the door!"

"I will."

As she did so and turned back into the room she saw the seltzer still untouched in its glass. *You did the right thing,* it reassured her. But her body was still aroused.

She had thought she would sit up all night, keeping watch. But after she undressed, she lay down across her bed and fell instantly asleep.

FIFTEEN

Wednesday morning Diana awoke to chilly winter sunlight, and a sense of empty virtue. She had slept heavily, but under the influence of strange dreams, dreams in which a judge with an animal's face kept scolding her. At least nothing terrible had happened to her during the night. She showered and dressed in a pair of wool slacks and a matching tan cashmere sweater, her best outfit. After tying her dark hair at the nape of her neck with an orange ribbon, she applied coral blush to her cheekbones, and added lip gloss. She knew she was doing it for Howard. The hell with it!

She was anxious to get to the office early to talk to Howard privately. By skipping breakfast and the newspaper she did, but Pearl arrived soon afterward. Marci followed, balancing her breakfast.

"You didn't start the coffee?" Pearl grumbled to Diana, stopping at her desk to put her things away.

"Was I supposed to?"

"You drink it, don't you?" Looking put-upon, Pearl picked up the empty pot from the coffeemaker and left the room.

Howard was the last one into the unit, pulling off his leather jacket as he crossed the room. When he saw Diana watching him, he immediately looked away. But he stopped by her desk. "Anything happen after I left?" he asked softly.

"No. I just fell asleep."

"No more weird phone calls?"

"No." She watched his face for some other sign.

"I guess I kind of got carried away. Too many gin and tonics. I'm sorry."

"Don't—" Before she could say anything else, Dolly was advancing on them from across the room, her pink face exasperated. She had not been friendly toward Diana since the episode with Infants Hospital. How much did she know of her husband's illegal activities? Maybe her membership in the DAR, sailing lessons for the girls, and anniversary gifts from Tiffany's were all built on sand. It was not an unpleasing thought.

But this morning Diana was not Dolly's target. Twelve-year-old Cassandra Smythe had been adopted as an infant through Heart's Retreat when her parents, late 1970s flower children, had not wanted the responsibility of a baby. But a few years later Jane Castle and Terry Forbes had married and become successful makers of film shorts.

Gradually their missing child became an obsession and they tracked her down to Crane Island. For weeks the Forbes watched their daughter, then finally called the adoptive parents. The Smythes threatened legal action. The Forbes, who lived in Manhattan, came to the agency to see if it would intercede for them. Howard had instructed Dolly to contact the adoptive parents. She had actually been able to negotiate a visit at Christmas, and permission for the Forbes to write twice a year and send gifts. She had complained about it ever since.

"What do the *artistes* want now?" Howard dangled his jacket from one finger. He looked tired.

"First, for Christmas, they gave Cassandra a VCR camera. It was probably an old one of theirs, but still . . . it completely turned her head. Now they want to make a movie about Cassandra's being adopted, and their reentry into her life. Get her reactions and the Smythes on film. You can imagine what the Smythes think of that!"

"That guy is so *pushy,*" Marci burst out, her voice rising. She looked lost in a huge top printed to look like a peacock's plumage. A silver cobra bracelet circled up her arm. "They think they can buy everything!"

Hannah looked up from her desk. "That's the problem with our society. People think everybody deserves a second chance."

"Do you think it *hurts* the child to know who her real parents are?" Diana asked. Would her life have been different if she and Earline had known and acknowledged each other?

"It can. Fortunately it doesn't happen that often."

"Why do they have a State Registry then?"

"That's for when they're adults, Diana. They can't be told anything until they're eighteen, and then only if their birth mothers register and want to be found. A lot of girls don't want to open everything up again. That's why they surrendered in the first place!"

Diana took a sip of tea. "But some kids must be curious before then."

She missed Hannah's answer, but heard Howard say, "Well, little Cassandra has had *her* curiosity satisfied."

"Yes, but look how," Dolly said. "Imagine finding out your father has a ponytail!"

"C'mon, Dolly, twelve-year-olds think that's neat," Howard objected.

"Mine doesn't."

"I'll bet she does. She's just not telling *you.* Wait till you see what she brings home in a few years."

"As long as he doesn't have an earring!"

188

"Just a tattoo of *Mom* on his arm?" Howard and Dolly grinned at each other, and Diana felt left out.

She was glad when the phone on her desk rang.

"Diana Larsen."

"Miss Larsen? This is Arlene Manning." The voice was tense, without expression.

It took her a moment to remember who that was, that Crystal's mother was remarried. "Oh—Mrs. Manning. I was going to call you. I'm so sorry about Crystal." *Why didn't I call? Because I couldn't imagine what to say to someone who had just lost her only child.*

"My beautiful little girl." Arlene was suddenly sobbing, her conflicts with Crystal forgotten. "The moment she got involved with Social Services, things went to hell! I hope you're brave enough to write the truth about that place."

"I'll try."

"You're the only one who took an interest in Crystal. You're the only one who called, trying to find her. But now I need your help. In getting her baby."

"Her baby?"

"Hank and I have talked it over, and we want to take him. I know they've probably put him up for adoption, but as the grandparents we have certain claims, too. Why should that baby go to strangers?"

"But—Crystal and the housemother both told me he was still-born."

"Oh, come on. That was just a story, wasn't it? I'll bet that baby is alive as you or me. And he's all I have left of my daughter. I want that baby! You can tell Social Services we'll do whatever we have to to get him. If I don't hear from them they'll be hearing from my lawyer." The phone slammed in Diana's ear.

Around her the office had gotten very quiet. She looked up and met everybody's eyes: Hannah's were curious, Dolly's wary. Howard at the coffee machine looked concerned. Even Marci, directly opposite her, had flipped up her head in alarm. Diana felt brushed by fear, the same fear she felt when she had gotten the threatening phone call. What did she know about these people, anyway?

Before she could tell Howard about the call, her phone rang again. She hesitated, then picked it up. "Diana Larsen."

"Hi, Diana! It's Caroline."

"Hi." She remembered that in one of her dreams Crystal had been Caroline's daughter. For a while. Then Caroline had been on downhill skis, waving and smiling, and before Diana could stop her, she had skied over a cliff. "I was just going to call you."

"Really? What's up?"

"I have another idea. Something we can do. Are you going to be home?"

"I'm always home. Now Joe's car won't be ready until tomorrow."

"Great. See you soon."

She was leaving several minutes later when Marci came running after her into the hall. "I have to talk to you," she whispered. Her narrow olive face, obscured by huge red-framed glasses, was tight with concern.

She's going to tell me what's really going on.

Marci glanced quickly back to the office to make sure that someone—*who?*—hadn't come out, then said, "Listen, Diana, you're friends with Howard, right?"

"I guess." She did not want to hear that he was mixed up in it.

"I know I'm older than he is, in years anyway, but that doesn't seem to matter so much these days," Marci said hopefully.

"No."

"Anyway," Marci put a tiny, bony hand on Diana's arm, "when you guys go out to lunch? I know you're just friends, and I wouldn't mind going along."

"Oh." *That's all I need, a cheerful threesome. Marci slapping the cakes on Howard.*

"It's usually on Thursdays, isn't it?"

"Usually. But I probably won't be around that much longer."

The fingers choked her arm. "Thanks." They weren't all that different, she and Marci. But at least she wasn't buying any illusions about Howard.

They sat in the greenhouse again, having coffee. "If I could somehow prove that Sidney Hazelton was in on it, would you believe it?"

Caroline shrugged. "I guess I'd have to."

"If we could prove it, then the police would have to investigate, right? Anyway, this is what I thought: If one of us called up pretending to be a pregnant teenager and offered him a baby, if he made a deal, then we'd *know* he's involved. The only trouble is, he'd probably recognize my voice."

Caroline leaned back in her chair. And waited.

Diana gave her an encouraging smile.

"He knows *my* voice, too."

"But you haven't talked to him in a while. Like I have."

Caroline put down her black-and-white cow coffee cup. "You want me to call up Dr. Hazelton, pretend that I'm a pregnant teenager, and ask him if he wants a baby. And then what?" *Not that I'd do it in a hundred years.*

"Just see what he says."

"But isn't that some kind of fraud? We've already impersonated the police."

Diana finished her cappuccino. "That's how things get done in the world."

"Not in my world! Want another cup?"

"It's a lot of trouble, isn't it?"

"It's just steaming the milk. The machine does most of the work. Why don't we just talk to the housemother instead?"

Diana shrugged. "I guess we could. But I don't think she's that involved. And then they'd know that we know about them."

"She couldn't deny coming here with those gifts!"

"Sure she could. Or she might just claim that someone asked her to deliver the basket. You can't really *prove* she did anything else here. He's probably just buying her off. Look, she can't even pay her phone bill. Maybe she thinks she's doing God's work." She sat up. "But if we could get him to commit himself on tape . . . It wouldn't be legal, but it could start an investigation."

The phone rang. They both jumped, then Diana laughed. "See? He's calling us."

"It's probably Joe." She went over and picked up the receiver. "Hi!"

"Mrs. Denecke? Rafe Millar here. We're set for tomorrow morning at six-forty-five."

"Tomorrow morning?" This was all the notice they were giving her?

"Meet me at the cemetery office a little before that. If you're still interested."

"Of course I am!"

"See you then." He hung up.

She turned to Diana. "They're doing the exhumation at six-forty-five tomorrow morning."

"Great!"

But she pressed cold fingers to her face. "I'm so scared."

"Don't be. You want me to pick you up, don't you? I'll come by around six."

Would Joe want to be there? If he did she could always call and cancel the ride.

But Joe wanted no part of the exhumation. Caroline brought it up when they were sitting together in the den that night. She explained why they were doing it, and pointed out that Rafe Millar would not be going ahead with it if he did not believe that an exchange of babies had actually taken place. Well, that was overstating it a little. But there was still no reason for Joe to sit with his arms crossed over his chest, refusing even to talk about it. *He just wants to keep*

Zach buried and get on with his life! That thought, terrible to consider, came to her about four-thirty A.M. the next morning. She turned her face into her pillow and pushed the idea away. *No, he just doesn't want to get hurt again.*

SIXTEEN

The exhumation party met at Greenhill Cemetery at six-thirty, just as the day was turning a grayish pink along the horizon. She and Diana were the last to arrive. Rafe Millar, Ernest Shockley, and a man she did not know were standing beside the Cudleigh monument. In the dimness the two white marble children, sitting on the steps of their parents' bier, looked fluorescent, as if lit from within. Poor little souls. Caroline was soon close enough to see the scalloping on the little girl's coat collar, and the button fastening her shoe.

"This is amazing!" Diana moved onto the bottom step for a better look at the youthful parents who were lying side by side on top, holding hands. Caroline turned away. *She doesn't even understand the tragedy of people cheated out of the chance of seeing their children grow up. Or children whose loving parents were snatched away forever.*

"Morning, ladies!" Ernest Shockley was resplendent in a tan houndstooth coat with a Sherlock Holmes cape, though his elegance was mitigated by a green John Deere visor cap. "Now the whole force is here."

Caroline held her breath. Rafe Millar just snorted and said something to the large, heavy-faced man in a navy trench coat. The man's sad eyes reminded her of the spaniels of her childhood. As she watched, he took a Pentax SLR camera from a case at his feet and practiced focusing on various spots.

"You're not videotaping this?" Ernest Shockley asked.

The photographer shook his head. "Nah. Not politically significant enough. They wouldn't waste the money."

Shockley looked affronted, as if it were a slap at his cemetery. "People videotape *funerals* these days."

"I already photographed the Greenhill sign with my watch next to it. Digital, with the date. It'll be fine."

"It'll be fine if we ever get started," Millar grumbled, disagreeable under a tan suede cowboy hat.

Caroline hugged herself against the March wind, remembering the promises to Millar that had made this morning possible. *Rumpelstiltskin.* It was a story she had never liked. But it was more frightening to think that all this machinery had been set in motion just on her say-so. *What if I'm wrong? What if Sol Maria Cruz was wrong in what she told me?* She imagined opening the small box and seeing the tiny flexed bones in a little suit, surrounded by stuffed woolly lambs and silver baby cups, or anything else they had stuck in to make the journey less arduous. No, that was much too nice, much too *Caroline;* more like rotting flesh, the stench of decay, a tiny skull. She felt sick.

"We're just waiting for the backhoe. They'll be here any minute," Shockley explained to the women.

The morning, though chilly, was overlaid with a fine gray mist. As the night pulled back, other monuments appeared around them, as if revealed on an Etch-A-Sketch screen. It was the kind of March day on Crane Island that she had gotten used to over the years, the kind in which the sun belatedly appears and beats down more strongly than anyone could have predicted. She could smell salt in the air, and remembered that the water was not far away. *No mat-*

195

ter what happens to you, the day starts up anyway. There were always enough people doing normal things to make life seem unchanging.

Diana had started to wander away to look at the other gravestones. Millar stomped his feet up and down on the ground. "What's the story?"

"The story is, they'll be collecting unemployment if they don't get their asses here soon," Shockley complained. He stuffed his hands into his coat pockets, removing the glitter of his fraternal rings from view. "This can't interfere with the normal business day!"

"There's somebody now." The photographer pointed his camera at a long Plymouth gliding through the gates and turning toward a machinery garage.

"Assholes," Shockley pronounced. "Come on, we'll meet them by the grave."

They started moving slowly through the oldest section of the cemetery in the direction of a newer area on the slope.

"This place is really fascinating!" Diana whispered to Caroline. She kept stopping to admire monuments. "Look at *this.*" She pointed to a tiny marble cradle which was poignantly empty. On the ground next to it was a worn carved lamb.

Caroline turned away. Why couldn't Diana remember why they were there?

"A lamb is for a little child," Ernest Shockley said cheerfully, dropping back to walk with them. "Broken columns mean cut off in midlife; wheat stalks like that one represent old age."

"Are all those stone urns for ashes?"

"No, they represent the soul."

"There's a whole world here that nobody knows about," Diana enthused. "How come the newer monuments are just plaques in the ground?"

"Makes mowing easier. We couldn't take care of this place otherwise."

Caroline trailed them, her feet sinking into the soft grassy ground. All she could think of was what lay beneath. No matter how beau-

196

tiful the monuments were, each one meant an empty place at someone's table. She let herself think of the baby she and Joe had buried over on Long Island. Whether he was Zachary or not, he was *somebody's* child. The Greenspans'—or someone else's. Maybe Joe was right to want no part of this morning.

The plot was a brown rectangle of new earth in the grass. Beside it stood a jelly jar holding a fistful of daffodils.

"No headstone?" the photographer said disapprovingly. He removed a series of small plastic bags and labels.

"Not for a year in this instance," the cemetery director apologized. "Jewish custom. But there's a sign identifying it." He pointed to a small white plastic marker with a number written in black grease pencil.

There was a rumbling from the road as the backhoe maneuvered its way next to the spot.

"Step back!" Shockley began directing traffic. "They'll dig down to the casket, then shovel around it to bring it out. You gotta be careful with wood, it can collapse."

"How far gone is he?" Millar asked tightly.

"The body without embalming? Like a cantaloupe in the sun." He paused as the dirt began to be tossed aside. "On the other hand, this one was kept chilled. The ground is cold and it's only been a week. You're very, very lucky."

Caroline looked around at the watching faces; none of them looked as if they felt particularly lucky. There was something so *wrong* about disturbing the coffin of anyone who had been laid to rest.

" 'Blest be the man that spares these stones, and curst be he that moves my bones,' " Diana announced. "Shakespeare's epitaph."

"Oh."

The digging continued. Then, as a corner of polished wood came into view, she grabbed Diana's arm. *Easy, easy. They're only digging it up, not opening it here.*

Diana turned to her. "Are you *okay?*"

197

"Uh-huh." But her stomach was churning, an uncharted sea of orange juice, coffee, and toast. She should have skipped the coffee. Millar's flat, broad face looked green as well.

"Hold it!" Ernest Shockley yelled to the backhoe operator. "You've hit oil!"

Caroline watched, unable to look away, as a man in a faded dark green jumpsuit edged himself into the hole and started digging a trench around the tiny casket; she winced as one corner cracked away. The man across from her kept snapping photographs.

"You didn't open it before you buried it?" Millar asked Ernest Shockley. His tone implied that all this aggravation could have been averted.

"No. Why would I do that? They never *go* anywhere."

"We'll see about that." He broke off as the worker in the hole hoisted the pine box in his arms and handed it up as far as he could. The backhoe operator, who had left his machine idling now and was standing next to Millar, reached down to grasp it. But perhaps he misjudged its weight; his foot slipped at the wet edge. The casket dropped back into the hole, the man falling on top of it.

There was a splintering crash as they landed.

Caroline heard Diana cry out.

Ernest Shockley cried, "Oh, my God. Oh, my God." He turned on the other policeman. "Don't photograph *that.*"

Bending over the excavation, the photographer clicked away.

One of the workers was swearing in a language Caroline did not understand. She put her hand over her eyes. *Why are we doing this?* Cautiously she peered through her fingers into the hole. The coffin was crushed. Tiny white flecks had spilled out everywhere on the dark earth. Maggots. Maggots already! She pressed her hand over her mouth to hold back a scream.

The worker closest to the coffin, perhaps disgusted, ripped away what was left of the top.

Caroline looked again. Not maggots. There were too many of them, too motionless.

Diana reacted first. "My God," she cried, pointing to the large orange plastic bags that had split open. "It's Uncle Ben's!" She started to laugh.

For a moment, no one seemed to know what it meant or what to do. Then Ernest Shockley ordered the men to fill in the grave. That is, his pudgy be-ringed fingers pantomimed shoveling dirt back in.

"You can't do that," Millar objected. "That's evidence!"

"Evidence of what? You've got it documented." Shockley pointed to the photographer. "He's got enough shots to fill a goddamn wedding album! This better not get to the papers!"

"Nobody's going to the papers. But cover it with a plastic tarp."

The cemetery director looked truculent. "Until when?"

"Until I say!" He turned to Caroline. "Now we'll have to exhume whoever *you* buried."

"Oh, no!" Joe would *never* allow that. *He'd divorce me before letting me dig up the plot with his mother's grave.* As she said it she knew she was being unfair; after all, in pressing for the exhumation, she had not given the Greenspans' feelings any consideration. Had they been upset? What would they say when they found out what had happened? "You already have the autopsy of the baby we buried," she pointed out. "You *know* it was Seth Greenspan." She had finally found out the baby's first name from Millar.

"Yeah. But we're still missing one!" He started walking toward the office, Diana and Caroline beside him.

She and Diana exchanged incredulous looks. Then Caroline gave Diana a quick shake of her head to keep Diana from responding.

It was too late. "Hel-lo-o." Diana said to Millar, making it into three sarcastic syllables. "This woman has been trying to tell you that for at least two weeks."

His flat blue eyes turned on Diana. "Who the hell are you?"

"The Voice of America. The press."

Now Millar's glance was trained on Caroline accusingly. "She's my friend," she said quickly. "But—what are you going to do?"

"What am I going to do? I'll send someone to check your yard again."

"I doubt that there's anything left outside *now.*" She could barely keep the bitterness out of her voice. "It's rained hard since then."

"When we dusted the bedroom for fingerprints, we only found two different adults," he pointed out defensively.

"Joe's prints and mine. But anyone else was probably wearing gloves."

He still looked dissatisfied. "You have other kids?"

"No."

"Rafe, I'm heading out." The photographer caught up with them. They had started to slow down as they reached the end of the grass near the cemetery office.

"Got everything you need?"

"What I need, but not what I expected. Where the hell's the body?"

"Stop by my office. I'll explain it to you." Then he turned to Caroline and stared at her for a long moment. His lips parted, then closed again.

She stared back. Was this the only apology she was going to get?

"Uncle Ben's rice. Christ!" He turned away, shaking his head, as if she should have arranged something better.

Caroline and Diana climbed back into the Sentra.

"So it's good," Diana said.

"What's good? *Where's Zach?* Who has *him?* The police won't be able to find him; they can't do anything!" *Don't cry.* "Even if he tried, Rafe Millar wouldn't know what to do. Do you know how long it's been? They say if a crime isn't solved in the first twenty-four hours, it probably won't be."

"Who says that?"

"I don't know. Somebody." She wiped at her eyes. "I read it somewhere."

Diana strapped on her seat belt and summarized. "We can't find Susan; we can't ask Crystal; Roxanne won't talk. The police don't have any imagination. I could put pressure on Roxanne, I guess, but she'd only implicate Dr. Hazelton. And you don't believe it."

"You're really sure about him?" She felt herself wavering just a little.

"He's the only doctor Roxanne knows."

"I mean, if you're sure, I'll do it."

"What? You mean call him? Are you really up to that?"

"If it will find Zachary. And I can't think of anything else."

Back at the house she was still determined to do it. "The house is a mess," she warned, unlocking the door and bringing Diana into the kitchen. Actually there were only Joe's breakfast dishes on the counter, but seeing it through Diana's eyes there seemed to be so many *things:* fifty or so refrigerator magnets, antique crocks, glass jars, patchwork, the penguin with a clock in his stomach. Her large white bookcase was filled only with cookbooks. Many of them had come from yard sales.

"Want a scone or anything?"

"No. Just coffee if you have it."

They stood in the kitchen to drink it. Caroline finally put her cup back on the counter. "I'm ready."

"Do you think he's in yet? It's not even nine o'clock."

"It may be a good time. I don't think he starts office visits until ten."

"We have to tape it." Diana pulled a small recorder out of her black canvas bag. "But I don't have my telephone attachment."

"We can put it on speakerphone. That way it gets broadcast into the room."

"Right." She made a space for the recorder on the counter.

Caroline looked up the number and started to dial.

"Wait! Do you know what you're going to say?"

"I think so."

After three rings, Sidney Hazelton answered himself, sounding a bit put out. "Doctor here."

"Hello?" She made her voice high and breathless. "Um—this girl

201

I know—I'm really calling about a friend who's going to have a baby? Anyway, this other girl I know said you might know someone who wanted a baby."

"Wait, wait, wait. You're calling me about a friend who's having a baby? Doesn't she have a doctor?" His voice was warm but cautious.

"I think so."

"Okay. Who's her doctor?"

"Uh—someone on Long Island. She lives on Long Island."

"When's the baby due?"

She looked wildly at Diana. "Uh . . . soon."

"Now, don't take offense at this, but I have to ask: Is your friend white?"

"Yes. Yes, she is."

"I assumed so. Her age?"

"Nine—nineteen."

"And you're sure she wants to give her baby up."

"Yes. She sure doesn't want to keep it!"

"Well, it's her decision, of course. But you can tell your friend that if she's still interested, she can call me after the baby is born. I know many very nice couples who would love to have a healthy baby. We can discuss it then."

Dr. Hazelton appeared to be signing off. Diana was mouthing something at her, then grabbed a pen spotted like a cow and drew a dollar sign in the air.

"Uh—wait! What about money?"

"Money?" He made it sound like an alien substance.

But she persisted. "Well, you know. For expenses and all."

"Well, anything like that is usually arranged by the couple adopting. They'll pay reasonable expenses, about three or four thousand dollars anyway."

"Wow!" She was a teenager again. "I mean, that's good."

"Is there a number where I can reach *you*, Miss . . ."

"No. My mother wouldn't—I have to go." She hung up the phone.

Then Diana was beside her, rubbing her back enthusiastically. "You were wonderful! You sounded good and scared."

"I *was* good and scared! After I started talking, I actually *became* that girl."

Diana looked interested. "Did it feel as if you were doing the right thing?"

"It felt like I was doing the *only* thing." She leaned against the counter, considering it. "That's what I'd forgotten. It's easy enough now to wonder why I didn't just tell my parents or why I wasn't brave enough to have the baby. But I wasn't." She had a memory of standing in the dorm bathroom a hundred times during those first few weeks, pulling down her pants, hoping to see some evidence that her period had started. Just the way she was checking constantly now in the hope that it had not. "That baby—if I'd had her— would be thinking about college now herself." Or himself. But she always thought of the baby as a girl.

"Wow." Diana turned toward the counter. "Let's listen to the tape."

"Why?" She wasn't sure she could stand to listen to herself as that girl.

"Because I think tone's important. His, I mean. The problem is, nothing really illegal was said. If he'd offered you twenty thousand dollars or demanded to meet with you *now*, it would be suspicious. Of course, if he'd said he wasn't interested and referred you to Social Services, we'd know something else."

"But he said to call him after the baby's born," Caroline objected.

"I know. . . . So we'll call him again in a few days. After the 'birth.'"

"In a few *days?*" She felt dismayed at the idea of another delay. "And then what?"

"He might want a meeting. We could really nab him then."

"Oh, *right!*" It was what her students always said to each other,

203

parroting older kids, teenagers; now she knew what they meant. "He'd recognize me the moment I walked in."

"No, no, I don't mean go there. We'd just set it up, and see what happens. And in that call you could press him to implicate himself more. We could plan out the questions beforehand."

"This is crazy!"

Diana leaned against the refrigerator. Caroline heard the crunch of dried poster paint as she pressed against the good-bye paintings. "He was definitely interested, though."

Caroline could not deny that.

SEVENTEEN

Friday night Diana waited in her apartment for Erik. Unmarried man or not, it no longer mattered. "Look, Erik," she would say, "this relationship is history." Last Thursday, when she finally got into the city, he had conveniently been on his way out, an invitation for a long weekend in Southampton tucked under his arm. The roommate had a visiting aunt from Ohio sleeping in Erik's bed. So Diana had spent two nights on her coworker Undine's couch, then limped back to Crane Island Saturday evening. Erik's not including her in the house party in the Hamptons had rankled all week.

There was also the little business about the changed phone number. The relationship was worn out, too stretched, like the elastic in old underpants, to hold anything up. The downside was that it was one of her longer relationships. Maybe she was just not destined for permanence.

Still she jumped when she heard his footsteps on the stairs, his hand turning the knob.

"What a shitty week," he announced, looking around and finally locating her by the kitchenette. He came over and gave her a long kiss. "I never want to live through anything like *that* again."

"What happened?" His lips tasted like straw. Tonight he was in denim: denim jeans, pale blue denim shirt, denim jacket with a shearling collar. He also had on the hand-tooled cowboy boots he had started wearing last month.

"Just a lot of craziness at the magazine. A lot of shake-ups."

"Do you still have your job?" What if he had been fired and expected her to *support* him?

"I *think* so. If I still want to work in such a madhouse. I may see what else is out there." He slumped into the sofa; she perched on the opposite arm.

"What's out there, Erik, is a cold, cruel world."

He looked sulky. "You do okay."

"I don't have your tastes. When was the last time you saw me buy anything? I have a twenty-dollar Casio, not something like that." She pointed to his wrist.

"This? It's from a client."

Ah. "But aren't they expensive?"

He brushed at his light hair with the heel of his hand. "They were showing it in a photo. They couldn't sell it after that."

"Who would know?"

He looked over at her with irritation. "They do have *some* scruples in advertising. Even though I know you don't believe it."

"I just can't believe you got something worth thousands because it sat on someone's wrist for five minutes."

"Try five hours!"

"Still. Is that how you got those boots?"

"No. I *bought* these." He turned and pushed his glasses farther up on his nose. "Is there a problem?"

"I don't know. You tell me."

"What's for dinner?"

"Dinner? Reservations."

He sighed and leaned back, closing his eyes. "Figures."

"Oh, really?" She pushed her hands together against her lap to keep them from shaking. "Tell me how it figures."

"It figures because you're too self-absorbed to ever think of doing something for somebody else. To cook a good meal for me when I'm tired and had a miserable week. If I want to eat anything around here I have to make it."

"Whoa, cowboy." She held up a palm. "Let's talk about you for a minute. Like your getting a nonpublished phone in an apartment that's half mine, and never bothering to give me the number!"

He opened his eyes defensively. "That was Jim's idea. He *is* paying your share now. But," he rallied, "you knew you could reach me at the magazine."

"Right. Why doesn't that make me feel better?"

"I don't know."

"When were you planning to give me the number?"

"Whenever I remembered. You make such a big deal out of everything." His voice was a whine. "You were a lot more fun before you started worrying about everything so much. Like making the streets safe for women. Or me."

"Making the streets safe for you?"

"No! Cross-examining me!"

"Holding your twenty-inch ass accountable? Is that what you mean?"

He twisted his mouth at her vulgarity.

"Because if it is, you're in luck. I've had a hard week too, Erik. And I've just been sitting here wondering what I need you for, on top of everything else."

He looked startled. "What are you saying? Are *you* telling *me* to go?" He sounded affronted that she had beaten him to it.

She smiled. "Don't trip on the stairs."

Sunday afternoon Joe insisted that Caroline come with him to a swim meet at Saint David's. His boys weren't participating; these were elementary school swimmers from local clubs he wanted to keep an eye on. Saint David's had an excellent reputation for the freestyle and the backstroke, thanks to Joe, and he was always on the lookout for scholarship recipients.

Caroline was glad for the invitation. In winter she enjoyed entering the pool room and being dazzled by the wet white tiles and hot, chlorine-filled air. Any competitive sports interested her. When she and Joe had first talked about having children, both had pictured raising little athletes.

As soon as they got in the car, headed toward the Carpenter Bridge, Caroline realized Joe had brought her along to talk. But he didn't start where she expected. "I'm thinking about leaving Saint David's."

"What? Why?"

His eyes didn't move from the road. A profile that could go on an ancient coin. "I won't get a pension till fifty-five, but we could sell the house and move to Florida. I'm sure I can hook up with someplace down there to do coaching, and if you wanted to you could always teach. And we'd have a lot more time to sail."

"But I don't . . . I understand what you're saying, but I don't understand . . . I mean, why now?" Was he trying to protect her?

"Why not?" Unlike Diana, he could talk and drive well. "I figure it's time to cut our losses. We *know* what makes us happy. Your parents are already in the South; we don't have anything to keep us here."

You didn't answer my question. "You think that running away will make things better?"

"Yes. I do."

"But what about *Zach?*"

"What about him?"

She shifted in her seat so she could see him better. "Do you think he's alive . . . or dead, or what?"

"Caroline, I don't know what to think!" He smacked the side of the steering wheel with his palm. "First he dies and the police are suddenly accusing us of murder. You get into this wishful thinking thing that he's really alive somewhere."

"But—"

"Wait!" He braked for a red light. "Then suddenly we're not under suspicion anymore because the police have dug up a coffin and it's full of *rice*. But they aren't running out and arresting anyone else. If they can't figure out what happened, who can?" A car behind him honked to signal that the light had changed. Joe raised his hand to show that he'd heard, and put the car in gear.

"But you seem to resent my even looking for him." Her throat felt achy.

"I don't resent it, I just don't know what to think!"

"Other people believe he could be alive," she said stubbornly. "The police, Diana Larsen, Sol Maria Cruz, they all think that." It was a short, but important, list. "Suppose, just suppose, that I walked in the door with Zach next week. What would you think?"

He took his eyes off the road for a moment and smiled at her. "If you walked in with him, and guaranteed that he'd grow up without any more mishaps, I'd be thrilled."

"Would you still want to move to Florida?"

"I might."

"Me too."

EIGHTEEN

Soon after Diana came in Tuesday, Howard stopped by her desk. "Are you getting everything you need?"

"Does anyone? More or less."

He hesitated. "How much longer do you think you'll be here?"

"Not that much longer." She checked to make sure Marci was not around. "We should do lunch."

"Maybe Friday. I have to sign some papers today." What had happened to Wednesday and Thursday? He was still putting her off.

Howard pounded one fist rhythmically over the other. "How's the long-distance romance?"

She smiled. "Funny you should ask. I gave him his discharge papers this weekend."

"You're really free and clear?" His dark eyes watched her, speculative and amused.

"That's me. How about you?"

"Almost."

"Really?"

He smiled. Her eyes trailed him all the way into his office.

Wednesday afternoon Dolly took a phone call, then moved to Diana's desk looking sober. "That was Fleur Senak." She lowered her voice to half-mast. "Nicole died."

"She *died?* How?" *It was Starry Night. She smothered her, I know she did!*

"They think she must have choked on her spit-up. The passage was clogged. . . ."

"My God! I never thought that would happen. The obvious things—the things you always worry about—they usually never happen. Shit! She had a real personality."

Dolly nodded. "I know. I was getting quite fond of her myself." She glanced around to see who else might be listening, then lowered her voice further. "Fleur said something very strange."

Diana put down her pen. "What?"

"That when they found Nicole she was cold and almost blue. That doesn't sound like they were keeping a very close watch on her." Dolly sighed. "And I thought Fleur was such a stable personality."

"Did they call the police?"

"The *police?* I don't think so. I'm sure it was natural causes." She glanced toward Howard's office. "I'd better tell him before he accuses me of withholding information. But I wanted you to know."

"Thanks."

She waited until Dolly had moved away, then picked up the phone. As soon as she heard Caroline's voice, she said, "It happened to someone else!"

"Diana?"

"A baby that the Adoption Unit placed with a family, the woman just called to say the baby died. And she's saying she was very cold. And blue."

"No." For a long time Caroline didn't say anything else. "Tell me exactly what happened."

Diana recounted Dolly's comments. "I'm going to call Fleur myself. After all, I was the one who brought the baby to the house." It gave her a claim to investigate further.

"Wait till I tell Rafe Millar. Now he'll have to do something! Can you believe he hasn't been out here *once?* He sent someone to take plaster impressions, that's all. What's the family's name?"

"Fleur and Michael Senak. Fleur like flower. The baby was Nicole, they live in Comsewogue. But I'm going to try and see Fleur, actually talk to her. Anyway, you guys should meet." *If Nicole was taken by someone unaware of her condition, I don't give her that long.*

"Diana? Let me know what she says. And *thanks.*"

But when Diana called Fleur, she got a machine. "Hi." It was the piping, self-important voice of Starry. "We can't talk to you because we're either not home or in the city. You can leave your phone number if you want."

Diana waited for the beep, then said, "Fleur? This is Diana Larsen. I was really shocked to hear about Nicole." She hesitated, then plunged on. "Please call me, about the arrangements and all. You can call me anytime." She gave her the office phone and her home number as well.

But when she hung up she was not content to leave it that way. Instead she dialed Directory Assistance for Manhattan. There was no listing under Senak. Maybe when they went into the city they stayed with someone else.

"Hello? Is Rafe Millar there?"

"Speaking."

"This is Caroline Denecke. I have something new to tell you."

"Shoot."

I'd love to. "I just found out, it happened to someone else! What happened to me."

"What happened to you?"

How could he ask that, as if he didn't even remember? "I mean, what happened to Zach. It happened to a baby in Comsewogue! You don't know about it?"

"Nobody told me." He sounded more interested. "I'll check it out."

"The family's name is Senak. S-e-n-a-k." She had already forgotten their first names.

"Okay."

"What about Zach?"

"We're working on it."

"Doing what exactly?"

He hung up.

Friday morning Shane Norman went into labor. This time, when Eileen called, Diana went immediately to the hospital. Nothing was going to happen to Shane and her child. This baby was going to be monitored every step of the way, from the descent down the birth canal to placement with an adoptive couple. Diana imagined the baby bobbing gently down a long bobsled slide with herself waiting, arms outstretched, at the bottom. Who else did Shane have to look after her?

Eileen was waiting on a gray vinyl sectional in the lobby. Her feet were up on the smoked glass coffee table, the worn-down heels of brown loafers crushing *Parents* and *Modern Maturity*. Diana was sure she was a familiar sight to hospital personnel. How many times in how many years had she sat in the same spot, waiting for news of a teenage birth?

Yet when Diana sat down, the housemother still managed to look excited. "Poor Shane thinks she's having her appendix out!"

"Really? I thought that she'd come around to admitting it."

"It comes and goes." She pushed a white box of miniature donuts across the vinyl. "Fresh out of the freezer."

Diana shook her head, then changed her mind and took one. "What did you hear from Roxanne?"

Eileen looked droll. "I got a postcard from her from the Catskills. I guess they ran out of money before they could get to Niagara Falls."

"That's interesting. I always thought it was all in her head about her boyfriend."

"Who knows? His building don't have all the condos rented, that's for sure. I just hope they're remembering to feed that baby once in a while."

"Aren't you concerned?"

Eileen looked at her. "Why? She fed herself, didn't she?"

Diana wiped powdered sugar from her mouth. Eileen was very credible. If Diana hadn't seen Roxanne in Bayhead, she might have believed what she was hearing without question. "What did you hear from Susan?"

But Eileen gave her a roguish smile. "Forget about Susan. I'm getting two new girls next week. You should come and visit *them.*"

"I can't stay here that much longer. That's why I'd like to talk to someone else who's already given birth."

"Well, if all goes well, she's right upstairs."

Diana nodded. *How much more can I pump her?* "I had a funny call from Crystal's mother, about the baby."

"And wasn't *that* a terrible thing!" She actually crossed herself. "I told that detective, she wasn't herself after the baby was born dead. But I had no idea she'd run off and—hurt herself."

"Eileen: You knew Crystal. Do you honestly believe she'd lie down on the tracks and allow herself to be mutilated?"

The housemother looked steadily back at her, faded blue eyes wise. "Ah, but that's what teenagers *are.* If they're miserable, they'll do something dramatic. They think that being dead is just for a little while."

"I don't believe that, not about Crystal. What about all her plans to model?"

"Just whistling in the dark, Diana, whistling in the dark. Want a cup of coffee?" She reached for her purse and pushed off the couch. "We adults have our drugs, too."

Just before noon they were summoned to the information booth.

214

Shane had given birth to a baby girl who weighed six pounds eleven ounces and had an Apgar score of nine out of ten. Perhaps the baby, despite her incestuous background, would be close to normal. There had been no complications, and Shane was on her way down from the delivery room. Diana watched Eileen hang up the phone.

They stopped first at the glassed-in nursery, finally locating the baby in a crib marked "Norman." She seemed too small to be real, curled in on herself like a kitten whose eyes were not yet open. "She's a little cabbage," the housemother whispered reverently. "And you know what I'm going to do?"

Make coleslaw. "What?"

"Find out if *I* can take her. Just until they put her with adoptive parents, I mean."

"But wouldn't that be hard on Shane?"

"Oh, she won't be there. She'll be going to a regular foster home."

So this was Operation Shane, the plan to get this baby. Once she was at Heart's Retreat, Shane's mother would, no doubt, make a cameo appearance and leave with her grandchild. She could imagine Eileen telling her earnestly about it the next day, pointing out that Shane must have been in touch with her mother all along!

What was a white baby worth, anyway? Twenty thousand? Thirty thousand? And after they had taken the baby, what if Shane asked questions? She didn't want to think about that.

"I thought it was against the rules to bring a baby to the maternity home."

Eileen gave her a conspiratorial wink. "So I'll bend them a little. It's not like Shane and the baby are coming there *together.*"

She had to try to warn Howard. Or someone else. But who in the unit would see anything wrong with Eileen's plan? Maybe the question was, who could she trust? Probably only Marci. Ditzy as she seemed, she was at least honest. And she was the only one beside Howard who had no prior connection with Heart's Retreat.

Meantime she herself could alert Jocelyn, to make sure that the hospital didn't release Shane and the baby to anyone except an agency caseworker.

Shane was in Martha's Vineyard, the room named after the ferry that ran between Port Jefferson and Bridgeport. The other bed was occupied by a woman who appeared to be in her thirties; she was absorbed in a talk show about interracial lesbian couples.

Shane's face was pinched white, her eyes closed. Seen without her burden, she looked tiny. Diana went over and brushed back her bangs; her forehead was clammy with cooled sweat. "Shane? Shane?" There was no response.

Panicked, she turned to Eileen. "Something's wrong with Shane!"

The housemother's face was implacable.

"Shane." Diana grasped a bony shoulder and shook it.

The huge brown eyes flew open. Shane stared at Diana as if she didn't know her.

"Shane, what's wrong?"

Her eyes rolled white, then slid shut immediately, as if an invisible hand had reached over and closed them.

"Nothing's wrong," Eileen said impatiently, crowding in against her. "She's tired, that's all; she just gave birth. Leave her be."

But Diana was at the doorway, signaling to a small Pakistani nurse. "This girl's unconscious. Get a doctor!"

The nurse took a brief look in, then ran.

Diana went back to Shane. A moment later she heard Sidney Hazelton being paged over the intercom. "Dr. Hazelton to Martha's Vineyard. Dr. Hazelton to Martha's Vineyard!"

If she dies, I'll kill him.

But it was another doctor, a heavy-set Hispanic woman in a white jacket, who pushed into the room. She saw Eileen and paused momentarily, then moved to Shane's bed.

Diana, Eileen, the little nurse, and the other new mother craned to see.

216

The doctor raised one of Shane's eyelids and studied her pupil. "Too heavy a dose of anesthesia for her size. Some fool in the delivery room . . ."

"Can't you *do* anything?" Diana asked.

"Oh, she'll be okay. It'll wear off."

"You can't give her something?"

The woman smiled; one upper tooth in her dark face was chipped. "I don't know *what.*" But she bent over Shane with her stethoscope and listened to her heartbeat in several places, then felt her pulse. When she pried open her mouth to check her throat, Shane jerked away. "Okay, Sleeping Beauty, you'll wake up pretty soon." She straightened up.

"I'll stay with her," Diana said firmly. Taking Shane's hand in hers again, Diana sat down in a navy blue sling chair and watched. Shane's skin was bluish white against the sheets, but she was breathing normally. Once she gave a whimper and shook her head strongly, as if to protest what had happened to her. At thirteen she had been sent on a journey not of her own choosing; of course there would be side effects. "Who was that who came in?" Diana asked.

"The doctor? Sol Maria Cruz," Eileen said.

The one who had delivered Zachary and had given Caroline the right information about the autopsy.

Eileen moved impatiently beside her. "We're only allowed fifteen minutes," she warned. "It's already been longer."

"I said I was going to stay. You can go."

"After a few thousand births, you learn not to worry. When she wakes up, tell her I was here."

"Okay."

By three Shane was able to be aroused easily.

"How are you?" Diana asked.

"My tummy hurts."

"That's from the baby."

"What baby?"

Diana pressed a gray stuffed mouse with red-and-white polka-

217

dotted ears from the gift shop into Shane's arms. "I'll see you to-morrow. Don't go anywhere."

Belatedly she realized that she had missed lunch with Howard. But with Marci in the office it probably would have turned into a threesome.

Saturday morning she arrived back at the hospital to find Shane alert and watching cartoons. Moving past her remains of breakfast—a paste of puffed wheat and milk, toast crusts, and a juice carton—she gave Shane a hug. "What's up?"

"Ow! My stomach!"

"It still hurts?"

"Yeah." Shane rolled her large brown eyes theatrically. "You wanna know something gross? They shave you down there, and when it starts to grow back it feels all prickly."

"I know. Have you seen the baby?"

But Shane didn't say *What baby?* "The one that looks like Miss Piggy?"

"No, she doesn't; she's cute," Diana protested. "Did you think of a name?"

"Yup. That's what I'm going to call her. Miss Piggy." Shane started to laugh and then suddenly she was sobbing bitterly, her face pressed against her stalklike arms. "I never wanted a baby," she wept. "And now I'll never see her again!"

Diana moved over to stroke Shane's hair, tears blurring her own eyes. If Shane thought there was any way of taking care of the baby, she would do everything she could to help find a home for the two of them. They could grow up together. "Do you think you want to keep her?"

"How can I? I'm just a kid!"

"I know. But you'll get older."

"I can't take care of a baby. Can't they give her to people where I could see her sometimes?"

"Maybe." There was such a thing as open adoption, she knew. "But you don't have to decide anything today. I spoke to this woman from Social Services yesterday, Marci Potamkin. She's really nice, and she's going to put her in a foster home this afternoon. That will give you a chance to decide." Because Shane was so young and there were no parents available to sign for her, the baby could be placed as destitute. Marci, of course, had been delighted. She was placing the baby in a foster home which was, she had whispered over the phone, childless and anxious to adopt.

"What about me?"

"She's finding a good place for you, too."

Shane pressed herself up on one thin elbow. "I'm not going back to Heart's Retreat?"

"Do you want to?"

"No! Big Mama smells in the morning. And she *lies.*"

"Really? What kind of lies?"

Shane considered. "I'm really not going back there?"

"That's what they said."

"Well . . . Big Mama said like, you were dumb, and not to tell you anything. That the social workers were going to put Crystal in a school for bad girls, and that's why we had to help her get away."

"How did you help her get away?"

Shane grinned. "You know that day when you came and she said Crystal ran away? She was really upstairs hiding. In her room."

"But I saw her room!"

"No, you didn't You saw the *junk* room. Big Mama heard your car and told Crystal she should hide."

"Then what?"

"She mostly stayed in her room."

"But you saw her."

"Sort of." She shifted uneasily. "But where am I going?"

"A foster home, I think."

"You mean with strange people?" Her brown eyes grew glassy with tears.

Damn! "You'll know them soon enough." It sounded like a line from *Anne of Green Gables.*

"Shit! Maybe I'll just hit the road." She went back to the TV.

"Shane, listen. If you go there and do what you should, maybe at Easter vacation we'll go down to Disney World—just you and me."

Shane looked back up, startled. "What?"

"I've never been there either. I'd like to see it." That wasn't exactly true; she could die happy without having seen Pirate Island and It's a Small World. But Shane's reactions would be worth the price.

"Really?"

"Really."

She pursed her mouth wisely. "I bet you're just saying that so I'll be good at the foster home and go to school. I *hate* school."

"You don't want to go to Florida?"

"I do!"

"Well, it's a deal." This next part would be harder. She stood up. "Why don't you say good-bye to the baby before Ms. Potamkin comes; wish her luck and all."

Shane shook her head, pensive. "I'd be too sad."

"That's okay. Sad's okay."

"Well . . ." Shane gave a huge sigh and moved slowly out of bed. Her stomach pouched slackly under the light blue hospital gown. Together she and Diana walked to the nursery, Shane leaning against Diana.

She stood by the glass for a long moment, then moved her hand in a small wave. "Good-bye, Miss Piggy," she whispered. For a moment she pressed her forehead against the glass. She turned quickly to Diana. "But we're *really* going to Disney World?"

"Really."

"Marineland too?"

"You drive a hard bargain. But—maybe. If you wash your hair."

"Deal."

NINETEEN

The summons from Diana came Sunday morning. Caroline and Joe were lying in bed, awash in newspapers. A metal TV tray between them held bagels, scallion cream cheese, lox, orange juice, and coffee.

Joe, closer to the phone, reached for it. He made his hello into three syllables, like chimes. After a moment he said, "Sure," and handed the receiver to her.

"Hello?"

"Hi. It's Diana."

"Hi."

"Listen, are you free today? I feel like . . . doing something."

She was about to say that Sunday was a bad day, that she and Joe had plans, when she realized belatedly what Diana was talking about. "I guess."

"It feels like it's time."

"On a Sunday?"

"Why not? You want to come over here?"

"I think so." She could not imagine calling Dr. Hazelton with

221

Joe in the same house. Maybe that meant it was beyond the pale.

"You know where Mario's Vacation Apartments are?"

"No."

"No?"

"No. They aren't exactly a landmark."

Diana gave her directions.

"I'll see you around one," Caroline concluded.

Joe smiled at her fondly. "You'll see who around when?"

"Oh, just Diana Larsen. You know, the writer. The one who went to the cemetery with me."

He poured more juice. "I thought maybe we'd go out later and look for a better refrigerator for the boat."

"You did not. You're just going to be watching swim videos," she teased. "I saw the stack you brought home."

He grinned, then reached over and played with her fingers. "But I like you in the house when I do. In case I get any . . . ideas."

"You'll just have to contain yourself till tonight, won't you?"

"Are Beth and Jackson still coming to dinner?"

"Oh, God." She had totally forgotten. "But I'll have everything ready to put in the oven. Did you start the puzzle?" Shifting to spread lox on her bagel, she felt a whisper of liquid slide out of her. *It's nothing, only discharge.* She had been checking for days, had been scrutinizing toilet paper for traces of pink. But there had been nothing; she was *sure* she was pregnant.

Mario's Vacation Apartments were not hard to find. Caroline could not imagine how she had missed seeing something so colorful. Who would have thought to transplant orange tile roofs and potted palm trees to Crane Island? And why?

Diana lived at the top of a narrow set of stairs. She pulled back the door and motioned Caroline in.

The room looked pleasant enough, it had a blue and white and emerald green color scheme, but it still seemed like living in a motel. It made her think of traveling salesmen's putting up family photos on transient dressers. Except there were no family pictures here, very little evidence of Diana herself.

Caroline sat down in a molded white chair beside the table. "We're really going to do this?" She felt edgy.

"Why not? If we can show he's guilty . . ." But she slumped down in the chair opposite Caroline's, pushing her dark hair back. "God! This whole situation is so elusive. It makes you think that people get away with a lot of stuff in life. Did you ever see that Woody Allen movie about the eye doctor? And in this case the police aren't doing *shit.*"

"I know."

"So we'll call and see what he says."

"You know he won't be in his office on Sunday."

"I know. We'll call him at home. I already found his number in the book. When he hears who it is, he should be glad enough."

Diana stood up and fastened a suction cup device to the phone receiver, plugging the other end into her recorder. They rehearsed what Caroline was going to say, then she dialed his home phone. Her stomach rumbled nervously.

"Hello?" It sounded like a young girl. She hadn't thought about him having *children.*

"Hello. Is Dr. Hazelton there?"

"Sure."

After a minute he came on. "Sidney Hazelton here."

It was too easy. "Uh . . . hi. I'm sorry to call you at home."

"Who is this? Did you try my service?"

"N-no. This is the girl who called you a few days ago. About having the baby?"

"Oh, yes. Yes, of course." His voice warmed several degrees. "Has the baby been born?"

"Yes."

"And you're in the hospital?"

"No. At home." Had she told him it was herself or a friend? It felt harder to do this time.

"Where's the baby?"

"Here." She could feel Diana frowning at her one-word answers.

"Tell me a little about the baby." His voice was soft and encouraging.

"Well . . . she's a girl. She's real cute. And healthy." *So why aren't you keeping her yourself?* "But she cries a lot."

He laughed gently. "That's a baby for you. Why did you think of calling me?"

"Someone told me you found homes for lots of babies." She tried to make her voice chirpy.

"Well, sometimes. I guess any OB does. We have couples coming to us constantly, desperate for a child, and we try to hook them up. But you're sure you want to do this?"

"Yes." It sounded weak. "Yes!"

"Let's see; it probably would be best for you to come to my office. Not today, of course, even doctors need time out! But tomorrow evening, about six?" He didn't give her a chance to respond. "Unless I'm making an unexpected delivery." The warm laugh. "If I am, I'll need a number to call *you*. What's your number?"

Panicked, Caroline looked at the wall phone and read the numbers out loud.

"And your name? Your first name?"

"Um . . . Wendy."

"Okay then, Wendy. We'll see—"

"What about the money?"

"Well, as I said, that will have to come from the couple."

"But if I'm bringing the baby, I want the money then!" She drew her insistence from her memory of Susan. "Ten thousand dollars. I know what people pay for babies." *I can't stand this. I can't stand even saying it.*

"Okay—Wendy." There was a different note in his voice, one she couldn't define. "We'll have the money for you. Just come."

She hung up then. She had been planning to apologize to Diana for giving her number, but Diana pounced on her first.

"Why did you give him *my* phone?"

"He said he had to have a number!" She knew she sounded defensive. Part of her still felt like a teenager.

"But he can trace it right to me! Eileen has my home phone!"

"But why should *I* be the one taking all the risks? You just sit there and—and orchestrate things."

Diana's gray eyes were flat. "Because we're trying to get *your* baby back."

Caroline looked down at the red-tiled floor. Diana was immediately conciliatory. "I should have expected he'd want a number. Just tell me what he said."

She did. "Tomorrow night at six. In his office," she ended. "Isn't that enough to contact the police?" She knew she was begging. "He went along with all that money." And yet . . . he hadn't sounded *happy* about it.

But Diana was nodding. "I think we should tell your policeman."

"Okay. Good! But I also think we should talk to the housemother. If we pretend we know all about it, she might tell us something, to save herself."

"You've seen too many old movies."

"Then *I'll* do it!" She put her hand on her purse, ready to stand up. What was wrong with her today?

"Wait, wait. Just wait. I'll go with you. I'm just trying to think. Eileen's probably really pissed because she isn't getting Shane's baby. But she shouldn't blame *me*. Okay. Your car or mine?"

Caroline pretended to check her watch. She was edgy but not suicidal. "We'd better both drive. I may have to leave from there."

"Follow me, then."

The driveway of the maternity home was now edged with forsythia, immoderate clouds of yellow as if the house had been abandoned. As she parked, Diana noticed that one of the upstairs shutters had come loose at the top; the chilly sun cast a skewed image of its sail-

225

boat shape cutout. She was glad to see Eileen's old Chevy station wagon parked to one side.

"It's huge," Caroline whispered, coming up beside her. "How many girls *live* here?"

"Two as of next week. But Eileen's home."

Caroline nodded. She looked tense to Diana.

"She's probably in the kitchen watching TV." Diana climbed the steps to the gray painted porch feeling Caroline close behind her. "I thought today would be warmer," she commented, ringing the bell. "Maybe it's because we're so near the water."

"I was offered a teaching job here in Comsewogue when I first came, but I didn't take it."

"Where *do* you teach?"

"Bayhead."

The door was already opening slowly. It was not thrown back in its usual welcome, but trapped after several inches by a chain. Eileen looked out at them.

Diana thought afterward that the blue eye had opened with surprise before Eileen slammed the door, but it happened too quickly to be sure. At the time she was expecting Eileen to slide off the chain and open the door all the way. Instead there was the metal scrape of an additional bolt.

They waited for another minute, but there was only silence. Diana banged again on the door. "Eileen, it's me!" Finally she said, "I guess she doesn't want to see us."

"Damn!" It sounded like the strongest word in Caroline's vocabulary. "Do you think she recognized me from when she came to my house?"

"I don't know. Let's walk around to the back. Maybe she'll change her mind."

Diana had never been behind the house. The back was even more weathered than the front. Several fire escapes had rusted and bled and one was hanging against the white shingles. The ground was a soft beige sand with stalks of beach grass. Although a sturdy brown wooden dock reached into the water, no boats were moored to it. "That's how they used to bring the girls in. It was all very secret."

"They even had stables." Caroline pointed to a long wooden shed with stalls, open to the air.

"No, I think that's just a garage. I can't exactly see them letting the girls ride! That cement building there is for cold storage." It stood directly behind the house. "They keep all their frozen food in there."

"What should we do?" Caroline asked.

"What—" She was pulled back into the present from a reverie of life here sixty years ago. "Go and talk to Rafe Millar, I guess. Tell him about tomorrow night. He could check and see if the Hazeltons have a Volvo."

"That sounds good!" said Caroline enthusiastically. But she was frowning at her watch. "Oh, Lord, I don't have time. I have company coming early and I promised I'd be back. Joe . . ."

"That's okay. I'll keep you posted."

"I don't usually go for tits that size—no, really, I'm an ass man—but she had bazoobis like volleyballs and . . ." The slender cop with the massive perm and rose-tinted aviator glasses paused when he noticed Diana staring at him. "Officer Jon 'Disco' DeWall here. Can I help you?"

Yeah. Get a life. "I'm looking for Rafe Millar."

The idiot turned to another cop, a small older man with the face of a weary accountant. "Rafe around?"

"He's off today. Be back tomorrow noon."

DeWall turned to Diana. "Sorry, hon, he's not here."

Is it the way I look, or are you just a pig? She looked beyond him to the other officer. "Can I talk to you?"

"What's up, hon?" DeWall was saying to her as she pushed past him and sat down in the chair beside the older man's metal desk.

"I have to reach Rafe Millar!"

"He'll be back—"

227

"No, no, today! It's about a kidnapped baby."

But the man was nodding. *That* case. The exhumation."

Of course. She should have known in a small department they would talk about that. "I have some new information."

"You can tell me."

But she shook her head. "It wouldn't make sense to you." She curled her fingers around the metal chair seat as he consulted a Rolodex, then dialed. "What's your name?"

She told him, but it was evident from his long silence that the phone was ringing without being picked up.

"Could you keep trying?" Now she felt anxious. "I'll give you the number where he can call me back." She hesitated. "There's one more thing. He was going to run a computer check on all Volvos on the island. But if he's not here . . ."

The man pursed heavy lips. "We're not real busy; I could do that. I'll leave the printout on his desk."

"Great! Thanks." If she called Millar right at noon tomorrow she could explain it. But hopefully he would call her at home before then.

As she was climbing the steps to her apartment she heard the phone ringing. Millar! Well, he would leave a message.

But when she unlocked the door the answering machine stared back at her with a solid red eye. Whoever it was hadn't wanted her to call back.

She poured herself a jelly glass of vodka from the bottle of Absolut Erik had left behind. Then pulling her jacket off, she sat down on the couch. Crystal was dead. Erik was gone, and her story was going nowhere. With her dwindling bank account she had promised to take a thirteen-year-old to Florida. She sat with her knees to her chin, arms wrapped around them without moving, for a long time. Finally she drained the glass. Sidney Hazelton, like the movie optometrist, was going to somehow slither out of it.

It was the phone's ringing that finally stirred her. Jumping up and moving into the kitchenette, she caught it on the second ring. "Hello?"

The line was open, but there was no response.

"Hello?" she asked again.

A crackling, then a deep male voice demanding, "Is George there?"

"George? No. You must have the . . ."

But the connection was already broken.

Damn, she knew that voice! Why had she said anything? Someone wanted to hear her voice, to identify it. Caroline had given Sidney the number; he was trying to find out whose it was. Yet she couldn't swear it was Sidney's voice even disguised.

It was time to stop drinking; the vodka wasn't making her feel better, it was only blunting her sense of danger. *They know who you are. Try to realize that.*

She had not felt warm since that moment at Heart's Retreat. Filling the tea kettle, she switched on the flame beneath. When it was steaming, she poured water over a Country Apple tea bag.

The scent of cinnamon made her think of Karin Larsen. "Diana, you never stop and *think.* You never stop to consider the consequences until it's too late."

"Yes, Deedee," Eimer added dolorously. "It's hard times ahead."

She turned to them. "What should I *do?*"

"Come home," he advised. "Go where that doctor can't find you. Those people called just now to see if you were home. They're coming over to get you."

Would he really have said that?

"And leave that other child alone!" her mother added. *"You* can't do anything for her."

That was definitely Karin. Diana left the tea on the dinette table and went quickly to the bedroom. Stripping off her clothes, she pulled on a set of long underwear. Over it went jeans, a red turtleneck, a patterned Norwegian sweater, and boots. Then, in case she had to sleep in the car, she stripped the comforter off her bed and

bunched it under her arm. Finally she located the Crane Island telephone directory under a pile of newspapers in the living room and
brought it with her.

What are you doing? I don't know. Just getting out of here. She could
always go to Caroline's and crash her dinner party. But Caroline
would hardly be happy to see her. Eileen knew where Caroline
lived, anyway. *I should get off the island entirely.* "Things always seem
worse at night, in the dark," she said, to keep herself calm. It didn't
work.

Caroline arrived home just in time to set the table and begin cook-
ing. But she felt shaky. Instead of getting a sitter, as Caroline had
expected she would, Beth had brought along two-year-old Rory,
who alternately squealed in frustration and interrupted their conversation. *I would never have brought a toddler to the house of someone
who had just lost a baby.* Then, removing a casserole of scalloped potatoes from the oven, she tipped them all over the kitchen floor. Beth
heard the crash and came running in from the den to discover Caroline scraping potatoes up off the tile and back into the dish. So serving them was out of the question, though she had considered doing
so.

Instead, she made Kraft macaroni and cheese, and they joked
about serving that with fine wine. There was plenty of gossip to hear
about school; but, spooning out lemon mousse, Caroline thought,
she doesn't really know me at all. It was hard to really listen to the conversation anyway. She kept thinking about Zach, thinking about
Diana.

She was still thinking about them when her company left. With
Beth and Jackson gone she had to face what she had been postponing
since the afternoon. There was no new baby coming. She went upstairs into the bathroom and slowly lowered her white underpants;
there, against the nylon, were rust-colored streaks, the evidence that
her period had begun. *It's not fair! Not after a delay of three weeks! Not
when I'm further from finding Zachary than ever.*

230

Sitting with her forehead against the edge of the sink, she might have expected to cry. But the tears that had flowed endlessly in the first few days were now frozen. Unable to move, she listened as Joe went into the bedroom and moved around.

"Caro?" He tapped on the door lightly.

"Yes. I'll be out."

"That's okay. I'll go down the hall."

After a minute she heard a shudder of pipes; he was using the bathroom near the nursery. *Zach's bathroom.*

Still she could not move. It was not until she heard him return to the bedroom that she reached under the sink and pulled out the package of tampons. Mechanically she unwrapped one; then she moved to the hook on the bathroom door where her nightgown and robe were hanging and got undressed.

Joe was already in bed, the lamp on his side of the queen-sized bed extinguished. "Good night," he murmured sleepily.

She could not say anything until her light was out and she was in bed as well. Then she pressed herself against his back. "I got my period," she whispered.

She felt him nod. "I thought you would."

"But I could so easily have been pregnant! I'm not that old, I'm fertile, the tests never found anything. And you've had kids."

"That was twenty-five years ago."

Tell him. Tell him. What if Diana ever asked if Joe knew and she had to say no? "It could be something else. When I was in college I had this—operation."

He shifted toward her. "You mean like a D and C?"

"Sort of." But she had to go on. "It was—I was, I was going to have a baby. And I just *couldn't.* Not then."

"You got pregnant?" His astonishment rang through the bedroom. "But you're so, I don't know, innocent. I mean, wholesome. I just can't imagine *you,* of all people, in that situation. You seem so interested in other things that your interest wouldn't even be in sex. Not then, anyway."

231

"It just—happened." *I wish I could say that it only happened once; that I was drunk. That I was raped.*

He shifted so that he was lying on his back, staring at the ceiling. "This was the guy you were involved with for a couple of years?"

"Uh-huh."

"But he didn't want to get married?"

"No. He didn't." That was the sad truth. "So I felt I had to do something, and I've been sorry ever since."

He reached out and put his hand on her stomach, gently tufting her nightgown. "You couldn't have a baby under those circumstances," he agreed.

"But . . ." *I thought you would hate me for having an abortion!* "You don't hate me?"

He sighed. "I'm disappointed, I guess. It changes my picture of you a little. But of course I don't hate you! You're my wife."

"But sometimes I worry that something was damaged inside. So I couldn't have children."

"Caro, you're the one who wants a baby so badly. Don't forget, it could be my age, too."

"It couldn't be that. You're so virile."

He laughed. "Flatter me."

"I know I should have told you. Before. But I thought, you being Catholic . . ."

"Well, I don't like the idea. But how do you think I had only two kids with Lorraine? Given her depression, even before Lisa, we *had* to use birth control. She wasn't happy about the idea, but there was no choice."

Caroline rolled over against him and he began stroking her hair. She closed her eyes. *If we can survive Zachary and the police together and survive his knowing this, I guess we'll be okay.*

TWENTY

The world was a dark and dangerous place. Diana kept checking her rearview mirror for the lights of someone following her, but the only illumination along the Martinville-Comsewogue Road was her own. A distant train whistle suddenly broke into her thoughts, evoking all the lonely moments of her life. *If I died right now, who would care?* Quickly pushing a Billy Joel tape into the deck, she turned up the volume: "She's a Modern Woman" bounced against the sealed windows and swirled around her, giving her courage. That's me, a modern woman. So modern that she was rushing through a prehistoric blackness, carrying her own music and lights.

Was it crazy to be driving along a deserted road? Maybe only less crazy than staying in the apartment. She would check the Hazelton house for the Volvo, then lose herself on Long Island. They would not be able to find her there. Passing under a traffic light that had been turned into a yellow blinker, she drove by a deserted gas station with the unearthly green glow of an experimental photograph. At the Carpenter Bridge Highway she followed a yellow sanitation truck to Logan Point.

Logan Point, on the water, was the most exclusive community on the island. A white-steepled Presbyterian church stood in the village square, surrounded by shops with names like *Say It with Flowers* and *Banbury Cross Books,* but there were also tiny weathered clam bars, and magnificent views of the sound. Typical that Dolly and Sidney could afford to live here—on the profits of gray-market babies.

The Hazeltons' address had been listed in the phone directory at 18 Jeremiah's Path. On her map the road ran parallel to the sound, the backyards sloping down to the water. Diana drove along Jeremiah's Path slowly, looking carefully at each beautiful home. Number 18 was a large white Victorian of eaves and gables with an extraordinary sunburst decoration on the front. The evergreens around it were perfectly groomed; the dark, glossy double front doors had identical spring wreaths.

Amazing what tainted money will buy. Dolly had been in the office the day Diana had said she was on her way to Heart's Retreat. She could have picked up the phone and called Eileen to tell her to hide Crystal. And Dolly herself had visited the Senaks and knew which room Nicole would be sleeping in. She couldn't quite picture Dolly or Sidney creeping through the window. No doubt they had accomplices. If she could find a silver Volvo here it would nail their connection to Susan.

She turned around at the corner and came back, then parked on the side of the road just beyond the house. The family cars were evidently parked in back. She switched the dome light to "off" and climbed out of the Sentra, leaving her door open partway for fear of making noise. The darkness seemed threatened by light at its edges, the horizon a sheet of black paper ready to burst into flames. But it was hours until dawn.

From the edge of the driveway neither car she could see had the squareness of a Volvo. But there might be a third car parked beyond her angle of vision. Stepping carefully onto the lawn, she moved toward the backyard. The grass was still thick, though the ground felt frozen. Then suddenly there was the menacing growl of a dog. Not one dog, a kennelful! Five or six spotlights on the house flashed on, drenching the front yard like a stage. Diana raced back to her car.

Slipping into the driver's seat, she collapsed against the freezing vinyl. Fear captured her breath. She fumbled in her jacket for her keys. But no one ran out of the house to confront her. And a second later the floodlights switched off and the barking ceased at the same moment. The darkness was unnaturally still. As she released the hand brake and let the car roll slowly backward to where she could make a turn, she realized there were no dogs. It was nothing but a clever burglar alarm. *I'll bet they have plenty to hide.*

A wave of fatigue made her drop her head to the steering wheel. She was suddenly much too tired to drive anywhere. On Long Island there were all-night diners and motels, but she knew she couldn't make it without a nap first. She could not go back to Mario's Apartments either.

Retracing her route to downtown Logan Point, she drove onto the large pier. Several pickup trucks belonging to clammers and all-night fishermen were already in a row; she slid the Sentra in between two. The water spread before her like a dark blanket. Setting her runner's watch for six-thirty, she climbed into the backseat. She checked again that the doors were locked, then pulled the comforter around her.

Diana woke abruptly, her body shaken by the sensation of falling. As soon as she tried to move, everything hurt. Flexing a stiff leg, she remembered that she had been dreaming about Crystal. She had been sitting in a rundown disco—the kind that kept their Christmas lights strung outside all year-round—waiting for Crystal to come out and perform. The show was delayed. Finally the teenager appeared at a stage door and beckoned to her. Diana ran after her through a maze of underground passageways and finally out into the parking lot. But she never found her. And she never would.

Pressing her hands over her closed eyes, she created a kaleido-scope. Crystal had planned all along to give away her baby for money and say it had been stillborn. "Money's no problem," she had said, presumably after she had been paid. So what had happened to make her change her mind? Certainly not a belated interest in motherhood. Then what?

She shivered and focused on the dream itself. What else had long secret passageways, outside lights, and a parking lot? A hospital, of course. Shifting painfully against the seat, she realized that she had never actually asked anyone at the hospital about Crystal's baby. If they said it was a live birth, it would be more evidence against Sidney. He hadn't delivered the baby, of course, but he had confirmed that the baby was stillborn.

She stopped at a diner in Martinville and called Jocelyn, hoping she was working an early shift.

The nurse came on the line right away. "Diana, hi! I understand that Social Services actually got this baby placed."

"Shane's baby? Good. Listen, I wanted to ask you about something else."

"Sure."

"Do you remember, about three weeks ago, a girl named Crystal Andresen?"

"Sure. Of course. I was so shocked to hear that she killed herself! I guess you never know. She had a little boy. Sol Maria delivered the baby. Sidney was supposed to, but he was sick or something."

"But the baby was okay?"

"Perfect."

"What do you think of Dr. Hazelton?"

"Sid? He's okay. He has the reputation of trying to handle too many deliveries, of course; I don't know if it's enthusiasm or just plain greed. You don't go to him unless you're willing to wait hours. But there are lots of women who swear by him. Underneath his gruffness, he has tons of bedside charm."

236

Tell me about it. "Would he ever do anything unethical?"

"Like what?"

"Oh . . . try to channel babies to adoptive couples and take money for it."

"Diana, lots of doctors and nurses make those kinds of connections! But they don't do it for the money. And I wouldn't exactly call it unethical."

"What would you call it?"

"Being helpful? Listen, I know Social Services places babies, too. But when Heart's Retreat was private, they used to be very picky about who got a child. And that left a lot of people who didn't meet their standards, but who deserved children too."

Not according to Hannah, they didn't. But she hung up feeling alarmed. If most people didn't consider what Sidney was doing to be wrong, would the police? *But it's not just making connections! It's criminal things, like leaving behind dead babies, and killing teenagers.*

How long had Sidney and Dolly been syphoning off babies from Heart's Retreat? How many babies had disappeared who nobody even knew about?

She decided that the Social Services office would be the safest place to be until she could talk to Rafe Millar. Even so, she waited until other people were entering the building and moved cautiously into the Adoption Unit.

Propping her head on her hand she tried to decide what she wanted to do.

"You look terrible," Howard announced, stopping by her desk. "Too much partying?" He asked it with a dark, wistful smile that made her heart contract. *You're the only one I want to party with.* "How's the family man?"

"Don't ask." But Howard, removing his leather jacket, let himself be steered in that direction. "You want to hear the latest? My son needs a trip to Israel to commemorate his bar mitzvah. To give him 'a sense of his heritage.' I offered him a train ticket to Park

Slope—that's where *his* roots are—but nobody liked that."

Diana laughed. "Just say no."

"Tell me how." He moved closer to her, putting his hand on the back of her chair. "You do look tired. Are you okay?"

I forgot to put any lipstick or blush on. Shielding her mouth with her hand, she said, "Who knows? I think I'm coming down with something."

"I hope it's not that flu." Hannah was unbuttoning her black watch plaid coat and removing a tam the color of Christmas boughs. Her short gray-blond braid bounced on her neck. "I had the shot this year, but everyone else is coming down with it."

"I hope it's not." The ache spreading painfully across her shoulders came from sleeping in her car. But she wished suddenly that she were one of Hannah's daughters, settled comfortably in a canopy bed and plied with catalogs and cups of hot tea. Knowing Hannah, the Earl Grey would be laced with rum. But there were worse things. *I need somebody to take care of me. The eternal cry.*

"You're sick, Diana?" Dolly asked, coming in and starting to unload her tote bag. There was criticism in her voice; Dolly seemed to feel that letting yourself get sick was just bad planning. As Dolly pulled out alligator pumps, *Vogue,* and a new jar of hand cream, Diana scrutinized her porcelain face for traces of guilt.

"I'm okay," she said, peering into her white coffee cup. It had an unpleasant residue left from last week. Tan streaks on the outside put the flowers behind bars.

When she looked up, Dolly, unsmiling, was advancing on her. *This is it.* She waited for her to pull a gun from her blazer pocket or hiss the words of a threat.

"How can you drink out of that cup?" Dolly demanded. "No wonder you feel sick!"

"I know." But she did not move. Was it a ploy to get her out into the hall or isolated in the ladies' room—or was Dolly just a member of the sanitation police? "I forgot to wash it."

But when Dolly turned back to her own desk, Diana refilled the cup at the coffee machine. She decided to stay close to her desk. Instead of working seriously she listened to other people's telephone calls. The only interesting one was Howard's. At the end he yelled, "Fuck you, Shelley, you can call yourself Little Bo-Peep for all I care! It's no longer any concern of mine."

After he banged down the phone, Diana took out her notebook. Although she usually taped interviews, she also made notes about the way people had looked when they said certain things, and the setting where the conversation had taken place. She flipped through pages. But the original story seemed boring.

Just before noon Marci approached her. Today she was vivid in an emerald green blouson sweater and matching slacks. *The human shamrock.* Diana noticed that Marci had traded her designer glasses for blue-tinted contacts, which gave her brown eyes a purple sheen. "Shane's baby is adorable!" she announced. "If you're looking for a happy couple to talk to—"

"Shane Norman had her baby?" Dolly interrupted, looking over her reading glasses.

"Over the weekend." Marci appeared ready to tough it out. "She's in an infant study home."

"Why wasn't *I* called? I'm the worker for the girls!"

Hannah joined the conversation. "Which home is she in?"

"I hope they know they can't *keep* her," Dolly warned.

Howard emerged from his office. "Before any blows are struck, the list is still in effect." He turned to Diana. "Feeling any better?"

Distracted, the others turned to her.

"I'm okay."

"You'd better take care of yourself," Dolly said. "That strain B virus is a killer!"

The word *killer* echoed through the room. Pulling on her parka, Diana promised the room that she would be careful.

But Howard followed her into the hall, raking a hand through his dark curls. "You're up to something," he accused.

"Like what?"

"I don't know. Let's go to lunch."

"It's only Monday!"

"You missed Friday."

"Howard, I can't today. Maybe tomorrow?"

"Maybe tonight?"

She hesitated.

"I think you're getting way too involved in things. You're going far beyond the scope of your article, Diana."

"How do you know that?"

"I can tell."

She started to lecture him about how uncovering the truth in a situation was never beyond her scope. Instead she just smiled and said, "Maybe you're right."

He wasn't fooled.

Oblivious to anyone passing, he put his arm around her tightly. "Diana, don't do anything stupid."

"I won't."

"You're just going out to lunch and coming back?"

"Uh-huh."

"Who are you having lunch with?"

"Howard."

"Okay." He pulled his arm away reluctantly. "See you later."

At the heavy front doors of the agency, she hesitated. Even getting in her car seemed dangerous. People who could kidnap children from their beds could wire bombs to car ignitions. There was a pay phone at the corner gas station. She started out walking quickly, and ended in a run.

The phone was by the air hoses in a traditional glass booth. Fumbling clumsily with a quarter, she got it in the slot on the third try. The plastic receiver was too cold to grip firmly; it burned against her ear.

"Precinct. Millar here."

She almost cried when she heard his voice. He was the *police*. She would be safe now. "This is Diana Larsen."

"Larsen?" He seemed to be consulting something.

"You remember. From the cemetery, the exhumation. Didn't they tell you I've been trying to reach you?"

"Yeah, I got a message. I didn't know who you were. Why do I have a printout of Volvo registrations on my desk?"

"I asked them to check," she admitted. "Can you see if there's a Sidney or Dorothy Hazelton on it?"

"Why?"

"Because he's involved in baby selling and this whole business of substituting babies. Like Caroline's! And the Senaks'." *They never called me back.* "We called him about a baby and he offered us ten thousand dollars!"

"*What* baby?"

"No baby, actually. We wanted to see what he'd say." She wasn't explaining it well.

"So you called and offered him a baby and he said to come to his office tonight."

How did he know that?

"I have to tell you, Miss . . . Larsen, that he already called me about it. There was a message when I got here."

"He called you?" Her arm holding the receiver felt hollow and frozen.

"He said when he got the call he was alarmed that a teenager would try to give her baby away for money. He first planned to get the child and turn it over to the authorities, because he didn't want to get her in trouble with the police. Then he thought he'd better call. I thought this was going to be a break in the case, someone passing babies around. I was going to be there! Now I find out it's *you.*"

She couldn't think of anything to say.

"You're not helping, you're fucking things up! This case is enough of a bitch all by itself."

"Is Dr. Hazelton's name on the list of Volvos?" Her voice sounded meek to her.

He sighed, but she heard a rustle of paper. "Grunthen, Hall, Hegeman. No Hazelton."

She felt the pang down to her feet. Had she been wrong about *everything?* "Could you read me the other names?"

A snort of disbelief. "Let me tell you, first off, that it's against the law to set people up. It's called entrapment." His indignation was ballooning. "Second, if you'd gone there tonight I would have arrested you!" He banged down the phone.

Well, he had a right to feel frustrated. Quickly she dialed Caroline.

The phone was picked up on the first ring. "Hello?"

"Hi. Forget tonight." She found she was talking fast. "Dr. Hazelton already called the police about it."

"What do you mean?"

"I mean, he reported to the police that someone was trying to sell him a baby!"

She sighed. "So it makes him look like the good guy."

"Caroline, he *is* the good guy. I guess. He doesn't own a Volvo, either."

"Well, in a way, that's good. I couldn't imagine him doing something like that. But in another way—"

"In another way, it's terrible. It leaves us with nothing."

"We still have Eileen Norris."

"Rafe Millar was going to be there tonight to arrest whoever it was." It almost seemed funny. "Yeah, we still have Eileen. She's actually our only chance. We'll *have* to lean on her. And it won't be easy. I tried it about Susan and she doesn't give."

"I could meet you there."

"Okay." A car pulled up close behind her, splashing grit. Diana jumped and turned around. A woman in a multicolored stocking cap gestured questioningly at the phone and Diana nodded that she was nearly finished.

"What time do you want to go there?" Caroline was asking.

"How about now?"

"Okay. I'll meet you there."

"Let's park out on the road and walk in. She can hear the noise of cars on the clamshells. I don't want to give her any warning."

She hung up and looked around. The woman waiting for the phone was still there. But she felt like she was being watched by someone else. Roxanne had definitely said "the doctor" in response to Diana's comment that the people she was involved with were dangerous. It was true that Roxanne had not identified the doctor by name, but . . . could it be that other doctor, that Sol Maria Cruz? And then she was ambushed by an idea so preposterous that she almost did not give herself time to consider it.

She began to run.

At the Social Services building she hesitated. Maybe she should go upstairs and tell Howard where she was going. But then she would have to try to explain the whole thing. And he would object again to her getting involved. Instead she walked down the side path to the parking lot in back. Someone had taken the trouble to plant crocuses next to the brick building; it looked as if the green shoots behind them might be daffodils. She expected that there would be people in the parking lot, going to lunch or coming for an appointment, but she saw no one. Still, it was broad daylight. Nothing was going to happen to her now.

Moving quickly toward the Sentra, she noticed a white pickup parked across the front of it, blocking the car in. Damn. She would wait a moment, then if it wasn't moved she would have to go inside to find the owner. No doubt it belonged to some client who was inside begging for housing or food stamps. No, this truck was brand-new with a green logo on the side. Something to do with gardening, or home maintenance. She was sure she had seen it around Crane Island before.

And then she remembered where.

Too late she heard the rasp of a shoe on the cement. Frantically she ran the rest of the way to the Sentra and jabbed at the lock with the key. Once inside she could blare the horn till help came. But before she could open the door, iron hands clasped her shoulders and twisted her around.

"Hi there." Michael Senak gave her a grim smile. She had seen that smile before, on Starry when she was approaching Nicole with the Pound Puppy. Despite the chilly weather Michael was wearing only a black denim jacket and jeans. His brown hair had grown longer, and instead of a shirt open to the naval he had on a white turtleneck sweater. The only remnant of his jazz musician days was a gold stud earring.

She opened her mouth to scream, but he slapped a leather palm against it. "None of that!"

In answer she thrust her knee into his groin.

It should have worked. It had worked in her self-defense class. But somehow, despite his yelp, he was grabbing her and thrusting a dirty handkerchief against her face. The sight of their struggle was blocked from anyone's view by the white truck. As she started to go under, she knew that her wild speculation had been right.

"This is so satisfying." She heard him talking from far away, from over the noise of the truck. "Here you are, one of the people who came to my house like the judge of the world, criticizing the way I raise my kid. I feel sorry for some of the girls—but not you."

She was trying to put it together. "You killed Nicole?"

"Nicole the veggie? That child is not easy to kill."

And then his voice was too far away for her to hear anymore.

TWENTY-ONE

As soon as she hung up the phone, Caroline brushed her teeth and located her turquoise jacket. Should she leave a note for Joe? But she would probably be back by the time he returned from school. She felt elated that she had talked to him last night; they had no secrets now. *It feels like I'm setting my life in order.* She shivered. Outside, though it was March, it felt very cool. She felt in her pockets to make sure her mittens were there before starting the Saab.

At Comsewogue Road she hesitated, then turned right. Before the routine of her life had been shattered, she had never paid much attention to where places were. Now she noticed everywhere she went. Even so, when she went down the road she thought Heart's Retreat was on and did not see it, she panicked. It would probably not be listed in the phone book! She turned down the next street, Bay Avenue, and was relieved to pass the tangles of forsythia from the day before.

Diana's car was not there yet. Caroline parked on the street outside the driveway and waited.

When Diana did not come, she wondered if she had changed her mind about parking away from the house, or had forgotten she told Caroline that. She got out of the car and walked down the curving dirt driveway. When the house came into view it looked even larger than she remembered—a shingled hulk of secrets. She crept closer. Diana's red Sentra was not there. But the housemother's station wagon was. And so was a silver Volvo. *The Volvo.*

She wanted to go over and look inside it, touch it, as if some essence of Zachary still magically remained. But she was suddenly wary about stepping into view. Pulling a tiny address book out of her purse, she wrote the license plate number down. Diana had just gotten delayed. She tiptoed back quietly to the safety of the Saab.

For several minutes nothing happened. There was the occasional sound of a car coming down the street behind her, but none of them stopped. And then a white pickup truck veered sharply in front of her and careened up the driveway. The tires shrieked. She pulled back hastily against the seat, though she was in no danger.

A few seconds later another car came down the road and coasted to an uncertain stop in front of her. Diana? But the car was the wrong color, and a man with a mustache was climbing out of it. She had the eerie feeling that they were gathering for something. *In olden days we would have ridden up on horses. Now we all arrive in our own metal armor.*

She froze as he slammed the car door and looked at her. Immediately she pressed the automatic door lock button, and with the click she felt safer. As the man approached her side of the car she could see the dark stubble of five o'clock shadow. Somewhere she had read that it was considered stylish now—but his worn leather jacket and baggy dress pants didn't make him a model from *Fashions of the Times.*

Then he was rapping urgently on her window. Maybe he was just lost. A tourist. Someone who had nothing to do with Heart's Retreat. She rolled the window down slightly.

"Hi." His voice was husky. "Did you see a white pickup turn anywhere? I was following it, then it was gone."

"It turned in there." She motioned to the driveway on their right. "That's Heart's Retreat. The maternity home."

"That's Heart's Retreat? In there? I guess it's been a while since I've been out here."

Caroline lowered her window a little more. "I'm meeting someone to talk to the housemother."

"Oh. I'm Howard Liebowitz. I supervise the Adoption Unit."

"Then you know Diana!"

"*That's* who you're waiting for? But—she was in the truck!"

"She was?" In the quick look she had gotten, there had appeared to be only one man inside.

He pulled at the side of his mustache nervously. "I thought so, anyway. She went out to make a phone call and then came back to her car. But she started talking to this guy in the pickup blocking her. He drove away and I didn't see her anywhere so I thought she had gotten in."

"She was supposed to meet me here."

"So let's go inside."

It was so dark and so cold that she wondered if she were in some altered state. Like death? *But people always think that. I'm not dead, I was just in that truck with Michael Senak.* She could almost remember his hoisting her out, her feet stumbling on a driveway that crackled like clamshells, then being led over a doorsill into a building. *He pushed on my shoulders and made me sit down against this wall and then I felt sleepy again.*

Wherever she was, it was cold as hell. And there were no windows. The darkness was so deep that she could not even see her knees. She patted around with her hand and found she was sitting on wooden slats two or three inches wide, with narrow spaces between them. She had to get out of here. Now. But as she started to push to her feet, she was suddenly yanked back, her feet slipping from under her.

Someone's holding me. Who else is in here? "Let me go! Help!"

No one answered. Gingerly she moved forward again, and once again was jerked back. *Jesus, it's my hair! It's like my hair is frozen to the wall!* Her stomach turned over. *I'm in the freezer, that's where I am. I've got to get out of here!* But she dreaded pulling away. *I can't stand that kind of pain.* Again her stomach churned. Placing a shaky hand at the back of her head she worked the hair loose as far down as she could. Then, squeezing her eyes shut against the agony she knew would come, she pushed herself up.

Lights, red, blue, silver, stars, a ripping sound. Tears of pain flooded her eyes, ran down her cheeks. She was thrown off balance, landing forward on her hands and knees. The back of her head burned. She did not dare reach around to touch it. *But at least I'm free! I'm free.*

Cautiously she pushed herself to her feet and took tiny steps across the slatted floor, her hands out in front of her. It was too dark to see where the walls were, or where the door might be. Once she stumbled against a tower of small boxes. *I can't stand the darkness; I'm going to scream. It's worse than a closet, worse than anything I've ever been in.* She made herself get back down on the floor. If she crawled on something solid, it would feel less like a void. The floor, despite its gaps, was the only solid thing in the world.

Waiting on the porch, Caroline wondered if Eileen Norris would refuse to open the door again. But if Diana were already inside, why not?

Still, when nothing happened right away, Howard turned the embossed brass knob. The heavy door pulled open slightly.

The housemother was there immediately. "I didn't hear your car," she apologized.

"Eileen? I'm Howard Liebowitz from Adoption."

"Yes, of course!" She smiled now, roly-poly, full of goodwill, looking behind him at Caroline. *Does she recognize me?* "Don't tell me you're bringing the new girls yourself now!"

To Caroline's surprise, he just smiled.

The foyer they were standing in smelled of the rotting wool rug and mildewed books. The smell of a thousand auction sheds. Before Eileen could say any more, a young man in a denim jacket and a white turtleneck came down the hall and joined them.

"We had an appointment to meet Diana Larsen here," Howard said.

"Diana the writer? I saw her Friday, at the hospital. But I didn't know she was coming here today," said Eileen.

"We haven't seen anybody," the man said pleasantly. Pleasant words—but there was an unfriendly shine to his eyes. *He wants us to leave.*

"Is her car outside?" Eileen asked.

"I didn't see it."

Caroline looked at Howard.

"Well, I'm sure she'll be along," he said. "Could we sit down and wait?"

"Sure. Except—this isn't a very good time. For once, I'm teenager-free, and I have company." She indicated the man with her head. Up close the shiny black of her hair seemed synthetic. Caroline noticed tiny broken red veins in her face that she hadn't noticed when Eileen came to her house.

"It's a little cold to wait outside," he pointed out.

Then a sound jolted Caroline. A baby was crying. *You've been hearing babies crying ever since Zachary. But this one is real!* Didn't the others hear it? She strained to identify where the sound was coming from.

"Excuse me," she said, letting her smile become apologetic. "May I use your bathroom?" *I do have to go.* "It may be a long wait for Diana." Before anyone could answer, she had moved around them and was making her way up the heavy oak stairs, past a massive newel post and a frosted amber window.

"Isn't there a bathroom down here?" the young man demanded. But Caroline pretended not to hear. *Don't let him come after me. Just let me do this one thing and I'll never ask for anything again.*

The crying was coming from behind a painted white door halfway down the long hall to the right. It had a soft, choky sound to it. As she got closer, she realized it did not sound like Zachary's wail at all. But she opened the door without knocking and stepped inside. The room was tiny, furnished like an old-fashioned college dorm room, with a metal-framed bed, tall maple dresser, maple desk, and captain's chair. The lack of curtains or pictures on the wall gave it the feeling of being between students. A woman dressed in a red crewneck sweater and a plaid skirt, her navy coat open, was bending over a car seat.

Caroline next saw the child on the bed. She was sitting cross-legged with a book balanced on her knees, and seemed about seven. Cute in a red plaid jumper, with blonde curls, she reminded Caroline uncannily of herself. Then she understood why. The child was sucking her thumb and clutching Tuggy. Tuggy! His bright boy face stared at her imploringly from over the girl's arm as if begging to be rescued, his faded red-boat body almost hidden from sight.

"Hi." The young woman smiled sadly.

She thinks I belong here. Do I look that young?

"I heard a baby crying. I wanted to make sure he was okay."

"That was nice of you. It's a she." Caroline realized that the woman, reaching in to stroke the baby's cheek, was fighting back tears. "We're just waiting for my husband. He had to run an errand before we leave for the city."

"I think he's downstairs."

"No rush. Believe me."

Now that the baby had stopped fussing, her breathing seemed loud and raspy. Not like Zach at all. But Tuggy! "I like your toy," she said desperately to the child. "Where did you get it?"

"She took it from a friend's house, that's where she got it," the woman said, channeling her sadness into something more like parental censure. "Starry isn't very good at knowing what's hers and what isn't."

"Daddy said I could have it! He said they wouldn't miss it."

250

"Well, that was *wrong* of Daddy, wasn't it? But we won't talk about it now."

Caroline pressed against the doorjamb, trying to deny the idea that was forming in her mind. A child that young surely wasn't capable of climbing through a window and taking a baby out of a crib. Even if someone were waiting at the top of the ladder to take it from her and hand her the other one? *Even the kids I teach would never . . . well, some of them might, if they thought it was a game . . . if they were allowed to take whatever they wanted while they were in there. . . .* She remembered Rafe Millar's question, "You have other kids?" when he was discussing the fingerprints found in the nursery. The answer had been right there. *But who would have believed it?*

There was the sound of someone coming down the hall. Panicked, Caroline stepped back out of the room as the man in denim approached her. There was no time to close the door. "Find the toilet?" He didn't hide his contempt.

"No. I guess I'll look downstairs."

He continued toward her. Was this Daddy?

For a moment Caroline thought he was going to grab her; she pressed back against the brown-papered wall. But he continued past her and into the room.

I didn't even get a chance to ask her where Zach was! And I completely forgot about Diana.

Despite her terror, she did not stay on the floor. Instead, she stood up and started moving slowly in what seemed to be a straight line, hands extended, until, without warning, she was hit in the face. She stumbled backward with a choking cry. But she hadn't been hit; she had walked into something herself, something solid and cold. It had been hanging up like the sides of beef and lamb that her father kept in cold storage on the farm. Was this a meat locker? What she touched was frozen stiff. Not . . . meat. She knew she wouldn't willingly touch it again.

251

For a long moment she could do nothing at all. She hugged her chest, tormented by images. They must have put Crystal in here until she froze to death. Then they thawed her enough to lay her down on the tracks. *That's what happened to her hair, it must have been ripped off when they pulled her away from the wall. Maybe they had to dye it black to hide the dark bloody scabs. It wasn't the train at all. I can't stand this!*

It was a shock to realize that Crystal probably never left Heart's Retreat. And neither would she. There was no inside latch on old meat lockers, and it would not occur to anyone to look inside this one. Caroline would know that something had happened to her. But by the time her body was found—God knew where—there would be no way to piece it all together. She needed to stay alive if only to tell people what she knew.

The good news was that she was dressed for the cold. Were you supposed to move around to keep up your circulation or stay still to conserve heat? *My God, I don't even know that!* She tried to remember her father's freezer on the farm. There had been a bare bulb in the middle with a string hanging down. Wildly she waved her arm back and forth, but touched nothing. Maybe by the door. *If I can only find the door.* She started moving again, moving straight ahead until she came to a wall.

Feeling her way, she found, finally, what felt like a doorframe. She patted it all over; there was no inside latch. But next to it, so chilled that it seemed to burn her fingers, was a metal wall switch with a thick coil of wire ascending from it. As she flipped it up, a light went on. She saw, first, stacks of white bakery boxes and giant packages of frozen vegetables. *At least I won't starve to death.* And then she saw something else sticking out from between the boxes. A leg with a white Reebok on the end.

Oh dear Jesus.

She was sure she couldn't look. But she made herself inch around anyway.

The girl was sitting against the wall in an alcove formed by the frozen food, her mouth twisted in a terrified grimace. Small, very thin, sharp-featured, she was dressed in a baggy gray sweatshirt and jeans. Diana studied her clothes as if to find clues to why she died. The girl's short black hair had the same bluish cast of her skin. *She looks like Cher. And she looks . . . freezer-burned.* The sudden bark of laughter was her own. If you don't wrap people properly, they will get freezer burn.

How long had she been here? But she knew the answer. Ever since she gave birth to Zachary.

It was Susan. It had to be.

It was all Caroline could do not to race back up the stairs and demand to know where Zachary was. But it would not be smart. She forced herself to smile at the others. But Howard seemed to sense that she had found something out. Instead of moving to leave, he settled himself further back against the entrance to the living room. Eileen frowned, shifting a yellow sweater cuff to look at her watch—a hostess expecting her *real* company soon. But Howard was her boss now. There was no way that she could order him out.

If Diana was there, why didn't she call out? Stamp her feet or make some sign? "How many girls live here?" she asked Eileen.

"None, right now," Eileen said. She turned to Howard archly. "I know I'm getting two, but I've never been down to *none,* even for a day."

He shrugged. "What can I tell you? You still get paid."

"Sure. But that's not the point! I like to keep busy."

There were steps on the landing and Caroline looked up quickly. It was the family. The little girl—Starry—looked like an English princess in her navy wool coat and red tam. She was still clutching Tuggy. Her parents followed, the woman holding the baby tightly. *Sad. She's very sad.*

Eileen turned to them, surprised. "I thought you were going to—"

"Later. It wouldn't be good tonight." The man was opening the

253

door with a quick look at Howard. "We'll see you in a day or two."

"But the family—"

"They'll have to wait. They can wait." He turned to the others. "I hope Diana shows up for your interview."

Do something. As the man and woman stepped through the heavy oak door onto the porch, Caroline reached out her hand to Starry. "I'll take that," she said. Few children could resist the pleasant, authoritative voice that had developed from years in the classroom. *If I can't have my baby, I want my toy.*

Starry's mouth dropped open slightly; as if hypnotized, she held Tuggy out.

"Thank you." Caroline made herself smile, but her heart was banging against her chest. She wanted to run after them, and demand that they tell her what had happened to Zach. But she knew she would get nothing from them. And she had the license plate number.

She turned back to the other two, pressing Tuggy against her. They were looking at her mystified, and she realized they had no idea what had just happened.

They must think I'm crazy, taking away a child's stuffed toy. But Howard was looking at her thoughtfully.

And Eileen with recognition.

She had stopped shivering. *I'm not really cold anymore. Maybe a miracle is happening.* But she kept her hands balled in fists in her parka pockets. Fingers were the first things to get frostbitten. Fingers and toes. *I'm not blue with cold, I'm white. I'm turning into marble like the couple at Greenhill Cemetery.*

She made herself think about something else. A can of soda left in a freezer will turn to ice and explode in less than an hour. Was blood like Pepsi? Shit! She tried to make herself think about the girls and focused on Shane and Disney World. She'd never wanted to go to Florida, it seemed all sun and retirees. Well, now she wouldn't have to worry about it, or about getting old.

She twirled her arms, and stamped her feet. She knew that the body shivered to generate heat. If she had stopped shivering, then maybe she was close to dying.

There were other things hanging from the ceiling and other bundles in the corner, things that she was deliberately ignoring. I guess when they aren't kept in storage at Greenhill they keep them here— or maybe until there's a match. *Who could imagine something this horrible? But I never thought I'd die at twenty-eight either. I didn't think I'd die at all. Howard . . .* But that was a hot knife slashing through the slush of her brain. She thought about Michael and Fleur. No wonder they could afford that beautiful house! But why tell that story about Nicole's being dead and exchanged? To get the Adoption Unit to leave them alone, maybe. But also because they knew that when Nicole's body turned up in someone else's crib and was autopsied, the condition was unusual enough for her to be identified. It was like reporting a car stolen when it had been used in a crime.

In the corner where she was refusing to look were two clear plastic boxes, the kind that you stored shoes or boots in. But maybe these held babies. *If I look and find bodies it will really make me crazy. If I look at Susan, it makes what's happening to me more real. Dear God I don't want to die. If you let me live, I'll stop doing stupid things.*

Somewhere to her right there was the creaking sound of the door being opened. *I knew it. I guess there is a God!* She started to move toward the door, slipping on the wooden slats, when the light was suddenly snapped off. There was a quick rustling, and the door closed again. "Wait! Come back!" She knew she was screaming it. "Wait!"

Down at her feet there was a rasping intake of breath, a startled cry. *What . . .* But she already knew. Stooping down, she touched something without feeling it. Her fingers were already numbed to senselessness. But she knew that breathing. The sound returned her to the inside of her Sentra. Plucky little Nicole. *My God. She doesn't even know where we are.*

Patting around awkwardly with her hands she picked the baby up, careful not to press Nicole's face against her frozen parka. She had a terrible image of Nicole's delicate skin being ripped away. *If I unzip my jacket and put her under my sweater she can stay warm a little longer. . . . If I can't save myself, maybe I can save her.*

"I'm Caroline Denecke." She looked at Eileen steadily. "You came to my house—remember?"

Eileen nodded, not even abashed. "You're the one with the old husband."

Caroline crushed Tuggy against her. "Where's Zachary?" she pleaded.

"You don't have to worry about him. He's fine."

"But he's mine!"

"Yours? What are you talking about? He was never your baby."

"Oh, really?" She took a step closer. "Well, I have a birth certificate with my name on it to prove it!"

Eileen's pale-eyed gaze did not falter. "I don't know anything about that."

"But you know where he is!"

"Look, Eileen, *I* want to know where *Diana* is." Howard reached out and took hold of her wrist. "I know she was brought here in that white pickup truck. I'm sure your friend was the one who drove her here."

"I'm telling you, Howard, I haven't seen her!"

"And I'm telling *you* that that guy brought her here! Because I followed his truck from the office."

Caroline blew her nose into a tissue she found in her pocket. "Could she still be in the truck?"

He moved to the door and pulled it open. The truck was gone. "Shit! If he took her away somewhere . . ."

They both turned and looked at Eileen.

"He forced her into the truck," Howard said. "She would never have left her car behind."

Eileen spread her arms innocently. "But why would he want to hurt her?"

"Listen, Eileen, the point isn't why. It's what you think he might do to her."

The housemother looked from one to the other. There seemed to be a war going on inside her as to whether she would tough it out and deny everything, or cast herself on Howard's mercy. Her job—her whole life probably—was at stake.

Howard seemed to be observing the same thing. "Look, I don't know what you've done or haven't done. I don't care. But if Diana turns up dead, we have two witnesses who'll say you could have saved her life—and didn't."

Caroline started to move in protest—*you can't let her die to prove a point*—but Howard held up his hand to still her. "Where's the phone?" he demanded.

Eileen put her hand to her mouth.

"One way or the other, I'm calling the police. Now."

"Why? *I* didn't do anything!"

I can't stay here and listen to this. Opening the heavy front door, she ran onto the porch and down the steps. If the other man—*the kidnapper*—had taken Diana somewhere, Howard could find that out. But meanwhile she would look everywhere else.

As she ran around the side of the house the soft sand accentuated her limp, but she didn't stop until she reached the stables. Diana was right; they had housed automobiles instead of animals. Although there was sawdust on the floors, there were a number of oil stains as well. It took time, but she looked in each stall. They were as empty as they had been for years.

There was also the chilly water below the dock. But if Diana was underneath it, there was nothing they could do for her. There was the other building, the freezer. But that was for food.

She turned back toward the house, then looked at the freezer again. Seth Greenspan was chilled from the Greenhill refrigerator. But what if . . .

The freezer door had a large brass latch. Caroline pulled it toward her and let the door open slowly. What she saw, her mind rejected at first: Diana standing, unmoving, cradling something against her chest. She tottered toward Caroline and started to fall as Caroline leaned forward to protect the baby in her arms. Somehow she managed to hold Diana up as well.

"I'm dead. I'm dead." Diana kept repeating it slowly, over and over again. She stopped only long enough to point at a back door and say, "In there." Staggering against each other, they made it up the steps and into a large kitchen.

Settling on a brown tweed sofa in the corner, listening to someone on the shopping channel selling seeds to recreate "Monet's Garden," Caroline had a new fear. What if the couple with the little girl had come back; what if he had a gun? She bounced the baby gently to keep her from crying out. They had to get out of there, to hide! But before she could work out any plan, Howard came in.

"Here you are," he said to Diana, as if she had been there all along.

"No, she was in the freezer! So was the baby, they both were. We have to do something! She's not . . . right."

"I'm dead." Diana spoke in the same monotone as before. "Nicole is not dead."

Howard rubbed the back of his neck, distracted. "I already called the police. Should I call an ambulance? I'd better call an ambulance!"

"Where's Eileen Norris?" she asked as he moved toward the wall phone.

"Locked in a bedroom upstairs."

"How—"

"Don't ask."

Diana's eyes were closed. Adjusting the baby, Caroline put her other arm around her.

When Howard came back, he looked upset. "We've got to *watch* her. We can't give her brandy, anything like that. The dispatcher said not to touch her or take her things off until they get here, just wrap her in blankets. There must be some upstairs." He was already moving. "And keep her awake!" He stopped, guilty. "I didn't even *think* about the baby."

"She wasn't in there that long. She's the same one the people upstairs had when they left. Diana called her Nicole."

"Nicole? Jesus Christ! Well—it figures. It really figures."

TWENTY-TWO

She sat, cocooned in wool, on the old brown plaid couch in the kitchen. She wished people would stop talking to her.

Caroline was next to her on the sofa. Why was she wearing that funny hat with dancing penguins? Was that her baby, Zachary? No, of course not. It was Nicole. She turned her neck to look; the back of her head burned.

"I can't believe nobody wanted her. She's a wonderful, responsive child. Look!" Caroline turned the baby toward her and held a faded cloth boat in front of the baby. "Look at her *reach* for it."

Diana nodded, trying to remember something. "She has something wrong." Her throat hurt when she talked.

"I know. Howard told me. And she hasn't been getting the care she needs. But I told him I was used to all kinds of children's problems." She smoothed down Nicole's light hair, her eyes sad and appalled. "Can you believe anyone would try and freeze a living baby, even one they thought was handicapped?"

"There are other things—in there." Her head was heavy, a water-soaked basketball; her hands and feet had started to throb.

Howard was kneeling beside her, looking up at her, asking something. She twisted her fingers in his dark hair and closed her eyes until the ambulance came.

At seven-thirty in the evening she was released from Jefferson Hospital with a list of instructions. "Your temperature was down to ninety-two point four," Howard pointed out, settling her in the front seat of his car. "I was worried it had damaged your brain. You kept stumbling around when you tried to walk."

"It *ruined* my hair."

"So? You'll grow more." He reached over and squeezed her neck. "It's amazing how people can go from worrying about life and death to things that don't really matter."

"Easy for *you* to say." She meant it to be funny, but it sounded plaintive.

"That's true." He turned left out of the parking lot. "The hospital is keeping Nicole overnight. Then your friend wants to take her."

"What's wrong with Nicole?"

He turned to look at her. "Are you okay?"

"Yes!" *But am I?* She felt a sudden chill. "Did they get Michael and Fleur?"

"As far as I know. Eileen folded like wet cardboard when the police came. That cop, Rafe Millar, said she gave him their Manhattan address, as well as the one on Crane Island. She tried to tell him she was trying to keep babies out of 'unsuitable' homes like the Deneckes. But I think it was just the money, the cut she got." He shook his head. "I can't imagine what Dolly was thinking of, giving Michael and Fleur Nicole! He's a *bastard*. Instead of paying the girls the four or five thousand dollars he promised them, he popped them in the freezer when they demanded it."

"Like me. But where did he get other . . . dead babies?"

Howard sighed. "You don't want to know."

"Yes I do."

"Well, as a landscaper he had free access to Greenhill Cemetery. One of his accounts. When infants came in for burial, before they finished filling the graves in . . . Getting hooked up with Eileen gave him access to the other freezer. She's saying, of course, that she didn't know anything about that."

"Of course not." But she giggled. "She was always going out to the freezer for donuts. And to say hi to Susan." But there was something else, something he wasn't saying, and something that she couldn't remember. "What is it?" she begged. "What *is* it?"

"Diana!" He pulled the car into the edge of a Hess gas station and turned it off. Then he reconsidered and turned it back on, pushing up the heat and opening the window slightly on his side.

"Why are we stopping?"

"Just to talk." He reached over and cushioned her against his arm. "Are you hungry?"

"No. Are you divorced?"

"Since last week. As I kept trying to tell you. I think I'm attractive as long as I'm in charge and unavailable. As soon as you have me, it's not as much fun."

"That's . . . true." She had expected to say the opposite.

When she didn't add anything, he prodded, "And? So?"

"It means if it doesn't work out, it's *my* fault. Something the matter with me, not with circumstances." She pulled back to see him better. "And maybe you're on the rebound."

"Maybe I am."

"See? This relationship's doomed!" She slumped back against the seat on her side.

But he started to laugh. "What? Why? Just because we're *talking* about it? I'm crazy about you. Knowing why won't change that."

"But—where's Shane? What happened to Shane?"

"Shane's fine. Marci brought her to a foster home this morning. But did you promise to take her to Disney World?" He sounded askance, as if such things weren't done.

"Yeah. But what about Roxanne?" Pieces of memory were returning. "Is *she* okay?"

"She didn't get frozen, if that's what you mean. Fortunately she didn't push Michael for money, Eileen said."

She finally listened to me. But Shane and Roxanne were not what she was still forgetting. "It's something to do with Caroline. And I can't *remember.*"

He brushed his fingers across her cheek. "You will."

"But it will be too late!"

"Diana, calm down."

"Wait. It has to do with this morning." She closed her eyes. *I stayed out all night and then I called Jocelyn. I found out later it wasn't Sidney Hazelton who was involved. So it had to be that other doctor—the one with the Spanish name.* "Who's the other doctor?" she begged.

"You mean at the hospital just now?"

"No. I've got to call Caroline!"

"Now?" But he looked around to locate the pay phone at the gas station, and pulled the car up beside it.

"What's the number?" Howard got out of the car and dialed it, then handed the receiver to Diana through the open window.

Be home, she prayed. *Be home.*

"Hello?"

"Caroline, it's me."

"How *are* you? I stayed at the hospital as long as I could, then I had to get Joe to take me back to get my car. I told him about Nicole. I *think* it's okay."

"That other doctor, that woman," she begged.

"Sol Maria Cruz?"

"Nobody's mentioning her, but she was in on it too! I didn't understand what Roxanne told me."

There was a long pause. "You're sure she's involved?"

"As sure as I am about anything." *Not exactly a ringing endorsement.*

"But she was out with an operation. Unless . . ." There was a longer silence. "You think that was just a story? A ruse so she could stay home with him until suspicion died down? Or until she could make arrangements for his care?" She was building momentum. "She lost her own kids to her mother; she has this poodle she puts *diapers* on."

"But why wouldn't she just keep Zach?"

"The money, Diana! So that they could collect the eighteen thousand from us. That was probably her deal with Michael Senak. After all, she only had to wait a week for the baby to be taken back and given to her."

"You think Zach was there when you went there?"

"Oh my God!"

"Maybe he's there now." She was starting to shiver. "You want to go there?"

"Yes! And I'm bringing the police."

"Rafe Millar?" Another name reclaimed.

"Hardly. There's another one, the helpful one. Donald."

Howard insisted on driving Diana there. What he really wanted to do, he pointed out, was put her in a warm bed and feed her. "You should be *resting*. You don't need any complications. You missed losing your feet to frostbite by this much." He held out his fingers.

"I did not! I just have to do this one thing. Then we'll eat."

He sighed. "What are we doing?"

"Picking up a baby." *Don't tell him that it might be dangerous.*

It was completely dark when they parked down the street from the large coral house. Caroline's Saab, across the street, was empty, but Diana spotted her sitting in the passenger side of a patrol car. Getting out of the station wagon a little unsteadily, Diana walked over to them.

Caroline was showing a piece of paper to the policeman and he was nodding. Both of them jumped when Diana knocked on the passenger window. Then Caroline got out and hugged her.

Diana recognized the policeman as the one who had stopped her car in Little India. She remembered that there was something funny about the shape of his large brown eyes.

"It looks like she's home," Caroline whispered, her arm still around Diana. She motioned toward the policeman. "Donald knows all about the freezer at Heart's Retreat; Rafe Millar told him. They already arrested the Senaks. So this should be easy."

"You're not scared?" They were crossing the street to the house.

"Are you kidding? I'm *terrified*. I've already told myself not to get too excited about Zach. The only thing is—Donald says we can't search the house."

"What? What are we supposed to do?"

"I know."

When the three of them reached the oval-glassed front door, no one moved to knock. Then Donald rapped hard on the wood. Immediately a dog began yapping. Diana started, remembering how the barking at the Hazeltons had frightened her.

"There's a dog?" Donald's hand went to his gun.

"Little. Don't—"

The door was opened. It was Dr. Cruz herself, dressed in a billowing pink robe.

"Dr. Sol Maria Cruz?" Donald asked.

She nodded slowly.

You have the right to remain silent. If . . .

"I'm bringing you down to the precinct for questioning. Someone will tell you your rights there."

"What are you talking about?" She didn't seem to have noticed Diana or Caroline.

"You've been implicated in certain felonies." He actually looked stern. "Baby selling and kidnapping. I have orders to pick you up."

"That's ridiculous! The only baby here belongs to my daughter. Ask anybody in town." She started to close the door.

Donald turned to Caroline and Diana uncertainly.

For the second time that day, Caroline pushed around people and ran toward the stairs. She felt a hand grab at her jacket, heard Dr.

265

Cruz hiss, "He's not yours!" before she broke free. But at the top of the landing, she hesitated. *Where is he?* She began opening doors, looking into bedrooms that were perfect re-creations of Victorian daily life. And finally, in one of them, a dark woman, an older woman, holding a baby beside a satin bassinet, looked up.

Caroline moved toward her, holding out her arms. She smiled her invincible smile, one that made reaching for Tuggy just a rehearsal. "I'll take the baby."

And the woman handed her Zach. His dark eyes found Caroline's and she insisted later—to Joe, who cried when he saw the baby, to Diana, who got tearful when Caroline asked her to be the godmother—that when he saw her he smiled.